The Fables of Odo of Cheriton

orgueil dicume ite trbuche·

The Fables of
Odo of Cheriton

Translated and Edited,
with an Introduction, by
JOHN C. JACOBS

SYRACUSE UNIVERSITY PRESS   1985

A relatively small but *crucial* part of this work was made possible through a grant from the National Endowment for the Humanities. The National Endowment is a federal agency whose mission is to award grants in support of a variety of humanistic activities — to the end that the goods of culture may become more widely accessible and more democratically shared.

Library of Congress Cataloging in Publication Data

Odo, of Cheriton, d. 1247.
  The fables of Odo of Cheriton.

  Bibliography: p.
  1. Odo, of Cheriton, d. 1247 — Translations, English.
2. Fables, Latin (Medieval and modern) — Translations
into English. 3. Fables, English — Translations from
Latin. I. Jacobs, John C. II. Title.
PA8395.028A25 1984   873'.03   84-24134
ISBN 0-8156-2325-9
ISBN 0-8156-2326-7 (pbk.)

Manufactured in the United States of America

For Margaret

JOHN C. JACOBS received his Ph.D. in English and medieval studies from the University of Chicago.

PARABOLIC IS IS IS LIKE AND: *Magistro Odoni*

For where your treasure is, there will your heart be also.

No, not this or this or that but also, look! This
& this & that & this & this &,
Similarly, this too. Wolf & fox & brother
As one, devouring its prey & slick slithering
Away (is the serpent now) to beguile & bite & bleed another
Child of Eve & beguile the wily Devil, too, & feed
Upon his heart—that he may pitward plunge and burn
While all Cains upward fly (like the dove & ant & cat who needn't
    learn
Like lawyers but know, like Our Lord, how easy liberty lies among wilds
    of blue
& peopled zoo) seeking—yes here, see!—their hearts & treasure too.

JCJ

Contents

Preface

IN SPITE OF its physical position, this preface is as much an end as a beginning. It is the last section of this volume to be written. As such, it brings me back to the feelings with which I began this project.

I started out delighted and intrigued by the little fables whose translation is now complete. I end with those feelings not just intact but intensified—an apparent indication that my understanding of Odo's art, integral to that delight, has grown and developed. But I'm sure the delight itself was what set me to translating in the first place. And I hope I have made it possible for this book's readers, Odo's new audience, to share a similar experience.

Moreover, Odo's fables as I present them here are enlivened by quite remarkable drawings. These were done at almost the same time as *The Fables*—by one Villard de Honnecourt, a thirteenth-century architect whose sketch book amazed me from the moment I opened it. True, none of Villard's drawings was originally intended to illustrate a fable collection. To me, though, that seems of little importance. I like the added dimension they give to Odo's narratives.

Of course I am not an art historian. But when Syracuse University Press asked me to find pictures which would complement this volume, I made what was (for me, in any case) a stunning discovery. It seems that most printed books of medieval fables—starting with pre-1500 volumes—have for centuries been illustrated with basically a single set of visual images. That set has been varied in many ways but, to my eye at least, almost every illustrated collection presents some version of a recognizably constant group of woodcuts.

This highlights a fact of immediate interest. Not only are Villard's sketches often wonderful in themselves—fluid and energetic and "naturalistic" in ways which run counter to a widely held view of medieval art. Their inclusion among Odo's translated tales signals the first time, so far as I know, that *medieval drawings* have been used to illustrate a printed collection of *medieval fables*. Other printed collections have used the woodcuts mentioned above—renaissance woodcuts, considerably more recent than the texts they illustrate. (As printed here, Villard's drawings are freely adapted from a fine, lithographic facsimile of his sketch book: *Album de Villard de Honnecourt,* ed. J. B. A. Lassus [Paris: Imprimerie Impériale, 1858].)

My delight in both Odo's narratives and Villard's drawings cannot rectify any of my errors in translation or interpretation. For such errors and mistakes of judgment, I am indeed responsible. The responsibility remains mine and mine alone. But its weight is lightened, in my case, by enormous gratitude to so many people that I cannot name them all. This translation started out as a little project and ended up making demands on a scale I had not anticipated—thus giving me the opportunity to appreciate all kinds of assistance along the way.

Yet this very opportunity now presents a problem. Were I to list the name of every person who has provided important, profoundly valuable help, this preface would begin to look like the Chicago telephone directory—amplified by numerous appendices for many additional cities in many states. So I hope that the majority of those who aided me in one way or another—and whose kind help and encouragement have certainly not been forgotten—will accept a generalized offer of thanks. It is sincerely and warmly meant.

Some of my debts, however, are so special that specific acknowledgment really is required. Theodore Silverstein, Michael Curley, and Bernard McGinn all backed my application to the National Endowment for the Humanities. Much later, Norman Spector offered generous encouragement. In a different but equally important way, assistance came from Myron E. and Ruth Russell and from my parents, Charles F. and D. Clair Jacobs. Susan Mango, quite beyond the requirements of her position as Director of the NEH Translations Program, never failed to tender aid where possible. And two dedicated humanists, Anthony C. Yu and Winthrop Wetherbee, went far past any obligations inherent in their formal appointments—each extending, in his own way, an enormously important kind of interest and involvement in my work.

Without the help of all these individuals, including those unnamed, I am not sure this book would have been completed. I am though certain as to my greatest debt—that owed the exceptional musician (my favorite cellist) to whom these pages are lovingly dedicated.

Chicago   JCJ
Summer 1984

Introduction

Fables—the very word betrays their confession of falsity—serve two purposes: either merely to gratify the ear or to encourage the reader to good works. . . . This whole category of fables that promise only to gratify the ear, a treatise on wisdom avoids and assigns to children's nursuries. The other group, those that draw the reader's attention to certain kinds of virtue, are divided into two types. As for the first, its content is grounded in fiction and the very telling of the story cloaked in lies. . . .

Macrobius

A fable is an oration fashioned so that it has a life-like form which manifests an image of truth. Thus the fable is the first thing that orators teach to children. . . .

Priscian

MANY YEARS AGO, an exceptional teacher warned me not to read the introductions to books like this—or at least to read the actual work first and then, perhaps, the introduction. By and large I found this good advice. For readers, and I certainly speak of myself, sometimes see in a work *only* those things they believe they ought to. In other words, an introduction can operate as a set of blinders. It can, contrary to the intentions of the introduction's author, turn a first reading into a process of documenting his assertions.

All this is a way of explaining something that can be put aphoristically: Dante is the best introduction to Dante, Aristotle the best introduction to Aristotle, and so on. I certainly do not know whether the humblest fable, lyric, or essay makes it to literary heaven more or less quickly than the massive accomplishments of our tradition. I do believe, however, that what is true of a Dante or an Aristotle — of a Homer or a Faulkner, for that matter — is also true of Odo of Cheriton. Odo's *Fables* or *Fabulae,* the work translated here, is its own best introduction.

Yet the fact remains that this volume marks the first translation of Odo, indeed of any medieval fabulist who wrote in Latin, into modern English. So while some readers may wish to turn directly to Odo's actual text — and I would neither discourage them nor suggest that they will fail to find rewards in so doing — this introduction is a rather unusual case. It has a special function precisely because Latin fables' medieval phase has been so long neglected (and, even when not neglected, treated indifferently). It would be a different matter had Odo and his colleagues, like Aesop and Dante and Dostoyevsky, a long history of familiarity among English-speaking readers.

Any such difficulties aside, though, Odo's fables are too good to remain the private property of specialists in Latin. Their author was as free and creative in his own way as was James Thurber when writing *Fables for Our Time.* Even so, the claim which points my comparison may do more to draw out problems than to solve them. For Thurber is very much our contemporary. The world in which he lived and wrote is pretty much our world, his intellectual and ethical assumptions are largely congenial with our own. Odo of Cheriton, on the other hand, did his writing in the thirteenth century. He died (1247) only two years after Thomas Aquinas had come to the University of Paris. Odo's was an age of vigorous (sometimes vitriolic) religious, philosophic, scientific, and social debate and conflict. In this sense, it sounds a good deal like the twentieth century. There is still a crucial difference, however. The varied conflicts I mention all took place in a context of belief rather different from the beliefs dominating our own "secular" age.

Modern speakers sometimes use "medieval" as a synonym for terms such as "unenlightened." And medieval beliefs, we may too easily tell ourselves, were superstitious and dogmatic — meaning, so far as I can tell, that those beliefs are different from our own and, therefore, make us uncomfortable, even annoyed. The twentieth century prides itself on surpassing the thirteenth in diversity and tolerance, yet we are not always of a mind to practice the tolerance we accuse others of lacking. Modern catalogs of heresies (normally compiled by men who do not call themselves religious) tend to highlight the commonest of commonplaces and orthodoxies from previous ages. This procedure recalls the humorous conjugation of an irregular verb: He is pig-headed, you are stubborn, and I am firm.

I suppose these observations alone will not give us much positive help, though all of them bear on Odo's achievement and the freedom from cultural bias which can enhance our ability to appreciate it. For some of the differences separating our time from his can act as barriers. They can keep us from seeing and delighting in the very inventiveness which makes Odo's collection remarkable.

My comments are based on actual experience. Having shown these fables to a wide range of people, I am particularly impressed by two aspects of their reactions. As it so happens, nearly everyone — from younger readers to adults with dramatically varied literary backgrounds — has found them accessible and fun. No special preparation is really *required* to read Odo. I can, nevertheless, testify to a second point. Many a reader has laughed or smiled, and then added: "But they're 'too religious' for me." Now the feeling that Odo's fables are "too religious" would be without literary importance if it did not mean, in practical terms, that readers who take delight in Thurber's freedom of invention and application may see in Odo little more than unenlightened "dogma" and benighted, egregious didacticism. (Indeed "didactic," like "medieval" and "dogmatic," has become a pejorative term.)

Granted, one could walk away from such responses — muttering all the while: "So much the worse for him . . . or her." But not only would this be smug, it would be foolish. It would block the very change this translation is intended to accomplish. Odo's powers as entertainer, commentator, and satirist merit more than a footnote in histories of literature. They merit an audience — an audience including professional students of medieval culture, to be sure. In addition, though, they should also draw in all other readers who (though lacking the specialist's grasp of Odo's language and culture) find a pointed tale engaging. Thus my aim in these introductory comments is hardly to tell anyone what they must see and appreciate in *The Fables*. In their strategies and effects, Odo's little narratives are too diverse to be pinned down in that fashion.

My real hope is quite modest. While this introduction has an organization and argument of its own, readers are encouraged to *use* my

3

comments in whatever ways best serve them personally—perhaps for the moment skipping whole sections, if that is what they find most workable. There are novelties in my treatment which I like to think some will return to later on. But since the translation is now complete, I and my readers are together members of Odo's audience. We share a common interest in *The Fables'* actual text. Having put that text in the foreground, I would merely suggest that my informal, largely non-technical discussion—however approached—may enhance many readers' understanding and pleasure as they go about discovering or rediscovering Odo of Cheriton's sophisticated but unabashedly moral, didactic art.

Literary Genres, Values, and Methods

There is a common-enough tendency to turn distinctions among kinds of literature into easily applied value distinctions. We have then ample reason to begin with the issues involved in calling a work "didactic"—and to glance, for a moment at least, at the place of fables as a didactic subspecies. Now one habit we noted earlier is the pejorative, deprecatory use of "didactic" (we might also have said "rhetorical" and "moral"—the latter often being taken to mean "offensively moralistic"). Its rough translation? "Bad." And what is "good"? Presumably the opposite, literature which is "wonderfully wrought" and "deeply felt"—"lyrical," "poetic," and "novelistic." Indeed labeling something a precursor of The Novel, even "the first novel"—here there are many candidates!—is a fairly popular promotional strategy.

Lyric poems and novels are certainly fine things—at their best, wonderful and moving. What they do most admirably, however, is not the only thing that literature can do. I admit, of course, that genre distinctions are not eternally fixed, that we *may* therefore use them to quickly sort what is "bad" from what is "good." The bother with this procedure is its consequences. Somewhat like static on the radio or television, it gets in the way. It makes it hard for us to hear an author's voice, hard to see much of what is in fact happening on the page.

If we are going to find instruction and delight in a work like Odo's *Fables,* we shall probably need to look freshly at the notion that first-

4

rate literature cannot be—or is diminished by being—rhetorical, moral, didactic. T. S. Eliot is remembered and honored for many things, sometimes for his grant of the very highest poetic honors to Shakespeare and Dante. In this connection it is worth remarking that Dante continues, today as in the past, to exert a profound influence upon the writing of poetry—paradoxically perhaps, given the epic proportions of his greatest achievement, upon the lyric. It is also true that he is most frequently thought of as a didactic author. And, indeed, he himself borrowed heavily from a tradition of didactic criticism (that of the medieval *accessus*) when writing about his *Divine Comedy*.

He described it as an educational book, a work intended to instruct men and change their lives. Now to be instructive is to be didactic, in the most literal sense ("didactic" going back to the Greek verb for "teach," "admonish"). There are admittedly limits in this approach to the *Comedy*, limits which critics have explored to a considerable extent. But the *Divine Comedy* itself is not our primary concern just now. I mention it simply to suggest that the experience of many of Dante's readers, over many generations, ought to loosen one's grip on the notion that "good" and "bad" are especially useful synonyms for "poetic" and "didactic."

Suppose we grant this. What follows? Must we claim that literary appreciation has no business making judgments? I merely want to affirm (as Aristotle might have put it) the role of the "middle." Insight, understanding must intervene—must actively *mediate*—if a reader's encounter with a text is to be genuine, his judgment real.

From my vantage point, then, it is important to note the *Comedy*'s great indebtedness to the tradition of epic poetry. I again ask readers to consult their own experience. Those who do will not feel hesitant about concluding that Homer is not Aesop, that an epic is not a fable; an attempt to systematically list the differences is hardly required. All the same, it is also pretty obvious that fables do share something with an epic like the *Divine Comedy*—namely, explicit didacticism. Indeed fables, especially the best known of them, are time and again capped by a proverbial saying or pointed aphorism: the "moral" of the story. In a moment we will expand on this and treat the genre "fable" more fully. As preliminary, however, we need to look at broader matters which promise to illuminate the positive side of moral, didactic literature.

Epic and fable—as well as a great range of other narrative and non-narrative varieties—have roots in the art of sophistry, rhetoric. Throughout a long history and amid shifting social and cultural circumstances, the art of rhetoric has had a continuous function as source of many things we value. Yet "rhetoric" and "sophistic" have suffered a fate similar to that of "didacticism." They have become pejoratives. Readers can easily test this by considering how frequently they hear statements dismissed by labels such as "rhetoric," "mere rhetoric," "sophistry." (It is hardly a compliment to call someone a "sophist.")

The early sophists were actually citizens of the fifth century B.C. They were teachers of rhetoric who left behind writings of their own. But the most influential portrait of them was painted by Plato. In the Platonic dialogues, Socrates attacks and ridicules their teaching as the art of making the worse appear the better. He claims that they practice a false art, one formed to serve the wrong end.

He did not deny that they were skilled storytellers. And by all accounts, defamatory as well as flattering, the early sophists were truly skilled tellers of tales—masters of public oratory. Of pointed relevance to our discussion is the fact that their speeches often gave prominent play to notable deeds. Laudatory and vituperative accounts of such deeds came to be known—once the Greek sophists' legacy found a place in the later systematizations of Cicero and other Roman rhetoricians—as "narratives." And a *narratio* had the role of recounting sequences of action in such a way that they helped an orator make his case.

The art of narrative, in a sense which goes far beyond oratory, continuously draws upon and enlarges its rhetorical origins. By late antiquity (the period sometimes known as the Second Sophistic) and the early Middle Ages, the marks of its influence pervade Latin letters: in histories, imperial biographies, saints' lives, laudatory poems, manuals on the art of interpreting texts (including the Bible), polemical and apologetic tracts, epics, schemes for educational organization, and sermons—*and in fables.*

For Cicero, Quintilian, and rhetoricians generally, there were various kinds of *narratio;* one of these was the fable, often explained as an account of things which neither happened nor could have happened. (A *fabula,* to put this a bit differently, tells of matters neither actual nor possible.) Yet such fables had a legitimate use in the grammatically and rhetorically based educational system of antiquity. Indeed, retelling Aesop's fables (i.e., recasting and amplifying Greek fables by turning them into Latin prose and poetry) was a standard classroom exercise. But Cicero not only opens a window through which we can view the schools of his and later ages. As the author of a *Republic,* a creative imitation of Plato's work of the same name, he provided the occasion for a widely read treatment of fables — that contained in Macrobius' late fourth-century *Commentary on the Dream of Scipio.*

As *The Dream of Scipio* is but one section (the conclusion) of Cicero's *Republic,* so Macrobius' account of fables is but a small part of his *Commentary.* Readers in the Latin West found the *Commentary* a source for many things. In it, Macrobius set forth neo-platonic teachings, a classification of the kinds of dreams, and also (in Book I, chapter ii) the observations of special interest here — his venture into what most of us would call literary theory.

What kinds of *fabulae* are admissible in philosophy? This is Macrobius' question. In the context of our discussion here, his answer recalls issues we ourselves were considering only a moment ago. For it implies a hierarchy of literary kinds running from low to high — and, ultimately, from bad to good. Macrobius marks each step in his analysis by mention of an illustration or two. Thus "fables" first divide into those which delight the ear and those which promote virtue, with the strictly delightful being turned out of the house of philosophy and assigned to nursery cradles! But fables prompting virtue get fuller attention. Some of these — fables in the proper, more limited sense — are such as Aesop wrote; though popular indeed, the point is that their content (*argumentum*) is grounded in fiction and set forth cloaked in lies. The remaining variety of virtuous fable fares better; its *argumentum* is at least grounded in essential truth. To communicate this (and now Cicero's *Dream* comes in as an illustration) it uses fiction as a means. A fable of this sort is not a *fabula* in the strict sense but a *narratio fabulosa,* a "fabulous narrative." Even here, however, the reader gets a warning. According to Macrobius, philosophers do not approve the indiscriminate use of fabulous narratives. They are not appropriate to all philosophic concerns. To put it more fully, in legitimate form a fabulous narrative has legitimate applications; but these do not include the Supreme God or Mind — both of which drive true philosophers to take a final step, to reach for and limit themselves to *similitudines* and *exempla.*

I cannot know whether my readers will find this a congenial scheme. It certainly has echoes in debates of our own day — when, for example, we hear poets argue that they lie in order to tell the truth.

7

However this may be, Macrobius' hierarchy already had — at the time it was set out in the fourth century — a striking backdrop provided by the long debate between poetry and philosophy. This is a debate whose opponents have never, to the exclusion of all ambiguity, managed to stay on their respective sides of the stage. It is also a debate which has never achieved a final, clear resolution. I urge my readers not to expect one either.

It is nevertheless a productive debate, one in which some of the positions used by the participants can be clarified. (1) In the gnostic tradition which traces back at least to Hellenistic times, fables broadly speaking are devices of concealment. They veil and cloak, protect and preserve especially lofty truths from uninitiated eyes, keeping transcendent matters safe for those elite intellects qualified to understand them. To cite Macrobius, Nature's "sacred rites are veiled in mysterious representations [*mysteria figurarum*] so that she may not have to show herself even to initiates. *Only eminent men of superior intelligence gain a revelation of her truths;* the others must satisfy their desire for worship with a ritual drama which prevents her secrets from becoming common." Even with these words' emphasis on concealment, we note that they also allot a place to revelation — which brings us to a second tradition. (2) In this, let us call it the didactic tradition, fables are primarily devices of revelation and instruction. They teach. And transform. This tradition traces back at least to pre-Socratic times. It emphasizes fables' powers of exposure and exposition — while *not* putting much stress on distinctions between transcendent and mundane truths or between elite initiates and common folk. Fables, to express the matter in slightly different terms, address a universal audience rather than one which is limited and particular, exclusive and exclusionary.

From this push toward issues which concern all or most men, a third tradition — one which we will term apologetic — emerges. (3) The apologetic tradition traces back most forcefully to sophistic performances (Gorgias' *Encomium of Helen,* for example) and to the later practice of rhetoric, especially judicial or "courtroom" rhetoric at Rome. The period known as the Second Sophistic (c. second-fourth centuries A.D.) is also the age of Christian apologists such as Tertullian. Fable is a pejorative and term of contempt in the mouths of these men. They adapt the devices of judicial rhetoric — Tertullian was a lawyer before he became a Christian — to religious debate. And Christians and their adversaries charge one another with belief in tales and deities which are "mere fables," that is, fantasies, childish fictions, fond and foolish notions. Fables are lies. (As we have seen, this tradition is reflected in one aspect of Macrobius' analysis.)

The apologetic view of fables comes close to that of (4) the philosophic approach, our fourth and final tradition. It is almost always Platonic in orientation and, indeed, traces back most obviously to the treatment of poetry and myth in Plato's dialogues. Here, fables are both a danger to serious inquiry *and* one of its necessities. As necessities, they come into play when the limitations of merely human speech threaten to keep the upward dialectic from encompassing the transcendent, the superhuman, at all. So fables corrupt minds, especially the minds of the young; they also enable one to speak about the unspeakable—the things which go beyond the powers of normal speech. Obviously, this is a tradition of paradox. Fables and the like are delightful but destructive, also welcome and essential for the higher levels of inquiry.

Traces of all four traditions are evident in Macrobius, and readers will probably spot them in Odo of Cheriton as well. As traditions, they are not rigidly distinct, and each tradition supplies materials which both poetry and philosophy can use in criticizing *or* defending fables. Now Odo of Cheriton was, obviously enough, a writer of fables. He was also a trained theologian. Yet whatever we imagine he might say— were he presented with our account of poetic-philosophic debate— one fact concerning fables stands out. They have, on a whole variety of grounds, been continuously condemned and praised throughout the history of the West. The debate about their value and status has been continuous, with this continuity being rivaled only by the continuity of actual production.

Odo of Cheriton was one of the producers, one of those who kept on writing. Though he certainly had his own way of reading and putting together fables, he left no theoretic account behind—nothing comparable to Macrobius' discussion. So far as fables are concerned, he seems not to have thought that orderly discrimination among kinds was crucial. He does not, for example, treat the distinction between parables and fables systematically. Most notably, his actual practice merges them. Thus he writes the collection which I have translated, *The Fables (Fabulae)*, yet characterizes it with reference to parables. "And because this is a parabolic treatise," he tells us in closing his prologue, "let us take our beginning in a parable from the Books of Judges." *Et quoniam tractatus est parabolicus*. . . . But prior to this—quoting the very verse of the very psalm which Matthew once used (see Matthew 13:34–35) to exhibit Jesus' teaching as the fulfillment of Old Testament promise —Odo had already explained himself, not many words back. Swift following a comment which makes *exempla* sound very much like aphorisms, he had told his readers: "I will open my mouth in parables [Psalms 77:2]; and I will set forth *similitudines* and *exempla.*" With that brief declaration, Odo collapses levels of discourse and folds together kinds of literature which Macrobius was so intent on separating. And indeed in Odo's treatise, any differences among *similitudines* and *exempla* and *fabulae* and *parabolae* (Macrobius made no mention of parables) seem insignificant. All are parabolic. This does not simply mean that Odo is depicting his *Fables* as a work which uses the Aesopian fable ("its content . . . grounded in fiction and the very telling of the story cloaked in lies") to teach religious truth—though in itself this fact is significant enough. For, even more strikingly, he is presenting his teaching *method* as nothing less than the method of the Bible, as the very method which the Truth Himself used to teach Truth.

All of this is so dramatic as to make further discussion essential. And it is worth mention that Odo's preliminary remarks imply a belief that literature can be especially valuable *because* it teaches, *because* it is didactic. Temporarily, however, I want to set aside literary form and method as the central focus of our discussion. Odo's little narratives again and again remind us that they are commentary on a social and natural world. So a direct look at our author and his time promises to let us feel more sharply the thrust of many a fable.

Odo of Cheriton (c.1185–c.1247): His Life and Times

Not surprisingly, Odo's biography touches multiple facets of the world in which he lived. Though many of the details are probably lost forever, the work of Albert C. Friend provides data that enable us to construct a fairly coherent picture.

Because of the circumstances of his birth and later education, Odo apparently knew both country and city life at first hand. It is speculation—though neither mere speculation nor a denial of the importance of literary sources and resources for Odo—to suggest that our author's youth probably involved watching the behavior of animals at first hand. But we also know that Odo was not a man of the countryside only; he spent a number of years in Paris and probably, through later travels, came to know the ways of many men and many cities. He was no stranger to life in either its rural or urban settings.

His birth can be placed about 1185, give or take five years either way. He was part of the fourth generation of a family which came to England from Normandy, probably fifty or sixty years after the Norman Conquest (1066). The family name derives from one of their properties, Cheriton Manor, located near the southeast coastal borough of Folkstone (or Folkestone) in Kent. Over the generations, the family had acquired a number of lands—though the ownership of real estate, to anticipate a matter we will be coming back to later on, was then a somewhat different arrangement than we are accustomed to. Nevertheless, it is clear that Odo was born into an affluent family. His father, William, was a man of property from the start; he inherited the family fortune at its height and became, in the late twelfth and early thirteenth centuries, a public figure of importance and power.

He named his son after the first "English" Cheriton, one *dominus* Odo who died some time before 1166; this choice of name made St. Odo of Cluny (879–942) our author's patron saint. There is real irony in this. Affluence marked Odo of Cheriton's family. Yet he, like Odo of Cluny, was a troublemaker—a reformer in an age when such activity often risked physical danger. Fortunately for us, the latter-day Odo expressed his anger and discontent (or important parts of them, at least) by writing well-barbed fables, many of which have lost none of their power to trouble and delight. Thus by his death in 1247, he had not increased the family holdings—though he had apparently maintained the ones he had kept. Still, whatever the magnitude of the estate inherited by his one surviving brother, Waleran, his broader and more enduring legacy is literary and specifically fabulistic. For not only were his fables widely copied (frequently, as an independent work) and circulated in his own day, they also were translated into both French and Spanish. No, the fables are not his only work. He indeed composed treatises, sermons, a commentary on the Song of Songs, and a penitential work—all this in a writing career beginning sometime prior to 1219 and extending past 1235. Even so, *The Fables,* probably written well into his maturity (after 1225), is the one complete work which does not survive—as a complete work—solely in manuscript. It is the one complete work which a printed edition, Hervieux's, makes available *in its entirety*.

Even the most casual reader will quickly see that the fables are the work of a man with a definable set of interests, largely moral and religious. Given his education and vocation, this is easy to understand. Paris had been an intellectual center long before the beginning of the thirteenth century, but 1200 has routinely been treated as the year when the University of Paris was chartered officially. There is evidence to suggest that Odo of Cheriton was at Paris by the charter year. In any case, he had become *Magister*—perhaps meaning he had completed the M.A. or Master of Arts degree—by a decade later, 1210–11. We know this, to quote Friend, because "in that year his father [William] paid a fine that his son *Magister Odo* might have custody of the church at Cheriton." (Custody, *custodia*, is a technical term; to "have custody" is to hold the office of "manager" of a church's patrimony—i.e., its wealth or endowment.) It is probable that Odo celebrated mass and preached some of his sermons at "his" Cheriton church, St. Martin's. Whether or not he did, before the close of another decade Odo was able to speak of himself as *Doctor Ecclesiae*, "Doctor of the Church." He had, in other words, completed his doctorate in theology (c. 1219). Although he may have gone on a pilgrimage during the years leading to his doctorate, Friend's evidence suggests that Odo probably spent many years in Paris, studying at both the Master's and doctoral levels with teachers of considerable prominence. From all we know of theological instruction in the twelfth and thirteenth centuries, one thing stands out. His academic work would have been focused on the Bible, the sacred scriptures. And he would have been exercised time and again in their interpretation.

In a different context it would be useful to distinguish among varieties of interpretive method. To my way of thinking, though, the point we need to make here is a good deal simpler. The central approach to scriptural study and explication was, for Odo's time, the figural method. This is fundamentally a way of reading which allows one to view both Testaments, Old and New, as embodying variations on common themes. Things appear in books of the Old Testament which prefigure—that is, present "in a figure" or *figura*—their later fulfillment in the New Testament. "Figure" and "fulfillment," "old" and "new," "ancient" and "modern" are constantly interrelated by biblical commentators of the Middle Ages. Thus Adam prefigures Christ, who is the second Adam. Eve prefigures Mary who (as a woman) is instrumental in making possible the world's deliverance from its fallen state —just as Eve was instrumental in creating that state. As one joyous carol proclaims via playful alphabetical inversion, what modern poets term a palindrome: *AVE fit ex EVA.* Which is to say that God (I render the line, slightly expanded, in English) "managed to bring forth 'Hail Mary' [*A-V-E Maria*] from Mary's antithesis, Eve [*E-V-A*]." The line may have been offered and understood more literally than we readily imagine, for a medieval tradition with considerable currency celebrated God as the poet of poets and His creation as the great poem or song of the universe.

However this may be, the central fact one needs to appreciate in considering figural method is the flexibility of interpretation it encourages. It not only allows one to relate things which, in controversy, would be severed and opposed to one another. But the relations set in motion are reflexive, they work backward and forward. That is, if Adam is a figure of Christ, then the god-man who is Adam's fulfillment reflects back upon and alters one's perception of Adam himself. The "second Adam" makes of the first a kind of "anticipatory Christ."

Reflecting upon this way of reading biblical narrative, we may recall the often-repeated claim that the Christian view of history is linear (a contrast is usually added which attributes cyclical views to pagan antiquity). Whatever the value of this claim and contrast, we may suggest that medieval Christians' methods of *reading* sacred history were not the flat, literal-minded procedure which the adjective *linear* may imply. And if some of us today find their methods and readings absurd, this is not necessarily a result of our superior intelligence or a consequence of unambiguous progress. More probably it results from changes in basic cultural assumptions, as well as further changes which have *decreased* the disciplined flexibility and range of ideas at some readers' command.

As for further clarification of figural method itself, John Donne's *Hymn to God My God, in My Sickness* is an example familiar to most students of English literature; and though the work dates well after the Middle Ages, I urge anyone wishing to go beyond these pages for a moving instance of figural thought to read its thirty lines. (For an extensive scholarly account, one ought first to turn to Auerbach's *Figura,* listed in the bibliography.) Yet at least part of the clarification we seek is open to all in Odo of Cheriton's text. On the very first page of his prologue to *The Fables,* Odo tells us that the Old Testament's Boaz signifies Christ (for both Boaz and Christ are variations on *strength*); and the New Testament's Christ—seen from this perspective—in turn reflects new light back upon Isaiah's Old Testament description (Isaiah 63:1) of one who is "beautiful in his robe, walking in the greatness of his *strength.*" Obviously, for the figural imagination lines of signification can be multiple; Adam need not be thought of as the only figure of Christ, nor Christ as the fulfillment solely of Adam.

But what is Odo's point is making this sort of discussion a prologue to his collection of *fables?* Fables are not scripture. And a *Doctor Ecclesiae* certainly would not have called his narratives biblical commentary (though some of them do, in their own way, take on a central function of such commentary). Our question can be answered rather simply, if only we are willing to generalize the sense of old and new. Just as figural thinking enabled readers to interrelate Old and New Testaments, it could also prompt creativity in the secular realm. It could encourage writers and readers to take *old,* received tales (derived from pagan and other fable collections, compilations of animal lore, oral traditions, etc.) and develop *novel* versions, further extended through analogies and contemporary applications—analogies and applications which themselves make for a new appreciation of the received material.

The figural method Odo's prologue applies to sacred scripture is also the dominant method of his fables. Readers who keep this in mind will find *The Fables* livelier and more "thought-full" than they would if they insisted on seeing Odo as a pious distorter of materials whose "real" form and meaning had been determined—once and for all—by earlier fable writers. After all, poets and writers in general are notorious for taking material wherever they find it—and for making of it what they will. It is *their* intentions which create and recreate form and meaning. Thus there just is no intrinsic conflict between Odo's roles as Christian teacher and as teller of tales, between earnest theologian-preacher and witty author. Those roles are mutually informing. (But again, we will fail to see this by regarding some classical or other version of a tale as its one, true form.)

So far, then, we have taken our author's life to the point where his doctoral work is complete—with a pause to expand upon critical links between his formal education and later literary accomplishment. However, a brief word about the years following 1219, along with a backward glance at additional aspects of his earlier days, will yield an even fuller sense of the actual person Odo of Cheriton. Here, his individual experiences begin to merge with the larger social experience — moral and institutional, private and public — of his age. I don't find this surprising. The habits of individuals are both the creators and the creations of the same individuals' larger selves — of, in other words, the institutional patterns or social structures which frustrate *and* facilitate the lives of men. Of course the picture is not always the same. In each particular life the most important points of contact between self and society are to some extent unique. In Odo's case, fortunately, his fables themselves guide us toward what is most significant for understanding their author.

References in a number of the fables probably reflect both pre- and post-doctoral travels (some of these being documented from external sources — the Public Records, an inscription in a book, etc. — and some being suggested or further confirmed by references and localized materials embodied in his sermons and other writings). On and off, Odo was in England throughout his life. But after a return to England for the two years following completion of his doctorate, he travelled in southern France and in Spain (c. 1221–25). Although a number of his fables target a seemingly remarkable degree of vice among the Cistercians, Odo may (as a student) have journeyed north to visit one of their houses near Rouen. (He himself has often been called a Cistercian, although there are no grounds for thinking he was a member of any order). In any case, his *post*-student travels definitely took him below the Loire.

While on the road, Odo apparently continued to write or at least to think through issues and gather materials which would, in time, find their way into his writings. His third collection of sermons (*Sermons for the Feast Days*) seems to have been influenced by practices and expectations most strongly associated with the southwestern French city of Toulouse. (The University of Toulouse had been established quite recently and was in competition with Paris for students.) As to the years following his southern travels, it is hard to say where Odo was or what he was doing. His father's death (1232–33), however, made Odo heir — as the oldest living son — to the family properties. Inevitably, this also made him heir to the burdens and responsibilities of overseeing their care. Partial records remain of his tax payments, from the year of his father William's death until that of his own. Thus, though seemingly reluctant to spend his energies in the direct management of real estate — he actually divested himself of some of it, thereby reversing the family's history of expansion — Odo was hardly a stranger to secular affairs. Not only did he pay taxes, but he had much earlier served as a tax assessor himself; and, in the year of his father's death, Odo apparently found himself liable for service with King Henry III in Ireland. (He was exempted and did not go.)

In 1234, Matilda (Odo's mother, William's widow) made arrangements for the continuing operation of the Cheriton family's primary residence at Farningham in Surrey. The Farningham manor, not much southeast of London, was not Matilda's home only *after* her husband's death. In spite of the derivation of the family name from Cheriton manor, the dwelling at Farningham seems to have been home to all of William's offspring during their childhood. This means that Odo grew up not in the agriculturally poor surroundings of Cheriton, but amid rich cropland where corn and fruit could flourish.

To expand on something suggested a moment ago, the marks of Odo's travels are scattered here and there throughout *The Fables*. As illustration we may remark the opening of Fable 14: "There lives in Spain a bird called the 'Bird of Saint Martin.'" One narrative (Fable 60) extends its initial interpretive analogy with a further analogy, this being introduced with the remark: "Such an event actually happened in our own time, in the case of a preaching brother in Spain." Others refer to places more specifically. There is mention, in Fable 98, of the foolishness of the king of a particular Spanish province, Aragon, and reference in another (Fable 1) to the Bishop of the Spanish city Toro. There are also a number of French references, and we may at least acknowledge the very funny account (Fable 19) of "a heretic in around Toulouse" (this city, already mentioned, is situated in the modern Département of Haute-Garonne which, on its south, shares a common border with Spain). Yet how much can all this tell us about Odo's life? Very little which is beyond question, though it is probable that our author had spent time in or near a number of the places to which he refers. I would quickly add, however, that lack of certainty in these matters is no barrier to enjoying his art. We can be grateful to Albert Friend for what we know of the particulars of Odo's biography — though inevitably, as with any life, most of these are lost. His fables remain.

The greater impress of Odo's travels through countryside and city — and of his rural childhood and urban university education, as well —

is not found in more-or-less datable and localizable details. His experience of the late twelfth and early thirteenth-century world had an impact on *The Fables* which goes far beyond mention of city and provincial names. For in that world, as in our own, the habits of men (their moral and intellectual virtues—and vices!) and their social institutions (often corrupt) wove the textured fabric of daily life. And while many segments might, as they emerged from the loom, be beautiful indeed when seen from a distance, coarsened strands were far from uncommon —with entire patches of fabric sometimes emerging in a state so flawed as to threaten the strength and splendor of the whole. These ugly spots, *maculae,* are targets of Odo's annoyance, disgust, anger and, yes, amusement throughout *The Fables.* Though it may go without saying that no author would bother to write such narratives if he believed his fellows were totally senseless, we yet may imagine Odo at times muttering darkly to himself: "There must be some redeeming qualities in these people, *some* spark of reason!"

Do I risk making Odo sound too much like a citizen of the twentieth century? Perhaps. Yet one of the prominently flawed patches in twelfth- and thirteenth-century daily life was hardly just a patch; it came closer to being a multitude of strands running through the fabric's every inch. I speak of fraud and force, violence. It is well to remember that the England and France of Odo's day were Norman England and, to a large extent, Norman France or Normandy. And all contemporary chroniclers of the partially "Frenchified" North Men—writers such as Dudo of St. Quentin, and the later William of Jumièges, William of Poitiers, Ordericus Vitalis, William of Malmesbury—picture them as people of enormous energy and vitality. The same writers also show us people who were not only strong-willed but willful, people used to getting their own way and not very tolerant of authority. As a consequence, they appear impatient—people rarely accustomed to fussing over "theoretical" issues such as the ethical character of a personal objective or its relation to the common good. In determined pursuit of their goals, the route running from persuasion through fraud to force could be traversed quickly. Violence and oppression were, at almost all levels of society, important facts of life. To this Odo's testimony is abundant, not in the secular realm alone but also in the religious. (The two were not so separate anyway, with many church officials holding secular rank.)

In large measure, the unpleasantries of English daily life had their

17

origin in the exigencies of William the Conqueror's rule from 1066 on and, also, in the feudal organization of society which William used to deal with them. (Feudalism, already established on the Continent, was imported to England from Normandy.) As an invader, the Conqueror needed to effectively contain any internal resistance put up by the native English. He needed, in other words, to assure internal peace as well as security against external threats. The quick fix, so to speak, was simple: buy the continued support of those who have already helped you by giving them lands "in fee." These were lands which previously had been held by the Saxon nobility, most of whom were now dead or in exile.

Here we must pause because the phrase "in fee" recalls our earlier allusion to peculiarities of land "ownership" in a feudal system. Land was not actually owned in our modern sense. Though ownership of land in the twentieth century normally brings responsibility for real-estate taxes, we do not speak of the taxes as the *cost* of the property itself. Contrastingly, the taxes were indeed the cost of an eleventh- or twelfth-century magnate's land. It was understood that the king was the ultimate owner of all properties in his kingdom, and ownership in fee meant that an "owner" was obligated to provide the king with services. These were the condition of "ownership." Now the obligatory services might take numerous forms: the supply of contingents of knights, payment of a monetary sum, provision of goods for the royal household, etc. No one, not even the greatest magnate, held his lands "free and clear"—nor was the inheritability of property a simple issue.

Even when such conditional ownership was obviously burdensome, a great man was unlikely to shirk his service to the crown. For the lands he held under this system—his "fees," known also as "honors" or "baronies"—were not normally contiguous. They were hardly lined up side by side. A man might have certain properties here, others there, and still others elsewhere. His holdings did not have continuous and easily defensible borders, which meant that secession or rebellion was extremely difficult. The security of one man's real estate was interlocked with the security of others'—and with the maintenance of a tolerable level of peace within the kingdom at large. This method of distributing lands appears, therefore, quite inefficient and odd at first glance. Actually it was quite efficient so far as a ruler's control of important subordinates is concerned.

But how would a land holder make good when his king demanded five or fifty knights? Often by granting *them* parcels within his own "fee"—even though they, in turn, might grant a section within their section to someone else, as payment for something further. This sequence could have been infinite except for one brute fact: there is an absolute limit to the quantity of land available for distribution. There were thus many landless knights—men trained for war as their one and only occupation. Some of their energies might be dissipated in the tournaments which were a fairly routine feature of late medieval life (and whose courtliness existed more in the literary romances than in reality). But tournaments did not provide land. Landless knights were still hungry for it and, so, were willing to sell their services to anyone who promised to deliver. As mercenaries, many knights' chivalric code came closer to honor among thieves than to the glowing picture constructed by later ages. As for the knight in shining armor, he was a literal impossibility since plate armor had not yet been invented. (In combat, a knight's body was protected by chain mail, a leather garment oversewn with metal rings.)

So much for the landless. What of the knights and others, higher up, who actually did "own" land? Since ownership was in fee, and since the *duration* of service owed and the question of property's transmissibility were both unclear, many a landowner—from the magnates on down—was less than content. When a man of property met his obligations over the years by repeatedly dividing that property, giving out a parcel here and another there, he might leave his heirs an inheritance much diminished from its original extent. Yet even when a man's prudence avoided this humiliation, the conditions of ownership under feudalism created persisting anxieties at the same time that they solved immediate problems.

The Robber Barons are not an original contribution of America's eighteen hundreds. The eleventh and later medieval centuries have bequeathed us a record of such men. Operating in various countries, they amplified their riches by preying upon anyone who travelled the public roads; sometimes their victims were pilgrims, sometimes itinerant merchants, sometimes members of the wealthier classes. The medieval countryside, in other words, was populated with thugs of varied social degree who pillaged and raped and murdered. Of course these activities were illegal. But even in criminal matters the law can be very remote, as any readers will know if they have traveled the unpaved public roads winding through national parklands in the western United

States. If today's traveller feels insecure in this kind of circumstance, he should not have much difficulty in imagining the feelings of medieval men and women, for whom almost all roads (in varying states of disrepair) presented a reasonable probability of danger—perhaps death. Nor was life for a villager necessarily better, since the same marauders could sweep down on his fragile home and take what they wanted. The inhabitants were frequently murdered in the process. Still, set murder aside and imagine. When thieves took a poor man's cow, for example, they might be stealing property which was critical for his livelihood. In other words, life outside a protected fortress or city walls was highly risky business. The powerful and ruthless found easy targets.

One should not, however, settle for the notion that *inside* the walls was all risk free or especially pleasant. Wastes, human and animal, were allowed to accumulate in the streets of medieval cities. Poor sanitation and sometimes-tainted foods made serious disease and illness ever-pressing realities. As for armed bullies, the countryside could claim no monopoly. And when pickings in the countryside were lean, one might encounter real wolves joining wolfish men on the streets of a city like Paris. A stroll after sundown was definitely not recommended. Should the traveller then stick to the comforts inside? Probably, though a medieval inn (regardless of country or city location) was itself not all that safe—thanks both to itinerant criminals who mingled easily with their prospective victims (especially when two or three men had to share a single bed for the night) and to avaricious and slippery innkeepers. Even allowing for the protection fortifications provide, life in the secular realm could prove tough going.

Nevertheless, I would not want to close these comments without mention of monasteries and abbeys and convents. Many of these housed men and women whose contributions to human life were positive and substantial. Yet monastic discipline, to a large extent essential to orders' effective activity, was hardly accepted with cheer in all quarters. Hence the number of monastic reform movements, initiated by the church itself, which sought to return fallen away religious men and women and their communities to observance of the rule which at least technically governed most of them. Three reform popes (Innocent III, 1198 accession to the papacy; Honorius III, 1216 accession; and Gregory IX, 1225 accession) gave great impetus to these movements for change. As one can see from a reading of the *Register* or travel chronicles of Eudes of Rouen (Odo Rigaldi: c. 1205–76), the problems were serious from the viewpoint of a man who—though neither sadistic nor cruel—took the ideals of monasticism and religious life seriously. But the patterns of conflict, sometimes violent, had been set in motion long before the time of either Odo—of Rouen or of Cheriton. (Taylor's *Mediaeval Mind* provides a good overview in "The Spotted Actuality," his study's twenty-fifth chapter.)

A single example will do. Abbo of Fleury (c. 940–1004), educated in one of the monasteries which had been influenced by the reforming work of Odo of Cheriton's patron saint (Odo of Cluny), was a man of learning who invested himself heavily in those earlier reform efforts. His life—and death—will sound a familiar chord for any who have already read Odo of Cheriton's actual text. Abbo visited a number of monasteries where monks were in conflict with their superiors, seeking on these journeys to resolve the difficulties so that a community might redirect its energies to genuinely religious ends. His final such visit was not final because he wished it to be. Rather, the monks of the La Réole monastery murdered him. It was a violent end, brought about by men officially committed to an institution and to values which provided no sanction for such an act. But the story gives the lie to one popular picture, that which displays medieval religious as emotionally lobotomized men and women whose only concerns were of heaven. Their lives involved much more than endless, hymn-singing processions. Neither emotionally nor intellectually were these routinely dull people. But there is obviously a negative side to vitality and energetic determination, whether we are speaking of secular or religious men. In countryside, village, and city, as well as in monastery and abbey (rural or urban), the ambitious and rapacious could enjoy good hunting and often make their kill.

That metaphor speaks to one pervasive flaw in medieval life. Often, as we moderns like to say of our own world, it was "a jungle out there"—or at least a forest. The actual forests and wildlife throw our attention to another of the aspects of medieval life, one which—like its metaphorical counterpart—involved real conflict and danger. As all land remained ultimately the king's (even when granted in fee), so too did the forests of the land. Here, however, the king's precedence was not just ultimate but immediate. The Norman kings and lords seem to have had a near addiction to hunting, and to preserve this pleasure the kings had the Forest Law which was laid down by William the Conqueror. The beasts of the chase—three varieties of

21

deer and the wild boar—were their property. And as for the chase itself, it was an elaborate ritual culminating in an elaborate "division" of the kill and procession homeward. (The ritual, even though clerical opposition to hunting was strong, was detailed in actual treatises on the art.)

Still, the Forest Law was widely hated. Much territory subject to the Law was on lands held in fee, land on which not only manors but whole villages were located. Yet a hungry man who needed the forbidden game for food could take it only at great danger to himself. Especially when it came to deer and the boar, the penalties were severe. Moreover, even the wolf was technically protected—although wolves were such a menace that killing one was no real risk on the legal side. Sometimes the king granted formal exemptions, thus allowing some subjects to take specified non-chase animals. Wolves were among these, but the fox, cat, and hare were also prominent on the list—presumably because they endangered both the beasts of the chase and domesticated animals as well.

It is worth mention that, when the fables of Odo are compared to his presumed sources, the wolf, fox, cat, and hare stand out especially—a matter whose significance I urge readers to consider. Whatever we make of this, though, a formal grant of exemption gave its recipient "rights of warren" in specified forest lands (usually those located on his own fees). What did such a grant mean, practically speaking? The freedom to hunt non-chase animals that threatened the recipient's own livestock and crops. Indeed in 1213–14 William, Odo's own father, paid so that he might have "warren" in the family holdings around Cheriton.

This transaction again drives home the interplay of the Cheriton family's activities with the customs and institutions of the age. But documented transactions can be supplemented by direct consideration of *The Fables.* Suppose readers could know Odo only through this one work. Suppose no non-literary evidence at all were available. Most readers, so I would guess, could not imagine *The Fables'* author having been restricted to a strictly bookish experience of the medieval countryside—the specifically English countryside and forests where the Normans loved to hunt, included. Their inferences would not be likely to stop there. What other things might they—might we—feel impelled to suspect?

For Odo to write as he did, he had to be aware of the perils and possibilities of religious life, both in its cloistered and non-cloistered forms. Moreover, we would judge he had to have an understanding of life within medieval cities and villages, and on the roadways connecting them as well. He had to have known and have thought about the character of men of property, and also the character of those landless men who aspired to ownership of property and enjoyment of worldly wealth. He had to know too that the rich and those aspiring to riches might be found among both secular and religious men. (Indeed where greed and its companion, oppression, were in the saddle, the "secular-religious" distinction seems to have been of slight importance to Odo — except perhaps insofar as a religious vocation made vice all the more reprehensible.) And if it might be too much to claim that our author had plumbed the essential depths of some unchanging human nature, it does not seem excessive to suggest that he had spent a lot of time observing the ways of men in a society whose dominant institutions were feudal and religious. Nor does it seem unwarranted, given the very existence of *The Fables,* for us to infer that Odo's observations were made from a stance which we may term "passionate disinterestedness" — a stance simultaneously entailing feelingful, involved perception *and* the "psychic distance" which saves a writer from immobilizing rage and allows his pen to move freely and comprehendingly. Thus many an entry in *The Fables* tells us that religious institutions were Odo's special preoccupation — and special target. Yet the same work clearly shows that this concern was part of something bigger. Page after page discloses an inclusive vision of human society, a vision informed by developed moral-religious commitments *and* by a sharp awareness that individual virtues and vices become actions with enormous consequences for all lives, all communities, all institutions.

In looking at Odo's life and times we have touched upon all the issues mentioned above. Before going on, however, we need briefly to note two matters which would be hard to fit in at any particular point in our historical account — yet which will stand out with special prominence for twentieth-century readers: the status of Jews and the status of women.

It is clear that Odo shared the beliefs of many Christians of his time with regard to Jews. While the period we are discussing saw great interaction among proponents of Christianity, Judaism, and Islam, this interaction did *not* produce widespread tolerance or a religiously pluralistic culture. On the Continent there were flourishing Jewish com-

23

munities. Yet Jews tended to be regarded in the same category as heretics, schismatics, "Saracens," "pagans," and "gentiles" (one of Thomas Aquinas' two *summae* is directed, in the tradition of missionary theology, *contra gentiles*). It is possible, of course, to paint a picture showing that this various category posed a substantial threat to the coherent survival of the distinctively Christian civilization which had emerged in Western Europe and England. I find such a picture less than persuasive. But readers may be helped by a distinction which is implied by Odo himself. He holds that a hard judgment, the judgment of a just God, will ultimately fall upon those who attack or are outside of the church of Christ. (One may better grasp the meaning of his position by a bit of translation, by thinking of such persons as unscientific or pseudo-scientific rather than — in a twentieth-century sense — as unchristian or heretical; Odo and his contemporaries tended to see these individuals as treating the one true basis of knowledge, reason, and morality either selectively or indifferently.) *He also holds that a Jew is a far more desirable neighbor than a corrupt priest.* Odo states this position in personal terms, and readers of *The Fables* will find in his text the basis for my ascribing it to him.

But if Jews and Judaism are not touched upon either frequently or with personal animosity in *The Fables,* what of women? This too requires a divided answer, one which continues to resonate in our own time. For Odo and many of his contemporaries, women embody both transcendent goodness and a deep, vicious sensuality. This sensuality emerges in Odo's pages as a continuing threat to a virtuous life. Women lure males to satisfy their appetites in accordance with nature, rather than transform those appetites so as to bring themselves into correspondence with Nature or God. Yet women are also seen as dangerous *to themselves.* Their sexuality-sensuality is a weakness which prompts them to forget the laws of God and the civil laws — those governing the sacrament of marriage, for example. In their weakness, then, women are to be protected (if need be, from themselves) in the same way that all the weak and impoverished are to be shielded from oppressors. When their weakness manifests itself as fiendish power, as a danger to men, they are to be shunned and even punished. When they seek virtue then their status, like that of Ruth, is a very different matter. Writing of the literature of Odo's time, Joan Ferrante reports that women "are not portrayed as 'real people' with human problems; they are symbols, aspects of philosophical and psychological problems that trouble the male world." (Readers interested in exploring this issue may turn to Ferrante's study, listed in the bibliography).

Regarding Jews and women, I have noted prejudices which many readers will dislike intensely. However it is important to understand that these views — distasteful and ugly as we may find them — were not peculiarly Odo's. From the perspective of our time and our place, they were serious flaws; but they were flaws common to the society at large. Saying this makes them no more attractive in their twelfth- than in their twentieth-century setting. Yet precisely because it is so easy to see which beliefs of other societies are prejudices — and so difficult to see the prejudices of one's own time — it is important to avoid being self-congratulatory. Telling ourselves that we live in a post-prejudicial age not only contradicts the record of our century. It also legitimates intolerance in the name of tolerance. What is more, it leads us to give certain aspects of *The Fables* disproportionate prominence and, perhaps, even to miss Odo's actual achievement and the delight it can yield. To make the point in general terms: if we banish (prohibit?) every work which contains disgusting "prejudices," there is an excellent chance that we will find ourselves unable to read — and think.

Yet the world of Odo's day was, in definite and striking ways, very different from our own. If we can avoid being censorious about the points of difference we react to most forcefully, we stand a much better chance of understanding what is really happening in *The Fables*. Such has been my main concern throughout this abbreviated history of life in the twelfth and thirteenth centuries. Now is the time, therefore, to explain what is special in my account.

What I have set forth is not, in spite of this section's title, an attempt to simply cover a "field" of data. I have not laid out what is usually called a survey of the times, an account of the medieval world picture, or the like. My concern has been to isolate those aspects of Odo's landscape which he himself brought to the foreground in his fables. Chicanery and nastiness and danger and violence stand out with a sharpness which would be — given different purposes, a different vantage point — quite exaggerated. Not *all* knights and barons were ruffians. Not *all* wanderers and innkeepers can have been venal and corrupt. And not *all* brothers and bishops were brigands in disguise.

The eleventh through thirteenth centuries saw a great burgeoning of trade and the revitalization of cities. (Which caused which is a matter of debate on which readers may consult the works of Pirenne and Mumford.) By most accounts, the free cities of the later Middle Ages—with their free citizens, trade guilds, merchant class, abbeys and churches, masters and students in the university towns; with, in other words, a great diversity of people and vocations—are one of the genuine glories of Western civilization. The same centuries saw, within many of these very cities, the rise of the historically primary professions in conjunction with the rise of universities. For while medicine, law, and theology were all very old even in Odo's day, the emergence of these *as professions*—backed by specialized academic disciplines (derived from the liberal arts) and self-governing like the guilds—is new. At the same time, literary activity flourished. Odo was not alone. His was the time of what has been termed "the renaissance of rhetoric," the time of Geoffrey of Monmouth's *History of the Kings of Britain,* of varied epics by authors such as William of Orange, of Beroul's *Tristan,* Chretien de Troyes's *Percival* and other Arthurian romances, Wace's and Layamon's treatments of the British-Arthurian material, Guillaume de Lorris' and Jean de Meun's *Romance of the Rose,* Bernard Silvester's and Alanus de Insulis' philosophic poetry—the time of often-distinguished historical writings, of lyric poetry, of the satiric *Mirror for Fools* of Nigel Wireker (or Nigel Longchamp). And of fables. To turn aphoristic once more, Odo of Cheriton lived in a time of great peril and great promise—the worst and best of times.

Some of the promises were realized. For the able and fortunate there were opportunities such as Odo found available *and used.* To be sure, this introduction's emphasis has fallen upon perils and abuses, upon the worst. It is these, after all, which are Odo's primary concern as a moralist. It is these which so frequently are targeted to receive the barbs of his art. Moreover, Odo is a special sort of moralist—at least in a number of his fables. Some of his narratives may be heard as straightforward cautionary tales. But many are properly (if loosely) to be termed "satiric"—that is, they are fictions designed primarily to attack. Odo's attacks should not be identified with those of a Jonathan Swift, for they do not go after specific historical persons. When a fable by Odo has attack as one of its purposes, the attack is invariably directed at a generic target or victim: a class of people, do-nothing rulers, an order of monks, a way of life. Odo's attacks seem not to be the sort which we read as primarily punitive (I borrow this, and the contrasting term, from Edward Rosenheim); they are more nearly persuasive —fictive commentaries on the abuses and abusers of his age, but commentaries and attacks which seek to transform the way men see themselves and their world and, therefore, the way they act. The goal is not simply to punish but to correct.

There is a logic as well as a rhetoric to this. The logic involves a correspondence theory of truth—a theory, Augustinian in its origins, which does not limit itself to verbal propositions but extends into the nature of things. Its working is well illustrated by the work *On Truth* by Odo of Cheriton's contemporary, Robert Grosseteste (c. 1175–1253). Taking the universe in which we live to be hierarchically ordered, Grosseteste writes: "The same thing can be true and false, as a true man is an animal, which is composed of body and rational soul. Augustine also makes the same distinctions: *if he is mendacious and vicious, he is a false man.*" In other words, man as man has a body and a *rational* soul; his nature in the order of Nature is defined by specific attributes and capacities. If a man's life and action are not governed by the nature which is specifically his, if his life-action is not ruled by reason, then his nature does not correspond to Man's proper nature. Just as statements are false when they fail to correspond with what is the case, so a man who fails of correspondence is a *false man.* Now the fabulistic point comes home. A false man's life and action may successfully correspond to the attributes defining a lower nature. They may correspond to those of an animal lacking a rational soul. They may correspond to those of a beast, and the *false* man may be disclosed as *truly* bestial—a wolf, a fox, a hateful serpent, etc. (One modification of this scheme is available to literature more easily than to philosophy, however. Some lesser creatures—sheep and oxen, for example—have a metaphoric value which makes them anything but bestial. Thus in certain fictive contexts, a man whose nature corresponds in some aspect—gentleness, for instance—to that of a sheep has not descended in the hierarchy. Far from being bestial he may truly be living in imitation of Christ!)

Nothing I have said denies that Odo's art is, in the most literal sense moral. To the contrary, my intent has been to affirm that characterization and expand its significance. For in an Augustinian framework, philosophy takes logic and ethics (God the Son being the *ratio intelligendi* of rational science and the Holy Spirit the *ordo vivendi* of moral science) as two of its three divisions. And in any case the divisions are mutually validating in *The Fables* since the logic—ultimately dependent upon a third philosophic division (God the Father, first person of the Trinity, being the *causa subsistendi* of natural science or

27

physics)—finds a basis in the nature of things. This logic, ontic rather than strictly verbal, thus provides the grounding for Odo's ethics or moral-religious perspective.

Although simply assumed rather than explicitly set forth in *The Fables,* all this appears to be at work in our author's collection—a collection which seeks to open men's eyes and reorient their lives toward prudence and wisdom and charity, sometimes by exemplifying these virtues and more often by exposing or attacking embodiments of their opposites. These are the vices of folly and, in a broad and not exclusively sexual sense, lust. Such is the thrust of Odo's varied fables; it has determined many of the special emphases in our discussion of his life and times.

The Sources and Art of Odo's *Fables*

To my mind, the usual approach to sources is not—with signal exceptions—terribly helpful. If an understanding of art is what we are after, it is at best a starting point. Yet there are texts which a fairly uniform consensus tags as specific sources for *The Fables.* Certainly there is a good chance that Odo had either read these or works clearly stamped by their influence: the tenth-century collection of fables known as the *Romulus,* and the animal lore and observation to be found in Pliny the Elder (his *Natural History,* Books VIII-XI), Isidore of Seville, and the various works known as bestiaries and *Physiologus.* Hervieux, moreover, was persuaded that Odo knew the works of the ancient fabulist Phaedrus (on which the *Romulus* is based) "in their totality." And Schofield—noting Odo's use of names like "Isengrim" for the wolf, "Tib" for the cat, "Reynard" for the fox—concluded that our author "shows acquaintance with" the *Romance of Reynard.* As I have already said, there is a good chance Odo had read most or some of these texts. Still, if calling something a "source" means claiming that it stood open on an author's desk as he wrote, then I do not see how we can claim to know Odo's sources at all.

This may be just as well. If we were to proceed as some have from time to time, we would go on to take the content of an author's probable sources and *subtract* it from the content of the work we're seeking to understand. Then we would conclude that the remainder—assuming something would be left by that point—represents our author's original invention. Although a good deal of critical work and editing has been done in this fashion, I may be picturing an extreme case. Frankly, I hope so. But however this may be, my point is that the approach I've characterized tends to be pretty mechanical and dead end.

Some scholars and medievalists might object that my comments fall short of picturing the real interest and complexity of current critical work on the literature of the Middle Ages—or, for that matter, on the whole range of literary achievement. There would be justification for their complaint, of course, since the approach described above (and tracing back to much nineteenth-century work) has been supplemented by work (its practitioners calling themselves "historical critics") which peels away the "husk" of a poem or narrative to disclose its nourishing, non-original "kernel" of doctrine. Here, the subtractive process is not expected to leave us with a remainder which might be called original, since historical criticism begins with the assertion that real originality was foreign to the genius of medieval culture (though verbal, expressive originality is admitted).

However interesting a more detailed analysis of critical approaches might be, and even granting their considerable influence, this introduction's argument suggests something more urgent. For us as readers —seeking to be moved and amused, challenged and changed—the question of how much is borrowed and how much is invented is not of much importance in itself. So far as our experience is concerned, what counts is a writer's art—his *use* of materials, his transformation of traditions. It is this which affects and alters our lives. And it may well be that what is genuinely original is an author's work, the aesthetic whole— not some separable or abstractable or subtractable part of it. Granted all the force of the creativity metaphor, writers are normally grateful at not being burdened with God's task in Genesis. They do not have to create out of nothing, and from the lifting of this requirement comes their special happiness. In need of creative resources, they regard tradition as a source of materials (and I use that term quite broadly). Tradition is not a heavy bundle which cripples the innovator. Far from being dead weight, it enables.

With these comments, we are on our way to discussion of sources of a much wider variety. This does not rule out the more specific kind at all, but now we are in a position to begin thinking about what writers do with inherited tales, images, ideas, and so on. So we will be well repaid if we give additional attention to sources of a less exclusive variety—to enabling *resources*. These are all writers' common property, a kind of communal storehouse filled with rhetorical-grammatical figures, useful conventions, and traditional forms (such as "the fable"). Discussion of this common store is specially to the point for us since Odo of Cheriton drew from it so freely.

One consequence of Odo's free borrowing is that his fables, taken together, read like an epitome of much Western literature. They summarize a generous range of literate experience and may, indeed, provide an introduction to that experience—even for readers inclined to follow Macrobius and assign the genre fable low rank. Though one commonly accepted picture of medieval life suggests that men of these centuries were dull authoritarians with little to read beyond the Bible and Aristotle, a different painting is uncovered when we read through *The Fables*. Odo delights in exploiting varied figures of thought and speech, numerous narrative conventions, and established "forms." Grammatical and logical schemata as well as verbal turns and puns; such conventions (though not "mere conventions") as were codified in how to books on the art of writing; aphorism and Senecan moral essay and courtly romance along with bluntly obvious beast fable and apologue —all of these and more mark *The Fables* in abundance.

The figures or schemata, like the narrative conventions, are important because Odo's handling of them gives individual pieces (whatever their source) a unique form which is recognizably traditional *and* novel. Here, in other words, our primary focus will be on things which clarify the particular form—the artfully realized structure—of the bulk of these narratives. To sort matters out in a rather rough and commonsensical way which should, nevertheless, ring true to many readers' experience, Odo's fables seem to fall into four groups: (1) apologues or "cautionary tales"—i.e., tales giving prominence to people rather than to personified animals (though animals may be included, but only on the periphery of the action or as occasion for its development); (2) beast or animal fables (these sometimes include people, but on the periphery of the action); (3) mixed fables, i.e., fables in which the interaction of animals and people is a central plot focus; and (4) virtually plotless but moralized animal lore. This is, I admit, no more than a simple subject-matter grouping. And the first three groups might well be treated as one, so far as form—in a strict sense—is concerned. They are three varieties of moral, instructive, didactic tale (perhaps distinguished by little more than their material content), three varieties of narrative organized for the purpose of stating an argument.

Yet it is also the case that we readers *do* respond to the deeds of persons—however much they are caricatured—in one way, and to the deeds of personified animals (and plants, too!) in another. For a twentieth-century reader, in fact, the word *fable* almost always calls up "animal fable"—usually accompanied, let us add, by a memory that the literature so designated is something we read as children. Thus the distinctions here introduced, however rough, may work as a useful starting point for drawing out the real diversity one encounters in a collection like Odo's—especially when we bring in the mediating role of "commentary" (traceable to the tradition of biblical commentary we discussed with reference to our author's theological education), along with the other items of "common property" mentioned a few paragraphs back, in giving his fables their particularized real world application and literary bite. These are fables that do not just address issues of the day. They do so with style.

Apologues

Even given our stress on Odo's knowledge of biblical commentary, it would not be particularly helpful to attempt to fit his fables into the format of one school of exegesis (say, the "fourfold method" as expressed by Thomas Aquinas in *Summa Theologica*, Part I, Question 1, Article 10). Indeed, only seven out of Odo's one hundred and seventeen fables begin a "commentary section" with the adverbial "MYSTICALLY. . . ." (Not all of his fables even have distinct commentaries.) The commentaries in those seven, moreover, are neither identical with one another in purpose or procedure nor markedly different from a number of other commentaries Odo wrote without benefit of the "mystical" opener. Yet nothing just said denies the power of Odo's art and method as a theological writer. The emphasis simply falls on *writer.*

Allow me to spell this out by way of example. Let us take a straightforward apologue—one without animals and, also, without any separate commentary. By and large, such commentary as there is, is built into the narrative itself. I have in mind Odo's tale of three homicidally inclined monks. We are familiar, from our treatment of Odo's life and times, with the real-life circumstances which form the background of "An Abbot, Food, and Some Monks" (number 6). Its argument might be paraphrased as an injunction: Think before you rebel, since those who now abuse you are likely to be succeeded by people even more abusive. But this statement is hopelessly "flat." The actual tale makes its point quite differently—grammatically, in fact—by showing us the conspirators in action. We have no idea what they look like, but note how Odo uses dialogue to put their manner of talking and thinking in the foreground.

Our monks endure a sequence of three abbots. The first permits three meals a day, the second only two, and the third but one. The first, from their point of view, is *bad*. (These are obviously gluttonous monks!) They ask God to arrange his death—though the text is quite ambiguous as to just how the abbots actually die. In any case, the first abbot is succeeded by one who is *worse*—one whose death brings, in turn, the third and *worst*. Odo has run his tale through positive, comparative, and superlative degrees of the adjective to bring us—and one grammatically astute monk—to a paradox and a question. What is the comparative of a superlative? What can conceivably be worse than the worst? Something "worse" than the "worst," like something "better" than the "best" or "greater" than the "greatest," is of course literally *in*conceivable (Odo's monks are experiencing the obverse of Anselm's so-called ontological argument!)—which is precisely the point. It makes the threat all the more threatening. "I can see that the first abbot was bad, the second worse, and *this* one the worst. I am terrified that, when the third is dead, yet another will come after him—someone even worse —who will use starvation to completely wipe us out." The plans to pray for the abbot's death are set aside and we, the readers, are stung with an English aphorism which states the argument we paraphrased somewhat laboriously when beginning our discussion of this fable.

Both tale and argument are simple enough. But the sparkle of Odo's initial conception, his use of dialogue, the way the abstract grammatical sequence is brought to the foreground (while matters of appearance, physical circumstance, and the actual dying of two abbots are kept present as part of an unobtrusive and largely implied background), the speed of presentation which results from the way foreground and background are manipulated, the dramatically paradoxical character of the sequence (not only are comparatives of superlatives

32

inconceivable, but as the narrative takes us "up" in the number of abbots the daily meals come "down" and the "progression" becomes a "regression"), as well as the effective closure provided by the explosive "pop" of what is apparently a piece of folk wisdom — all these are far from simple. They are the delightful complexities of art.

There is no need to claim that Odo is equally successful every time. But among the entries I would count as apologues, "Walter's Search for the Happy Place"(number 40; this reads like a condensed version of Dr. Johnson's eighteenth-century *Rasselas*), "The Fraudulent Scheme of a Count" (number 76), and "Playing Chess" (number 55; though very different in artistic conception, this one rivals "Some Monks" for brilliance) are very much deserving of attention. Odo's successes, however, are not limited to apologues. He is fully capable of taking a traditional animal fable and retelling it with special point and force.

Animal Fables

Take "The Wolf and Lamb Who Were Drinking," subtitled: Against oppressors of the poor. (Technically, such a "subtitle" is the promythion.) This fable (number 37) is so short that we may cite it in full:

> A wolf and a lamb were drinking from the same stream. And the wolf said: "Why are you muddying my water?" "I'm doing nothing of the sort," the lamb replied, "for you are drinking upstream; and the water flows down from you to me." The wolf came back at him: "Curse you! For you are contradicting me!! Who are *you* to be so arrogant?!" And he immediately devoured the lamb.
>
> Thus rich men, for no cause at all — and regardless of how the poor respond — devour them.

I can't imagine how this could be improved upon, and it is unquestionably one of my personal favorites. It is also a fable with sources upon sources: Aesop himself, Phaedrus (who wrote in Latin verse), Babrius, Odo's near contemporary Berechiah ha-Nakdan (the "Jewish Aesop"), the tenth-century prose paraphrase of Phaedrus we know as the *Romulus,* antecedent and/or contemporary folk "literature," and many others. Anyone wishing to discover how abundant these sources actually are can consult Joseph Jacobs' "Synopsis of Parallels" (in his *History*), B. E. Perry's "Analytical Survey" (in his Loeb *Babrius and Phaedrus*), and — in conjunction with Perry — Stith Thompson's *Motif-Index*. Fortunately for our purposes, it is likely that Odo had an identifiable *immediate* source for "The Wolf and Lamb Who Were Drinking," namely the *Romulus*. This work, viewed in contrast to Odo's version, may clarify the decisions which give the telling in *The Fables* its peculiar force.

Here is the *Romulus* "Wolf and Lamb" (I, ii) which, we note, bears the subtitle: "Aesop told this fable concerning the innocent and the depraved":

> Being thirsty, a lamb and a wolf each made their way to a stream (though from opposite directions). The wolf was drinking his fill, and the lamb was far downstream from him. When he saw the lamb, the wolf spoke as follows: "You've been muddying the water which I have been drinking from." The patient lamb replied: "How have I been making the water muddy for you, the water that runs *down* — from you to me?"
>
> The wolf did not blush at the truth. "You're cursing me," he said. The lamb replied: "I spoke no curse."
>
> "Now your father," said the wolf, "was here six months ago, and he did the same thing to me."
>
> "I wasn't born then, was I?"
>
> The wolf with his depraved jaws said: "And you'll keep on talking even now, you brigand?!" And he immediately lunged at the lamb and ripped out the life of the innocent one.
>
> This fable was told with reference to those men who maliciously lay charges against others.

There is no point in pretending that the *Romulus* gives us an unskilled narrative. Yet Odo's version may be superior and is certainly quite different. To my eye, two contrasts (closely related) stand out. First, Odo's version of the fable takes aim at a far more specific target than that of the *Romulus*. (Arnold Henderson, in studies to which I am much indebted, has explored this issue in detail.) The *Romulus*, true to the general drift of the animal-fable tradition prior to Odo's time, makes a general moral point. In contrast to Odo's piece, the *Romulus* version of "Wolf and Lamb" seems to *exemplify* the evils of depravity and slander. This is not to suggest that it commends either. Yet it does not "take aim" as does Odo's little narrative. "The Wolf and Lamb Who Were Drinking" specifies its target more narrowly and with greater concrete immediacy. It draws a bead, not on a broad category of vice but on a particular social class—on abusive men of wealth. Hence it is, by contrast, a piece built more to *attack* rather than simply exemplify an evil.

My second observation is intimately tied to my first. The gross signal here is the differing lengths of the two fables. The *Romulus'* "Wolf and Lamb" is just shy of being three-fourths longer than *The Fables'* parallel account. Length of course has no significance in itself, but it is worth mention here because the difference is a consequence of a special reshaping and transformation. Odo appears to have worked out particular changes *because* he is on the attack. He has increased the velocity and precision with which his narrative impacts upon or hits the mark which is his chosen target. In short, Odo's variation on this old and often-told fable has a new form because he made that fable mean and function in a novel way. The question is, how? How did he do the job?

Intent to narrow the tale's focus is clear from the onset due to the contrast between the two versions' subtitles (promythia). I suspect this is obvious. Not so obvious, perhaps, are the systematic changes in detail which make Odo's transformation effective—which draw a new argument into the foreground.

Odo has eliminated redundancies and extraneous matter. Thus he does not *tell* us that the lamb was downstream from the wolf and then, in addition, *show* us the same point by having one of the characters make mention of it. Neither does he bother to tell us that both wolf and lamb were thirsty (most readers will take this for granted), or that they got to the stream from different directions. (Is anyone really likely to think they came arm-in-arm?) Since Odo has eliminated matters of minimal relevance to his point, he opens his narrative with the two characters already involved in taking their drinks at the stream. Then immediately, rapidly we are moved into the central conflict. And this is itself developed with great speed. The lines of dialogue (not so many as in the *Romulus* version) fly back and forth, quickly shaping the situation. Further, the *Romulus* conveys the personalities of wolf and lamb by description—mentioning the wolf's failure to blush and terming his jaws "depraved" (*improbus*), referring to the lamb as "patient" or *patiens*—and then fills them out by bringing in the things these characters say and do. Not *The Fables*. Odo economically discloses his characters' personalities through their statements and actions alone.

Consonant with the newly drawn target of Odo's recounting, the entire business of the wolf recalling what the lamb's father once did, all this is dropped. Odo simply renders the wolf as a master of instantaneous translation—or *mis*translation! The lamb expresses disagreement with the premise underlying the wolf's question ("Why are you muddying my water?"). And the wolf promptly translates expressed disagreement as expressed arrogance—*et es ita audax?*—then swiftly proceeds to further translation. This time the (mis)translation is not done in words but action. We readers may say that in the wolf's mistranslation "arrogance" equals "deserving of death." But that is an inference. Odo's actual wolf doesn't bother to *say* anything. He doesn't speak. He simply eats the lamb.

In all of this, nothing the poor lamb says or does is rendered as a plausible provocation or cause of the wolf's action—which is of course Odo's point precisely. "Thus rich men, *for no cause at all*—and regardless of how the poor respond—devour them." This, the fable's moral (more properly, epimythion) has the sting of an aphorism, partly because of its brevity and partly because of the artfulness of the little narrative from which it follows. And, also, partly because of the rapidity with which it uncovers the fable's specific target. If we wish to think of one line as a compressed "commentary," we must certainly say that it is aphoristic commentary which effects a shock of recognition. It moves us abruptly and disjunctively—there is no transition beyond the simple *ita*, "thus"—into the fully human world in which rich men are obviously false men because they act with all the rational moral subtlety of the worst of predators. (To replay an issue we touched upon earlier, readers are unlikely to think of this fable's poor men as "false" even though their conduct—like that of rich men—is rendered in animal terms; for the specific animal, the lamb, has a range of associations —gentleness, meekness, humility, innocence, indeed the virtues of the Lamb of God—which make likeness to a lamb an "ascent" rather than a "descent" in the scale of things. Of course, some creatures like the serpent have diverse associations which can push either up or down, toward good or evil; in such cases, everything depends upon the specific fictional context.)

Odo's retelling of this tale derives its effect largely from a remarkable compression and economy. A great deal of exposition is folded into the fable's dialogue and action. The new figure which communicates his point stands out sharply, etched with sparing yet vivid lines. The inclusiveness and diffuseness of Odo's source (the *Romulus*) have been replaced by a more daring, more pointed plot and argument. To give general and genial moral advice is one thing. To risk the truly parabolic, to cast a spear at a whole class of men who are conscious of their status as a class, is another. And to carry out an attack with such skill that even those being attacked might well respond with laughter (and even with a recognition that common goods exist for some purpose other than being looted, that, too, one's fellow creatures exist for some purpose other than being devoured?) is both high comedy and high art. The skillful compression and economy we have observed well serve the strategy of attack or, moderating the point a bit, of chastisement. The fable moves as swiftly as an arrow loosed by a master archer, making "The Wolf and Lamb Who Were Drinking" not only a construction in language but also (in a sense) a reasoned action which seeks to affect both perception and action.

This is so because seeing the world and oneself differently *is* an action with the potential to rectify subsequent action. When a parabolic fable is adequately internalized by a reader, then it is not mere hyperbole for us to claim that *the fable as verbal construct "self-destructs."* To quote Wittgenstein's explanation (from earlier in this century) in closing out a work which he, like Odo, termed a *tractatus:*

> My propositions serve as elucidations in the following way: anyone who understands me eventually recognizes them as nonsensical, when he has used them — as steps — to climb up beyond them. (He must, so to speak, throw away the ladder after he has climbed up it.) *He must transcend these propositions, and then he will see the world aright.*

In one way, then, the conclusion of a fable — like the conclusion of a practical syllogism — is not a verbal proposition, a moral or epimythion, but an inner transformation which does away with summary words as it gives birth to novel action and capacity for vision.

This brings us to an issue whose discussion does not neatly fit into any particular fable group among the four already distinguished. Yet we can hardly avoid noticing, as we read *The Fables'* various entries, that there are "conclusions" and "conclusions." That is, different fables communicate their meaning, conclude, and effect a sense of closure in quite different ways. And the differences cut across all four of our groups. Even the two pieces already looked at do the job differently. Odo's tale of monks and abbots gives us the "sense of an ending" by citing—first in English, then in Latin translation—an aphorism probably drawn from folk sayings. Our author's tale of wolf and lamb closes out with even greater brevity; its single concluding sentence has, we justifiably recall again, the sort of sting which makes it aphoristic. That single sentence, let us further add, turns the tale into a unique whole by making it a miniature allegory of sorts. It becomes a complete fictive proportion: the relation of wolf to lamb is that of rich man to poor. Now since both fables' conclusions reflect back upon, illuminate, and produce wholeness of meaning in the narratives that precede them— the first does it by *universalizing* meaning, the second by explicitly "translating" meaning into the world of human beings while simultaneously *particularizing* that meaning—we may understandably wish to speak of these conclusions as a form of commentary. In some sense, so they are.

On the other hand, most readers of Odo will quickly observe a difference between fables with brief, pithy "commentaries" (such as the two just replayed) and fables with commentaries elaborate enough that the text itself seems to call one's attention to two distinct sections: fable proper and discussion of the fable. Even if we view the two sorts of commentary as identical in function and say, for example, that both work to communicate the full impact of a tale, *our experience as readers will continue to insist upon a distinction.* This suggests that before finishing with animal fables and going on to others, we need to digress for a few moments and talk about those of Odo's commentaries which we perceive as relatively elaborate (and, therefore, as obviously commentaries). As it so happens, there really is no single animal fable with a commentary very fully illustrative of Odo's range of strategies as commentator. And I have, in consequence, selected several for discussion—acknowledging in advance that my accounts make no claim to exhaustiveness.

However, no such claim is needed to call in question the conviction which Ben Edwin Perry expressed (in the introduction to his *Babrius and Phaedrus*) by quoting with approval Joseph Jacobs' 1889 assertion that the Middle Ages' Latin fables are "Phaedrus with trimmings." Perry amplifies this by saying that the trimmings "were numerous," although the observation still seems to miss the point. Even so, the metaphor is interesting enough. As used by Jacobs and Perry, it draws its power from the assumption that the substance of a meal — the main course, or something along this line — is one thing, the trimmings something quite different. And quite dispensable.

This is at best only one way of looking at things. As we all know from experience, trimmings are not necessarily superfluous additions — inessentials attached to an already coherent whole. Frequently, we speak of those trimmings as *making* the whole (and not in the sense assumed when we think of a whole as the result of adding up or combining independent parts). Common idiom has it that simple arithmetic is inadequate, that a whole is more than the *sum* of its parts. Whatever that expression's exact meaning, our habits of speech often do imply that we see each part as a potential whole — as containing, so to speak, "the whole." People will say of the cranberry sauce or dressing or gravy, "it *makes* the meal." Our freedom to subtract all of these items, while leaving the remainder untouched, doesn't turn the solitary turkey into a turkey dinner. It doesn't make the trimmings extrinsic to the integral dining experience. Indeed, without the alleged trimmings we will feel that the turkey dinner isn't really a turkey dinner at all. We will feel it lacks the qualities that create an experience which is, in all senses of the word, *singular* — which is truly, as Dewey would put it, *an* experience. (Dewey's point is basic to the critical sections of this introduction, and some readers may wish to consult "Having an Experience," the third chapter in *Art as Experience*.)

Perhaps it will seem forced to join food and fables in discussion, though the analogy of eating with knowing is very old. Moreover, Joseph Jacobs' particular use of the phrase (it comes from the opening sentence of his *History of the Aesopic Fable*) has stood for roughly a century as the dominant characterization of medieval fables. Thus when Perry edited selections from Odo of Cheriton in his *Aesopica*, he printed fable after fable with all or part of the moralizing commentaries — the trimmings — removed. But if we are going to find nourishment and delight in *The Fables*, we will need to reconsider the reading habits which the Jacobs-Perry metaphor has prompted. Indeed, it is likely that successful dinners and successful fables are not put together through an additive procedure, through the combining of simple parts—some of which (from a culturally and scientifically more "advanced" perspective) deserve to be labeled unnecessary, extrinsic, and dispensable so far as the integrity of a whole as *an* experienced whole is concerned.

Odo's commentary sections are not, in Jacobs' and Perry's sense, trimmings at all. On the other hand, looked at another way, they are the kind of trimmings we spoke of as "making the meal"—the parts which make and are made by the meaning of the whole. However, the view I'm advancing needs to be filled out by direct discussion of several selected fables with prominent commentary sections. To give my conclusions in advance, these all seem to be fables whose commentaries *extend, explore, expand, and fill out* thematic meanings by articulating a new range of relations; regardless of how pointed and witty a particular piece's final line(s) may be, fables of this variety tend to emphasize a special concern for theological matters and the significance of sacred history. In contrast, fables with brief "commentaries" most often *apply* thematic meanings quite pointedly and aphoristically; however universalized or particularized, and however complex, the relations stated or implied by the conclusion may be, fables of this variety tend to emphasize the practical and immediate—i.e., the moral and social-institutional abuses of the time.

As we turn directly to the texts, our discussion will focus on four fables: "A Certain 'Bird of Saint Martin,'" "The Complaint of the Sheep," "Of the Rose and the Birds," and "The Dog and the Scrap of Meat" (numbers 14, 35, 81, and 91).

To start with, let us pick up "The Complaint of the Sheep." Its narrative can be summarized easily enough. Because the wolf has been eating up the sheep, they take their case to the lion who convenes "a royal council." The pigs give testimony on the wolf's behalf, since he has regularly cut them in on his "profits." The sheep then tell their side of the story, and the lion renders judgment. He has the wolf and the pigs executed. End of tale.

Or is it? Odo goes on to develop his narrative further, not by extending the chronological sequence of events but by developing an interpretation which doubles and transforms what has been given already. He establishes what some would call "allegorical correspondences" (though that expression—and indeed the whole notion of allegory—has acquired misleadingly static connotations). Thus we get literally couched phrases: "The wolves are," *lupi sunt.* "Christ's sheep (i.e., poor men)," *id est pauperes.* "To the pigs (i.e., to other rich fellows)," *id est aliter diuitibus.* Logicians and linguists sometimes worry over what *is* is. But to many readers these will look like simple, unambiguously literal, one-to-one identifications.

Whether this is an adequate description of what these phrases actually do, we should note that they are supported by verbal parallels. This device, technically termed "assimilation," is one of Odo's favorites and he uses it again and again (usually more extensively than here). Thus we are told in the fable's narrative that "the wolf frequently invited the pigs to join in feasting on the lambs and rams that he had seized [*rapuit*]"—and in the commentary that rich men "plunder [*rapiunt*] and ravage Christ's sheep." Once Odo has established these parallels—and, in fact, we will want to say more about their nature and the manner in which they *are* established—his commentary takes a notable turn.

Without warning or benefit of any special transition, we are thrown both forward and upward. The commentary presses toward the transcendent, the eschatological. The handing down of judgment becomes Judgment, the Last Judgment. There is no *est* or *id est* to identify the lion (ruler of the beasts) with God (ruler of the universe and its creatures). By now, apparently, we are supposed to make such connections without help. All alone, verbal repetitions and the relations they suggest convey the functional identity of lion and God: "And the lion said: 'Let judgment [*iudicium*] be given. Let the wolf be hanged [*suspendatur*]'"; "but the Lord will come to give judgment [*iudicium*]. . . . The Lord will order the wolves and pigs hung [*suspendi*] in hell." By this concluding sentence, of course, we should see the wolves as rich men and the pigs as their cronies—or, perhaps equally or even more to the point, we should see rich men and their cronies as wolves and pigs! The commentary, then, is no mere addition imposed upon the narrative but an artfully constructed extension of the analogies or proportions which structure it; the commentary fills out the narrative to its proper magnitude. (And the narrative, we must now add, fills out, transforms, and enhances the commentary's analysis. Narrative and commentary are mutually informing.)

Simple enough to read, this fable—I refer to the whole piece, both parts—is rich indeed. As we have seen several times previously, Odo is sharply conscious of grammatical distinctions. One particularly important here and used with considerable frequency throughout *The Fables* exploits the voice of verbs — active (as in *I hit* him) and passive (as in *I was hit* by him) — and their potential for distinguishing action from "passion," what a man does from what he suffers, what is done to him. Most commonly, perhaps, Odo presents a situation in which the hunter becomes the hunted. "The Complaint of the Sheep" gives us a somewhat different variation. The wolf (singular) acts, he preys upon the sheep (plural).* The sheep do nothing, they suffer. They do, however, *say* something. They lodge a complaint with the lion, with God. Since speech and action are merged in the Godhead — as in the opening of Genesis, where the mode of action *is* God's speech — His judgment is an action. And the wolf suffers. The passive sheep have, by speaking, been genuinely active. They have "brought an action" — and won! — in court.

We might say more about "The Complaint of the Sheep." Still, it is probably best to let any added illumination be a reflection from our treatment of three remaining fables. As a narrative, "The Dog and the Scrap of Meat" (number 91) is even easier to summarize than the one previous. A dog is crossing a stream while holding a scrap of meat in his mouth. He sees the scrap's shadow, grabs for it, and therefore loses the scrap. (As the meat drops, its shadow or *umbra* of course disappears.)

My paraphrase is hardly briefer than the original. In contrast, Odo's commentary runs several times the length of his narrative. As a commentary, though, this one presents an interesting mix of literal, analogical, and merely implied correspondences. Its first transition is a simple *sic*: "Thus there are many men who have the assurance of grace." Spelled out, we would say that many men are like the fable's dog. The reason for the likeness is that both have something — but in what sense are the things they have alike? How is the assurance of grace like a scrap of meat? (Note that the correspondence of "grace" and "meat" depends upon the relation of the thing "had" to the "holder"; this correspondence of relations is much elaborated but never *stated*.) It is, one might reply, as though our author were remembering Paul's

---

*Obviously this fable's singular-plural ("one-many") distinction is also grammatical and — even though the wolf becomes wol*ves* in the commentary — significant. For it drives home the contrast of rich exploiters, who are relatively few in number, with the poor exploited who are numerous.

contrast of "shadow" and "substance": "Let no one, then, call you to account for what you eat or drink or in regard to a festival or a new moon or a Sabbath. These are a shadow [*umbra*] of things to come, but the substance [*corpus*] is of Christ" (Colossians 2:16–17).

The pertinence of the shadow-meat contrast, given our purposes here, is relative "substantiality" and "reality." Compared to an utterly insubstantial shadow, the meat is obviously firm and solid and a potential source of nourishment—it is the *assurance* of grace. Shadows are utterly without substance, while even their appearance (and appearance is their only reality) lacks independence. Like reflections—in Phaedrus' first-century version of this tale the stream's surface acts like a mirror, so that the dog grabs not for a shadow but a reflection—they depend totally upon an "original" and upon a source of light external to themselves. Their being lacks an internal principle. The relation of meat scrap to shadow, then, is like the relation of grace (and a range of other things as well) to . . . ?

Let us remember that the dog, however deluded, *sees* the shadow. Men, however firm their hold on grace, *see* the shadow of this world— Odo's *umbra istius mundi*. But how are we to speak of the shadowiness of the world and worldly things? (A simple *scilicet* meaning "that is" or "namely" introduces, by the way, a list of concrete instances.) While the metaphor is so common as to have lost much of its metaphorical impact, the question is worth asking. And the answer comes from Odo's citation of the Bible. As for worldly affairs and goods, the Book of Wisdom (5:9–11) teaches that "all those things are passed away like a shadow [*umbra*], like a messenger who runs onward, and like a ship that passes through the waves . . . or as when a bird flies through the air, of the passage of which no mark can be found."

This answer itself sets forth a further series of correspondences. In particular circumstances, a bird is like a ship is like a messenger is like a shadow. All have in common a kind of insubstantiality, for whatever their substance they are transient. That which these images share, however, demands our visualizing the bird *in* the air, the ship *in* the waves—the meat scrap's shadow *in* the stream. The reason these new correspondences accomplish something, actually driving Odo's account forward, is to be found in this dependence. With great forcefulness, they draw out the poetic potential of the fable's stream. It becomes, as it were, the flux of human experience. And in that experience men see—seemingly just below the surface—apparent substances which they mistake for bigger and better offerings of the actual substances they have "in their mouths." (We all know what it means to believe in and desire something so much that we "can *taste* it.") They see lovely foods, voluptuous women, worldly dignities, and the like.

Suppose we take a moment for summary; so far, we have the following correspondences. The fable has assimilated most men to the dog, most men's experiences to the stream, their free assurance of grace to the meat scrap, and the worldly goods they willfully grasp for to the scrap's shadow. Granted the assimilations have been managed in several ways. But if the formal completion of a statement is what really counts, we now have a proportion that looks more than adequately filled out — and Odo's fable can end right here with the quotation from Wisdom. In fact it does not, and the reason why is worth asking.

Even at this point it is a nice question whether the citation from Wisdom illuminates the fable or whether the fable illuminates the words of scripture. Actually both processes are at work. And as Odo bridges quickly to an evocative water passage from Jeremiah — its imagery identifies living water with God, dry cisterns with transitory things — we are in transition from the Old Testament's didactic books to those often termed "prophetic." The truth of both acts to confirm the truth of the fable; it also sets us up for a further transition. Now our progression takes us to the *New* Testament, and to St. Augustine. This is not a matter of simply "adding" instances to some sort of expanding catalog; as Odo's earlier shift within the Old Testament might have led us to anticipate, we are moving toward a "higher" confirmation. (The teaching method of Jesus was *parabolic*. But I Corinthians 12:31/ 13:1 presents Christian charity as a literally *hyper-bolic* way which, like the cognate geometrical figure, "casts beyond" or "above," which "transcends" or "overshoots"— although for good reason, Paul's term is commonly rendered "more excellent.")

The quotation from Augustine is given first. According to this, men who prefer death to life, chaff to seed, etc., are false men. They are men — and now we have gone on to Paul's letter to the Romans — "who changed the truth of God into a lie," *qui commutauerunt ueritatem Dei in mendacium.* This comes from the quotation which rounds out the final sentence of Odo's fable. In stressing a kind of experimental verification (a logical procedure), Paul's words are like Augustine's. Both men's formulations turn on the distinction of true and false and — in the context Odo has provided — merge that distinction with the rhetoric and grammar of the Wisdom and Jeremiah passages. If we are focusing on function, the stress of the passage from Wisdom is rhetorical amplification. Jeremiah brings in a grammatical stress on the contrasting plurality of worldly things (cisterns are many) and singularity of the one God, "the fountain of living water." Sacred history, though, includes both testaments, both B.C. and A.D. Moreover, Augustine is clearly post-biblical. Why is it important that a reader take note of all this? Because the full verification or falsification of the fable's truth, its thorough testing against the accumulated or common experience of human beings, requires the attempt to merge it with the truth of history as a whole (not with that of one period only). It is thus that Odo's recasting of an ancient tale, "The Dog and the Scrap of Meat," emerges—not only rhetorically and grammatically but also logically—as a valid whole. The logic is historical and the history rational. History and fable, commentary and narrative fill one another with meaning.

Much the same kind of interplay informs "A Certain 'Bird of Saint Martin'" (number 14)—except that here it is given a somewhat different twist. A distinction we noted earlier in "The Complaint of the Sheep" is now recalled by our present fable's promythion ("Against those whose daring in *deeds* doesn't match their *words*"), thus signalling that the contrast will once more play an important role. And again we are looking at a text whose narrative is brief, easily summarized. A small, delicate Spanish wren (the Bird of Saint Martin) goes forth and lies on its back. The sun is blazing down and a tree is nearby. (We know the season is fall since the bird's venture is placed "on a day near the time of the festival of Saint Martin"—November 11.) He raises his spindly legs and boasts that he could hold up the sky were it to fall. Then a leaf drops from the tree and the bird flees, crying out, "Oh Saint Martin! Why don't you protect your little bird!?"

There is but one character in this narrative, so the commentary can treat both his and the situation's significance while still moving along quickly. In addition, because of this fable's similarity to the one we just discussed, many points can be left for readers to explore on their own. Matters that are uniquely handled, however, deserve comment.

The words-deeds distinction immediately comes into play, in the very first sentence of the commentary section. As we think about this we will want to remember that to believe, in an ecclesiastical context, is (among other things) to make a statement—to say "I believe." This is what *credo* means. Now our movement into Odo's commentary is managed deftly. A simple indication of likeness does the job: "Such are the many [men]," *talis sunt*—and Odo continues with delighted wordplay: "the many who believe [*credunt*] for a while—but who, in a time of trial, draw back [*recedunt*]." Like the wren, such men express confidence, *say* "I believe." Like the wren, in the face of "danger" they say something very different and *do* nothing —except flee (hardly the action they promised).

This correspondence established, another "such" quickly shifts us from "the many" to a particular instance, drawn from the New Testament —namely, Peter's denial of Christ. Peter *said* he would remain faithful to his Lord; then, seeing Him suffering and himself being recognized by a maidservant, Peter *said* he did not know Jesus at all. Like the wren, Peter affirmed then denied. He did not do what he had said he would do. But Odo's commentary does not stop with this, an instance drawn from a single period. The events of the New Testament may be overwhelmingly significant, but thoroughly measuring the fable against history requires attention to the Old Testament as well. Thus the next biblical citation reminds us that "the sons of Ephraim practiced bending and shooting their bows." Done in public, this is a kind of statement, a boast. "Then," Odo continues, they "turned their backs in the day of battle"—this being the equivalent of exclaiming while fleeing, "Oh Saint Martin!"

As in "The Dog and the Scrap of Meat," sacred history and fable illuminate one another. Even so, we are *not* moving through that history in chronological sequence (contrast our previous fable). In "A Certain 'Bird of Saint Martin'" the New Testament instance is first, the Old Testament, second; and the third and final instance is not, chronologically, a middle fitting between the two which are presented prior to it. So far as our present fable is concerned, chronology seems irrelevant to the function of the historical examples. It is as though we are being confronted with a moral dilemma—the split of words from works —to which the *content* of history is important, but not the *chronology*.

The fable's third example thus comes from well after New Testament times. (Indeed it is simplest to take it as roughly contemporary with Odo's own life.) Now we encounter soldiers. When drunk, they boast—they *say* they have the "power to withstand and war down three Franks apiece." But here Odo caps his tale by giving these do-nothing soldiers a line nearly identical to the wren's final words. Confronted with a real danger they *say,* "Oh Saint Martin, protect your little bird!"

True to its initial promise, this fable takes on those who say one thing and do another. It indicts men who claim the power to handle events of catastrophic, sometimes *unnatural* proportions — such as the falling of the sky — men who, in spite of their claims and "creeds," scream for help when they face something of *natural* magnitude (something to which their powers are in fact proportionate). And the indictment has, as noted, an historical dimension. Citations from sacred history illuminate the fable's meaning; reflexively, the fable illuminates the history and folk wisdom of the commentary. Literature and history and the folk wisdom embodied in the comic cry uttered by both bird and soldiers: all merge in a single piece which states a truth about human beings. But the eschatological interest of "The Complaint of the Sheep," along with the quest of "The Dog and the Scrap of Meat" for progressively higher levels of confirmation for the fable's truth, disappear in "A Certain 'Bird of Saint Martin.'" They are replaced by a quite different merging of history and fable, one that is turned to the exposition of an "eternal" — and therefore contemporary — ethical problem: the split of words from works, speech from action, saying from doing. The exposition is whole, completed, when this problem has been set forth with the historical comprehensiveness required for establishing its status *as* an "eternal," perennial problem. (Since the exposition is against, *contra,* there is a persuasive point too; the push is toward resolutions of the problem, however persistent it may be.)

Now to close this digression on Odo's commentaries and head us back toward the two fable groups we have so far only mentioned, nothing rivals "The Rose and the Birds" (number 81). It is one of our author's snappiest performances and more ambitious than anything yet seen. Perhaps just because of this, it promises to cast light back upon each of the three commentary pieces discussed over the last few pages.

The promythion signals what it is about in advance: "And this tale applies to all who strive to possess honors" ("honors" being *dignitates*). Those who strive for worldly honors could include just about anyone, but Odo is especially concerned with clerical vice. From this flows his particular handling of the owl — obviously the bird of darkness, but a bird even more apt here because iconographic tradition treats it so unflatteringly. (To mention a rough parallel, Arnold Hen-

47

derson observed in his treatment of fables as social criticism, "perhaps not every bishop enjoys being likened to a snail or an ox, but those who lived in England in the thirteenth century had opportunities enough to get used to it.")

Turned prominently upon one of Odo's variously expressed but much favored distinctions, that of beauty and ugliness, the tale runs as follows. One day, the birds find "the most beautiful primrose" and, after an argument, decide it should go to the most beautiful bird. They are arguing over who is truly most beautiful when the owl proclaims himself the most beautiful—hence entitled to the rose. The rest of the birds dissolve in laughter and put off a decision on the "most beautiful" until morning. But in the night the owl steals the rose and, with the coming of a new day, the remaining birds pronounce sentence on him in absentia: "Let the owl never fly by day. Let him not live among the other birds. (But let him use his eyes *very* clearly in the dark!) If he dares come out by day, however, let all the birds set upon him, screaming and inflicting wounds."

If we pause we may note that this tale could carry a number of morals: avoid pride, vainglory is for the ugly, thievery merits banishment. It does not actually do so, however. And Odo's commentary, giving the fable an even sharper application than the promythion suggests, explains why. We may first remark the commentary's establishment of critical correspondences. Provisionally at least, we may say that the fable's owl "is" impious men, the rose "an ecclesiastical benefice, the care of souls," and that the rest of the birds "are" just men. Of course I have, in order to tidy things up in this way, ignored *how* Odo creates these relations. (Both "is" and "are" are in quotation marks due to the ambiguity of the distinction between "is" and "is like," etc.— between the literal and analogical—which comes to the fore in any parabolic context. Thus I cannot resist urging readers to consider Scott Buchanan's "fabulistic"—and parabolic?—report in *Poetry and Mathematics* that "the copula 'is' is a weasel word.") Yet the how, the way it is done, is very much the point so far as art is concerned. Unavoidably, my statement of correspondences (the owl "is" impious men, etc.) makes Odo's commentary sound mechanical and static. It is emphatically the opposite. In the course of its development, this commentary merges an analysis of contemporary moral-institutional issues with one of sacred history's most powerful events and its figures—then sweeps up present and past together into a single whole. The past is present here and now in the intersection of fable, history, and the cosmic. This remarkable closure is effected by our narrative's final shift to a perspective which is radical, eschatological, and transcendent yet also an intensification (rather than a denial) of the concrete present.

As for the correspondences already mentioned, the commentary's opening is quite straightforward; it sets out the identity of the "rose" and "an ecclesiastical benefice." But the initial complications of the fable's narrative are glossed over and, rapidly, we are thrown up against the question which is central to the arguments within the flock of birds: "So who deserves this rose, this office of care [or ecclesiastical benefice]?" The answer is immediate. And immediately it throws us— without assistance from any transitional "like" or "likewise," any further assertion that something "is" something else—into a world with insistently, though not completely, human features. "Certainly," comes the response, "the most beautiful of the birds—the one who has the picture of *virtues within,* the beauty of *good deeds without."* (There is no need to tell the reader that the birds under discussion here "are" human beings.)

The same sort of internal-external characterization we've just seen, above, next establishes the identity of the owl as beauty's opposite. "But along comes the owl, the bird who is ugliest—i.e., impious in *vice* and defiled by *evil deeds."* The transition from animal to human worlds is so smooth, managed without recourse to the more explicit devices of linkage, that movement into a context which is not only clearly but *fully* human is something we hardly notice. And Odo's very next sentence, clear in its reference back to the impious owl, should get the credit. "He [i.e., the owl] declares that the rose ought to be his. Then *just men* double over in laughter and ridicule." There is no statement that "the rest of the birds" either are or stand for a group labeled "just men." The assimilation is accomplished solely by the fictive context itself and the repetition of one key term. "All the birds were moved to laughter [*in risum*]" of the narrative section's second paragraph finds an obvious parallel in "just men double over in laughter and ridicule [*rident et derident*]."

While it is true that the order of the commentary recapitulates the chronological order of the narrative proper, the commentary does manage a shift of emphaisis. It amplifies the theft and its significance. "Yet while the just men are sleeping," the text warns, "back comes the owl." Why do I stop the quotation at this point? Because of what follows. *We* know that the owl steals the rose. But what Odo works out is no simple analogical account of the theft, for he has already situated us in a clearly human world. Now, through a much-expanded and expansive discussion, Odo draws us into a specific segment of this—into a world of corruption and chicanery which is emphatically ecclesiastical. The owl is, in a resonant phrase, "the son of darkness"; he is someone who "best knows how to handle the business of dark places."

What this consists of is filled in with blunt detail. The owls are debased ecclesiastics. What do they do in their "business"? Put it over on simple men, garner land and property, get their hands on abundant supplies of money. They are as well adept at flattering bishops and, hence, at getting benefices (we already know what they go on to do with such a "rose"). "And they do not enter in by the door (that is, through love of Christ)," Odo continues, "but by another way—their deeds thus making them thieves and robbers [*fures . . . et latrones*]." This of course picks up on the literal theft we witnessed in the narrative proper, when the rose was stolen (*furata est*). Yet the implications of Odo's words do not stop here. The assimilation of "thieves" and "thefts" to one another is hardly over and is, indeed, to receive additional amplification—not only by way of all the odious particulars put on display (the lower clergy have hardly been flattered in this, even if they are good at flattering bishops!) but also by a pointed allusion to John 10:1–16. "And they do not enter in by the door" recalls the counsel of Jesus (itself both informed by echoes of Old Testament accounts of the good shepherd—Isaiah 40:10–11, Ezechiel 34:22–24 and 37:24—and informing many medieval descriptions of the relation of a ruler or authority figure to those he rules):

"I say to you: He who does not enter by the door into the sheepfold, but who climbs up another way, the same is a thief and robber [*fur . . . et latro*]. But he who enters in by the door is the shepherd of the sheep. . . ." This proverb Jesus spoke to them. But they did not understand what he said. Jesus therefore said to them again, "Amen, amen I say to you, I am the door of the sheep. All others, as many as have come, are thieves and robbers [*fures . . . et latrones*]: and the sheep heard them not.

"I am the door. By me, if any man enter in, he shall be saved; and he shall go in and go out, and shall find pastures. The thief does not come except to steal, to kill, and to destroy. I am come that they may have life, and may have it more abundantly. . . . I am the good shepherd, and I know mine and mine know me — even as the Father knows me and I know the Father; and I lay down my life for my sheep. And I have other sheep which are not of this fold. Them also I must bring in, and they shall hear my voice and there shall be one fold and one *pastor.*"

As most readers will probably intuit, Odo's allusion to the above is far from being nonfunctional decoration. It works to cast us and the issues of the fable into a new context, a context in which clerical corruption is hardly forgotten but instead seen from the perspective of sacred history and the cosmic.

This shift does not, let me risk repeating, mark an abandonment of immediate, contemporary concerns. It is rather a new beginning, the establishment of a higher and enlarged vantage point for their consideration. In fact the very sentence which follows Odo's catalog of dark deeds makes owls clearly thieves and robbers. The sentence even opens with an explicit transition word! *Similiter* — this might be rendered "likewise" or, as I preferred, "it is much the same." But the question is, precisely what is "much the same"? An answer comes from Odo's subsequent talk of monks who lie and spread rumors within a cloister and, so, work their way into positions of authority. "Such men," the text of *The Fables* informs us, "are not choosing *Christ* but *Barabbas.* Now Barabbas was a robber [*latro*]; and indeed the worst of robbers succeed in getting benefices from kings, from. . . ." Engaging as this is — at least for readers who enjoy vituperation — it is important to ask why Odo's text treats everyday perfidiousness in such stark terms. What is the justification?

It seems reasonable to suggest that we are being drawn to view the temporal (i.e., a problem of Odo's own time and place) from an eternal, cosmic, eschatological perspective — from the vantage point of sacred history. One might even rephrase this and assert that we are now capable of seeing the "owlishness" of power-hungry monks because they appear against the backdrop, the circumstances, supplied by biblical history. Yet our questions demand a fuller, more discriminating answer. And it is perhaps pertinent to remind ourselves that in *action* — men do *choose,* the point of emphasis in Odo's words — the two levels and two perspectives come together. The temporal and eternal merge. To express myself as directly as possible, when a priest or other religious chooses to operate a scam which takes in a poor man or a bishop or both, then he *is choosing* (present tense) Barabbas. He is re-enacting one of the most compelling events of the past in the present. Hence comes the extraordinary force of Odo's conclusion which turns the judgment or sentence handed down from the court of the birds into the Final Sentence handed down by the awful Judge of the Last Judgment. Fable, contemporary problems, sacred history and the transcendent perspective emergent from that history, that collective human experience — all these test, validate, and illuminate one another. The utterly thorough interpenetration of materials so extensive in their range ("A Certain 'Bird of Saint Martin'" comes nowhere near "The Rose and the Birds" for comprehensiveness of thought) is what effects narrative closure and makes a witty tale about a flock of birds into a unique, artfully realized whole.

Enough said, I hope, to suggest that Odo's commentaries are best understood as more than decorative trimming. But before finally closing this digression, I want to draw out another aspect of "The Rose and the Birds" through a second, complementary reading. Our just-completed account started with the fable's characters and emphasized their developing narrative function; it stressed sacred history's role in providing a special perspective on the narrative. The brief reading now proposed will start with empty "points" and emphasize the emergence of a pattern; it will stress sacred history's role in transforming and making that pattern an "eternal object." To repeat, the two readings are not rigidly opposed, yet their complementarity is best illustrated simply by moving ahead.

At this stage of our discussion, it is not exactly news if I say that "The Rose and the Birds" manifests three primary points of attention: the owl, the rest of the birds, and the disputed primrose itself. It is however notable that the primrose receives far less *direct* attention than either of the other two — that expansions of its meaning are largely reflections bounced back from the systematically enlarged significance of the owl and, also, the birds. True, the rose's significance is the first to be stated by the commentary — but its subsequent amplification or growth in meaning is accomplished indirectly, by implication. The rose or primrose is like a fixed center, a point about which two other points of interest — owl and other birds — turn in ever widening and ever more inclusive circles.

Because of the commentary's opening words, we know early on

what the rose is ("an ecclesiastical benefice, the care of souls," etc.). But the owl and the birds? As we are aware by now, each is not one but many things, developed by way of a sequence which discloses many aspects of character. And it is this sequence itself which I want to examine for the moment. The commentary, consistent with its initial treatment of the primrose, focuses attention on what *is* — on what is most beautiful (the bird "who has the picture of virtues within," etc.) and what is ugliest (the bird who is "impious in vice," etc.). Specification of what is, however, turns out to require specification of what the emerging characters *do*. Virtue and vice turn active and external as good deeds and evil deeds. (The content of a man's soul cannot be observed directly, but all of us can see what a person does.) They do not end here, of course, but re-emerge in what characters *say*. The owl boasts, says that he merits the rose. And the rest of the birds? Their "speech" is first laughter, then the more articulate form, ridicule, and finally a legal judgment.

Odo now turns us back to what characters *do* and has the flock go to sleep (easily, we may assume, since just men are not kept awake by guilty consciences) — while the owl returns to . . . to do what? From the narrative proper, we know he steals the rose; but in the commentary, Odo never mentions this directly. Instead, we are "told" of his deed through the amplification already discussed in our previous reading:

> back comes the owl . . . who best knows how to handle the business of dark places, how *to despoil* simple men and farms and land, *to get and keep* great sums of money, *to flatter* bishops. This is how such men labor.

With this, the owl has become explicitly plural: "*their* deeds thus making them thieves and robbers." What is more, Odo's account of what characters do has returned us — though in a much enlarged sense — to what each one *is*. We must glance back to get the full contrast, but the more numerous birds "are" just men while the owl "is" (though one must not actually think in the singular) thieves and robbers. The sequence ("being-doing-saying") moves back and forth across the fable narrative like a shuttle upon a loom. What characters are, do, and say — and what the same say, do and are — weaves the substance of their motivation (i.e., what they *think* is valuable, whether these objects men

53

prize and pursue are ultimately real and rewarding or not) and also the emerging substance of the work as a whole.

Hence as we move back from what our characters at this stage are (respectively: lovers of justice, thieves, and robbers) and again look toward what they *do* we encounter the phenomenon of choice. Precisely targeting those monks who are little more than bandits, Odo, we recall, asserts that "such men are not choosing Christ but Barabbas." His reference is to the events of Matthew 27. And it is significant that choice, while a form of action, is not only expressed in people's subsequent overt actions but also in what they say. In Matthew's gospel, Pontius Pilate (Judea's governor) is described as observing a custom which allows for periodic freeing of a prisoner of the state. Pilate asks the crowd to state its choice. Whom do they wish set free, Christ or Barabbas? Their will is expressed in what they *say*:

> The governor addressed them [i.e., the crowd] and said to them, "Which of the two do you wish that I release to you?" And they said, "Barabbas." Pilate said to them, "What then am I to do with Jesus who is called Christ?" They all said, "Let him be crucified!" The governor said to them, "Why, what evil has he done?" But they kept crying out the more, saying, "Let him be crucified!"

With the allusion to this passage, Odo merges saying, doing, and being. For what one does and what one says are not simple consequences of what one is; they also create one's substance, what one is. To choose and state one's preference for Christ or Barabbas is *to be* a just man or a thief, is *to be* a bird of beauty or an ugly owl, is *to be* Christ or Barabbas. Moreover the process, to call back our earlier reading, is of a dimension we have already termed "cosmic." Odo gives the whole a transcendent push; judgment becomes Judgment as saying, doing, and being undergo a final transformation in the context of Judgment Day. *Quid erit in die iudicii?* "On that day, sentence shall be handed down: Never, in any manner, shall the owls fly among the birds of heaven. But they will dwell perpetually in outer darkness where there shall be weeping and gnashing of teeth." With this final merging at the highest possible level, our "circle" spirals upward — and downward, too! — toward the infinite. Infinity being infinity, there is thus a sense in which the events of the fable do not, in this reading, truly end.

They do however (on account of a commentary which is no mere decorative trimming but the active agent which draws out the narrative's merging of what is, what is done, and what is said) achieve their own kind of closure in a resolution of thought which makes the fable whole.

Mixed Fables and Moralized Animal Lore

These comments close out both our "digression" and, at the same time, our discussion of Odo's animal fables. Remaining are two final groups, mixed fables and moralized animal lore (what may be called *Physiologus*-type pieces). Since the mixed fables—with or without commentary—do not differ in fundamental strategy from either apologues, on the one hand, or from strict animal fables on the other, a direct analysis of one or more would do little to take our appreciation of Odo's art beyond the point already reached. So I would like to leave the mixed pieces for my readers' own examination and round out our account of the art of *The Fables* by turning to the final group, the entries I have termed moralized animal lore.

Odo's text actually gives us a number of these *Physiologus*-type pieces—"The Hornet" (number 8), "The Panther" (number 90), and "An Exemplum: The Serpent and the Crocodile" (number 28), for example. (Parenthetically, readers may be interested to know that Odo's "The Panther" shows significant parallels with *Physiologus'* panther—number xxx in Curley's translation—and that our author's "The Serpent and the Crocodile" also has significant parallels in both Pliny and *Physiologus;* see, respectively, VIII, xxxvi–xxxvii and xxxix. The role of the serpent here, when contrasted to the same creature's role in other of Odo's fables, brings home a matter touched on earlier: a creature's role is sometimes quite variable, because of diverse associations which enable an author to push it toward the good or the evil. Everything depends upon the specific fictional context an author creates, his *selective use* of *some* meanings of a creature to serve specific ends.)

Among pieces like this is an especially striking instance—one which will, by the way, add something to the digression just completed. I speak of "The Wild Colt" (number 56). The mark of this and other pieces in the same category is fairly obvious: they lack a story. Or to put this another way, the story they relate is explicitly, and in the etymological sense, typical. They don't inform a reader that "one day the fox encountered the wolf on the way to market and said. . . ." Their stories are themselves eternalized as types; everything is cast in an "atemporal" present tense. Thus "there is an animal known as the antelope. Using his horns he engages . . . " (number 27). "The fly is unpredictable—sometimes biting, sometimes befouling, and sometimes agitating us" (number 25). "When the pelican's young chicks raise their beaks and strike at him, he kills them. Afterwards . . ." (number 20). "There is an animal known as the serpent which enfolds itself in mire . . ." (number 28). The story of each, such as it is, relates the one characteristic deed of the particular creature—the act which discloses its essence. (In a way, these fables seem roughly analogous in their working to that remarkable category of English sentences —e.g., "He's the guy who talks as though he *has* a cold," "He's the guy who talks as though he *had* a cold"—in which the verbs' tense markers drop their normal function as a speaker eternalizes the distinguishing characteristic of someone or something, posits an attribute which listeners take as relatively persistent, enduring, and unchanging through past-present-future and, hence, as "eternal.")

For sure, these little pieces are not lacking in interest. But since I promised to deal with "The Wild Colt," let me begin by quoting its narrative in entirety. "A wild colt throws himself into the water or into a pit, unless he is held back by a bridle." That's it. The *whole* thing—at least the whole "narrative." Odo's commentary, however, turns this bare one-sentence description into a kind of allegory. He takes the colt as a man's "fleshly nature" and implies that the bridle must be used, i.e., the colt reined in, by a man's non-fleshly nature or soul. (This entry in *The Fables* begins to sound like a reminiscence of the myth of the charioteer in Plato's *Phaedrus*.) Still, more important than an enumeration of the various correspondences Odo sets up, is the way these are handled by his commentary. The commentary turns the one-sentence description into a kind of genuine narrative. Put another way, the commentary itself *becomes* a narrative—which, in turn, becomes the occasion for a further commentary. Fortunately, that part of Odo's commentary section which takes on narrative functions is brief enough to permit citation:

> Assuredly, your fleshly nature will thus cast you into the pit of
> sin and hell (through drunken binges, fornications, and the like)

unless you apply the bridle—evidently, the bridle of Christ's restraining nails. If you wrongly rein the bridle toward the table (i.e., toward a great feast) then you must not be forgetful of Him while at table, lest your horse throw you.

Thus does the first part of Odo's commentary change non-narrative animal lore into a parable, a narrative (and one couched in future tense, please note), in the process of moralizing it.

The second and final part of Odo's commentary—one might call it a "commentary on a commentary"—is at least equally engaging. Of course, many aspects of the passage reproduced above will be evident to readers who have participated in our discussion of other fables and their commentaries; it makes most sense, therefore, to move on to something not dwelt on previously. What the commentary (and I speak directly of the commentary section's second part) which closes "The Wild Colt" does most pointedly is as follows. It seizes upon the moral virtue —strongly implied but never explicitly mentioned in our above quotation—which a man *must* have if he is to take control of the reins and successfully bridle his horse. The virtue is constancy, *constantia*—the virtue which, so to speak, keeps a man's eye on the target regardless of the abrasions and temptations that beseige him from within and without. Odo's dilation upon this necessary virtue could well be printed alone under the title, *De Constantia.* And some readers may recall that the "moral essays" of Seneca (c. 4 B.C.–A.D. 65) contain a work, with precisely this title, showing that the wise man is immune to both injuries and insults—though its content and scope are in marked contrast to *The Fables'* counterpart. This, like the first part of Odo's commentary, is so brief that the most economical procedure is to quote it in full:

Constancy is necessary, lest you be a soldier who falls from his chariot at the buffeting of a breeze. Such winds are the words of slanderers, of flatterers, of men who incite you to wrath; and anyone hearing these words, *if* he is a fool, falls into anger or hatred or sadness. Such a man is not constant. Be therefore constant and firm, lest you fall and flee from the chariot of charity. "Whatever shall befall the just man, it shall not make him sad" (Proverbs 12:21).

This leaves no question as to Odo's focus. And the assertion of *constantia*'s necessity is followed, we note, by a statement spelling out what happens when someone lacks it. But what comes after this turns the stated consequence—"lest you be a soldier who falls from his chariot at the buffeting of a breeze"—into another miniature allegory. For what is "a breeze"? "Such winds are the words of slanderers," while the "soldier" must be the human soul—working, in a parallel with the immediately preceding commentary-narrative, to control a man's vulnerable nature.

In case this analysis has obscured the fact, it is worthwhile to insist that the moral advice of Odo's little essay has a lively tone—in part because of its concentrated brevity and pointed expression, and in part because of the playful patterns of alliteration and assonance which make it a delight to read aloud. In addition, its proverbial cap provides a conclusion which is final indeed. It *feels* final—not only because it comes from an authoritative, higher source (the biblical book, Proverbs) but also because of its aphoristic conciseness. Hence animal lore, material from both Old and New Testaments, Senecan moral essay, and biblical-proverbial saying come together in a work which is, after a fashion, quite different from the other pieces we have examined. As to that quotation from Proverbs which effects closure, we may ask whether it acts to provide a final insight into the meaning of the animal lore or whether the animal lore functions to illuminate the biblical proverb. The two processes are reflexive, of course, and it is not a question of choosing one *or* the other. Scripture is commentary on the fable and the fable is commentary on scripture. The two test and verify one another in a performance which gives a piece of *Physiologus*-type animal lore the vitality and sparkle we have come to expect from Odo of Cheriton's art.

It is true that we might explore that art in much greater detail and at far greater length. But we have, I think, said enough. Surely we have said enough that readers will not (should any feel inclined to do so) look at Odo's text condescendingly—or with a conviction that Odo simply "misunderstood" a whole body of material from antiquity and elsewhere. Even if we do not share Odo's religious and historical outlook, we are unlikely to be so irritated by his distortions and misunderstandings that we neglect their artistic *function*. We're unlikely to see them as the ignorant product of an inadequate philology (inadequate tending to mean that twelfth- and thirteenth-century philology is not twentieth-century philology). As dispensable trimmings. In short, we have come to a point where readers—perhaps especially those with a fondness for introductions—should turn directly to Odo's own words. These, as I urged early on, are their own best introduction. Where *my* introduction proves helpful, use it. There's no denying that I will indeed be happy if you do. Still, the greatest and most rewarding help will come from Odo himself. He may sometimes be puzzling at first glance. Yet he has provided me with many fine moments, and I know he will not do less for you.

Original sources and scholarship I have used and occasionally cited in this introduction, along with other materials employed in annotating particular fables, will be found in the bibliography at the end of this volume. What follows immediately as the final introductory section is a discussion intended for readers with a special interest in the art of translation and the purposes which have governed the making of this particular translation.

The Principles and Strategy of this Translation

> Good translation is grounded in practical formal criticism.
> Paul Goodman

In preparing my translation of Odo of Cheriton's *The Fables,* I have used Léopold Hervieux's text from his *Les Fabulistes Latins,* 5 vols., IV (1896; rpt. Hildesheim: Olms, 1970), 173–250. The translated fables are printed in an order that is nearly identical to the order of the Latin originals in his edition (exceptions are explained in a note to Fable 3). The complicated appearance of Hervieux's number-superscript designations has, however, been eliminated. I have instead identified each fable by a simple Arabic numeral—in addition, of course, to its title. Where it was both possible and useful, I have supplemented Hervieux's text by consulting Ben Edwin Perry's *Aesopica,* I (Urbana, Ill.: University of Illinois Press, 1952), 625–57. I say "where possible" because *Aesopica* contains a far smaller number of Odo's fables — and, frequently enough, fables *not* printed in their entirety — than does *Les Fabulistes Latins.*

Some few terms in Odo's text, let me add, are best left untranslated — or translated with the Latin term immediately following the English term or phrase selected as its equivalent. When dealing with such matters, I have observed a double practice. If the term (for instance: exemplum-exempla, paterfamilias) is entered in the English language section of the Merriam Webster *New Collegiate Dictionary* (1977), I have treated it as "English" and not italicized it. But terms not regarded as "English" by this, one of the most commonly used English desk dictionaries, have either been italicized (substantives and modifiers in a nominative form, singular or plural) or — where Latin terms are not readily defined by the context — placed in brackets and italicized (again, in a nominative form). As indicated above, these immediately follow the English word or phrase that translates them.

In addition, other matters deserve comment. First comes the issue of how to render Odo's scriptural quotations. Here, I have been guided by three versions of the Douay-Rheims Bible — for the obvious reason that the Douay-Rheims was done from the Latin Vulgate. Yet due to revisions, the three versions I have used are not always identical. These three are: (1) the "New Catholic Edition" (New York: Catholic Book Publishing Company, 1949); (2) the version published by the Douay Bible House (New York [n.d.]), this containing James A. Carey's 1935 revision of the Rheims New Testament; and (3) the *Douay-Rheims New Testament,* a 1976 reprint of that section of the Bible as originally published by the John Murphy Company (Baltimore, 1899). The reprint, however, is issued by Tan Books and Publishers, Inc. of Rockford, Illinois.

I have, as I said, been *guided* by these. Yet, since Odo's references to the Vulgate sometimes differ from the texts which would have been used in producing and/or revising the Douay-Rheims, and since I have wanted to make the tone and thrust of his quoted passages appropriate to the surrounding fable — and to the quotation's seeming function within that fable — I have often altered these three versions for the sake of preserving the flow of Odo's own narrative. And jumbled quotations, in which the lines occur out of sequence, have been translated with an eye to preserving that same narrative flow. Whether Odo was quoting from a faulty memory or whether his Vulgate differed from ours is, for purposes of this translation, of very slight importance. Hence I have seldom bothered to comment on his "mistakes" in my notes.

Next comes the problem of identifying these translated quotations from scripture. I have chosen not to distinguish between Odo's own identifications, those added by Hervieux, and those which are my own. For my primary purpose has been to produce a readable text in idiomatic English—while remaining true to the sense and effect of Odo's own language (though not always to his precise sentence structure or wording).

This brings us to a final set of issues, the handling of Odo's *non*-scriptural quotations. For those taken from poets of antiquity, I have checked and reproduced Hervieux's identifications; and my translations of lines from these poets have been guided (yet, again, only *guided*) by the versions in the Loeb Classical Library. But Odo's citations from church authors and medieval Latin poetry are another matter. I have not normally added identifications beyond those supplied by the author himself (though I have at times expanded these, so that a simple reference to "Gregory" may become "Gregory the Great"—a form of the name which allows a reader to use the Biographical Names section of a dictionary intelligently). What I *have* worked to give my readers, on the other hand, is an English rendering of the rhyme patterns of Odo's verse quotations. Thus a line of leonine verse such as that which rounds out Fable 67 ("The Fox")—*Puppe canis latus[,] pro munere reddet hyatus*—retains the distinctive internal rhyme which is the formal mark of a "leonine": "Give a dog passage aboard your *stern,* he'll pay you nothing in *return.*"

In other words, I have set out—in this introduction, the actual translation, and my annotations—to do things in a way which makes Odo's witty, sophisticated, sometimes metaphysical art as fully available as is possible for modern readers who are not likely to know the Latin original. (My bibliography includes a selection of works which have played a role in thinking through the issues of translation touched on but lightly in this section of my introduction.) So, as already suggested, I have indeed attempted literal fidelity to the sense of these tales, to the spirit if not always the letter. Expressed in the terms of a hardy medieval distinction, the "literalness" I have sought is not so much *verbal* as *real.* My aim has been to keep the vitality of Odo's tales in the foreground. Given this intent, certain kinds of annotations would have proven more intrusive than helpful. They would have added

61

too little to a reader's instruction or delight. And these together, we may want to remember, were the literary values which Odo of Cheriton clearly prized.

To verify my deepest hope is, I confess, impossible. But I like to imagine Master Odo opening this English "reincarnation" of his Latin *Fabulae,* hearing its voice as his own, then smiling with pleasure.

The Fables

The Prologue Begins
To Master Odo's Parables In Praise Of Him
Who Is Both Alpha And Omega

I WILL OPEN my mouth in parables, I will reveal the mysteries of long ago" (Psalms 77:2).

Hence we read in the Book of Ruth: "Let fall some of your handfuls on purpose, and leave them, so that Ruth may gather them without shame" (2:16). Thus Boaz commanded his reapers. Boaz embodies strength; and he signifies Christ, in whom there is the strength of divinity and the strength of omnipotence—Christ, who binds the strong one, namely the Devil, strips him of all his weapons, and distributes the spoils (so we read in Luke 11:22). This is He who, as we read in Isaiah 63:1, is "beautiful in his robe, walking in the greatness of his strength"—since his body's apparel was more beautiful than the moon, more radiant than the sun. He *descended* from heaven to earth, assuming flesh, and from earth into hell, liberating humankind; he *ascended* from hell to earth, recovering flesh, and from earth to heaven, there sitting at the right hand of the Father.

Now this Boaz has his harvest hands (namely apostles, disciples, and prelates) to whom the care of souls is committed. These men ought to reap the stalks proper to souls (namely the authorities and exempla of the sacred scriptures), by means of which souls are nourished and sustained. And then they ought to harvest the souls themselves and offer them to God—concerning which we read in Luke 10:2: "The harvest indeed is great, but the laborers are few. Pray therefore the Lord

of the harvest to send forth laborers into his harvest." For no sacrifice pleases God so much as the zeal of souls. If you offer up a single soul to God, He will say to you: "Arise, my good servant, etc."; for God values a single soul more than the entire world.

But many men are deeply afraid of the corporeal stalks (namely tithes and worshipful offerings) and they offer their souls to the Devil through depraved lives or through negligence. Concerning such men, the Book of Wisdom (6:6–9) tells us: "a most severe judgment awaits them that bear rule. . . . The mighty shall be mightily tormented . . . and a greater punishment is ready for the more mighty." It is as though the Word were saying: "It will be a hard judgment for Jews and Saracens; a harder one for heretics; but the hardest judgment will be that of false prelates—though it will be equally hard for those who glory in a multitude of riches, in showy horses, in delicate foods."

Now Ruth should be interpreted as "lacking" and she signifies the laity who, in themselves, are lacking—unless they are nourished by prelates. For, if someone sends these laity away hungry, then they will be "lacking" on their way (see Mark 8:3).

Therefore, you rulers of souls, let fall some of your handfuls, so that Ruth may gather them without shame—not only in the church, but in the court, the drawing room, at the luncheon, the banquet, in whatever place she may be while journeying upon the way. And let the paterfamilias bring forth from his storehouse both new and old words and exempla, with which faithful souls may be nourished. Thus speaks Ecclesiasticus 9:23: "Let all your discourse concern the commandments of the Highest." And this will be a greater gift than filling up the body. Whence Gregory the Great reminds us: "It is better to restore the sustenance in the immortal soul with a morsel of the Word than to stuff the fleshly belly with deathly, earthly bread." Therefore, seeing that Gregory also says that exempla are more stinging than words, I will open my mouth in parables; and I will set forth similitudes and exempla which are both more willingly heard and more securely committed to memory than are words. Understanding these similitudes and exempla, the man of wisdom will be wiser.

Whoever has ears for hearing, let him hear; whoever has eyes, let him look upon the things I have written; whoever has the spirit, let him address the faithful—so that everyone may yield to instruction in morals and the transformation of souls. And because this is a parabolic treatise, let us take our beginning in a parable from the Book of Judges.

1 How the Trees Elected a King

The trees assembled so that they could appoint a king to rule over them. They said to the olive tree: "Rule us." To which he replied: "How can I give up my oil, used by both gods and men, just to be elevated among the trees?"

Then they approached the fig tree; and they said: "Take up the task of ruling over us." "How," he replied, "can I abandon my sweetness and my mellow fruits—just for the sake of being elevated among the trees?" Next they came to the vine, in hopes that he might be one to rule them. But he answered their request: "How can I abandon the wine which delights both God and man?" And he had no wish to be elevated. At last, the trees said to the thorn: "Rule us!" The thorn bush responded: "If you truly want to make me king, come and rest under my shade; if you are unwilling, a fire will come forth from the thorn and will devour the cedars of Lebanon" (see Judges 9:8–15).

MYSTICALLY—the trees signify rustic men, monks, a congregation without a pastor. They assemble to elevate the olive tree, a man of justice. And he, refusing them, explains that he does not want to give up the oil of charity and be elevated to this worldly dignity.

The fig tree signifies the just man who, through frequent contemplation, both tastes how mellow and sweet the Lord is and, also, produces sweet fruits through his own good works. And this man—because there are many bitter things, many tumults, that go with worldly dignities—has no desire to exchange his own sweetness for such a position.

The vine is another just man, one who finds delight in spiritual joy, one who says: "Our joy is the witness of our conscience." Seeing that many bitter things and many tumults go with pride of worldly rank, such men have no wish to be elevated.

Thus the Canon of Toro, when he refused election, quickly moved

to another jurisdiction and explained himself to a comrade. That is, when asked why he did not accept the bishopric, he replied: "Should I have been counted among the bishops, I should have been counted among the damned." Again, when Master Hugo had been made Bishop of Meaux and was visiting his Parisian brothers, he told them: "If I had a mortal enemy and wished the worst for him, I would pray for God to make him a bishop. For I would consider this the worst possible curse." Nevertheless, since bishops are the pillars of the vault and the very beams supporting the cathedral, they govern and sustain the Church of God—while just men bring forth, into eternal life, the noble fruit of souls.

The useless thorn bush accepts the bishopric freely. This thorn is a prickly bush, lacking shade—whence, on account of too much dryness, it sends forth fire out of itself. Thus the impious man, the man who does not have the shade of refreshment or consolation, says: "Take your rest in my shade," for he promises many good things. But then, from out of himself, he sends forth the fire of avarice, of pride, of luxury. And thus, through his depraved example, he burns up the trees (that is, those in under him).

Thus did the Shechemites elect Abimelech who burned them up (see Judges 9:20).

2   The Ants

The ants likewise elected a tree as their king, and they urinated all over him. Then they elected a serpent—and *he* devoured them.

3   The Frogs Elect a King*

In like manner, the frogs convened a council so that they could make themselves a king. They then elected a certain tree and elevated it to the kingship. A while later, when they were crawling up over it, the frogs came to despise the tree. And they said: "Since our king is without dignity, let's depose him!" "So who do we select now?" Then, by popular assent, they elected a serpent who tore into and devoured them all.

4   The Chicks Elect a King

Once upon a time the hens elected, as king, a serpent who devoured them. The chicks then proclaimed an ordinance so that they could elect themselves another king. And one who was wiser than the others said: "Let us elect the dove, a simple animal who neither rends nor tears nor devours." So they did, and the simple dove lived among the chicks. But then the chicks said: "Our king is worthless, for he neither wounds nor tears." Said other chicks: "Let's depose him. And who, then, shall we elect?"

"Let us," they told one another, "elect the kite." And they did just that. One day—having been established as king—the kite tore a chick with his beak and talons and, then, devoured him. Then he did the same to a second, then to a third. Thus a people was afflicted by their depraved king.

Likewise, many are not content with a gentle king, a simple bishop, an innocent abbot. They elect a perverse leader who destroys everyone. For this reason, it is sometimes necessary to vex and wound one's subjects, at other times to pierce them, but at yet others to anoint them—so that they neither swell up with pride, nor turn sullen under too much affliction.

5   The Birds Elect a King*

The birds announced a council, so that they could elect themselves a king. Then one of them said: "Let us select the dove, a simple animal, because it neither pecks at nor tears at nor devours others." And they did precisely what this bird had suggested.

The dove indeed kept to a simple life among its chicks. Hence the birds took to saying "Our king is worthless, for he doesn't engage in killing or tearing others to shreds. Let's depose him and elect the kite!"

And they did so. Now the kite, once he had been established as king, one day tore into a chick with his beak and talons; and he devoured the youngster. Following this, he took a second chick, and then a third, and so on.

MYSTICALLY—there also are many men who are not content under the rule of a gentle king or simple bishop or innocent abbot. So instead they elect one who is perverse—one who destroys his subjects.

6   An Abbot, Food, and Some Monks   🌿

And this is applied to bad administrators and their worse successors

There lived an abbot who allowed his monks three meals a day. "This fellow," said the monks under him, "gives us too little. Let us ask God to have him die shortly." And whether for this or some other reason, he soon died.

Another was put in his place, one who gave them only two meals. Then the monks, angered and downcast, said: "Now even more prayers are in order, since we've had a meal taken away. May God take away his life!" And, in time, he died.

A third abbot was put in his place, one who subtracted *two* meals. Enraged, the monks declared: "This character is the worst of all since he is killing us with hunger. Let's ask God to make him die soon!!" But one monk said: "I am praying to God that He give him a long life and, for our sakes, protect him with His hand." The others, stupefied, asked why he said this—to which he replied: "I can see that the first abbot was bad, the second worse, and *this* one the worst. I am terrified that, when the third is dead, yet another will come after him

—someone even worse—who will use starvation to completely wipe us out."

Thus the customary aphorism: *Selde cumet se betere.* Which is to say: Rarely does a better one come next.

7 The Hawk, the Dove, and "the Duke"

This applies only to those who act belligerently, not to the doers of justice

Once upon a time, a hawk seized a dove and devoured it. The rest of the doves sought out their counsellor and complained to him, loudly. "Duke!" they shouted. For the Duke is a bird with an enormous head, and he is bigger than the eagle. And so the doves complained to him about the hawk—hoping that the Duke might (since the hawk had killed their comrade) do justice. Once he had heard their complaint, the Duke gave a reply accompanied by lots of noisy gurgling: "Cluck!" On hearing this, the doves said: "How wondrously he intones! He is certainly going to make himself a tasty morsel out of that hawk!!" Meanwhile the hawk came and seized another dove.

The doves again came to the Duke, imploring him to do justice. And he replied: "Cluck!" "Behold," said the doves, "how manfully he proclaims his warning! He truly will have justice done." The hawk took a third dove.

For a third time the doves came to the Duke, intent on having him take revenge. And his reply? "Cluck!"

Hearing this, they said to one another: "What is this 'Cluck' that he is always *saying*—while, at the same time, *doing* nothing for justice? Let's secede from his kingdom, and attack him as a pretender and a fool." And so when the doves and other birds saw the Duke, they set upon him.

Thus, when the poor call upon kings and prominent leaders to right injustices by doing justice, many of these noble fellows say: "We will. Yes, we will!" And so they pronounce a solitary "Cluck." Yet they

73

do nothing. More broadly, this fable concerns all men who make false promises, who say: "Cluck, cluck; I will do something, I will take action!" — men of the sort who never come forth with anything except that one lone "Cluck!"

8   The Hornet

Using his wings, the hornet likewise creates a noisy uproar. It's as if he were saying: *"Frai bien, frai bien."* Then at length, he drives himself into your eye.

Certain men of this sort say: *"Frai bien, frai bien."* They promise you salve, then drive home a sting; they pledge roses and deliver thorns.

9   The Crow

Against those who boast of having what they lack

Once upon a time, seeing that he was ugly and black, the crow complained to the eagle. The eagle told him that — on loan — he could wear feathers from various birds. The crow did so. He took from the tail of the peacock, from the wings of the dove; and thus he pleased himself by borrowing from other birds. Indeed, seeing himself so beautifully adorned, he began to ridicule and mock the rest of the birds. So the birds got together and, before the eagle, lodged their complaint concerning the crow's pride. Replied the eagle: "Let every bird you can think of be accepting of its own feathers, and then the crow will be humiliated." And when the birds did precisely this, the crow found himself abandoned — ugly and unadorned.

Thus does wretched man swell with pride on account of his adornments. But let the sheep be accepting of his wool, the earth of its mud, the cows and goats of their hides, rabbits and lambs of their fur; let all this happen, and the miser will be left alone — naked of adornment and ugly. And in any case, it is thus he shall be on the day of his death — the day when he'll be unable to take anything along, out of all his worldly goods.

Similarly, this exemplum directs its force against rich men who boast because of their abundant wealth. For the Lord, in due time, disposes all things. And thus the rich are reduced to the point of suffering humiliation.

10   The Buzzard and the Hawk's Nest

A buzzard pitched one of her eggs into the hawk's nest; and, from that egg, a chick was hatched. Now the other chicks in the nest, being noble, did their dirt outside. But the buzzard's chick always fouled his own nest. Seeing this, the hawk wanted to know: "Just who is defiling this nest?" After a bit, the chicks told her about the buzzard's chick. So the hawk took heed and grabbed the son of a buzzard and pitched him out of the nest — declaring as she did so: *Of on egge y the brouzgyt bytt of thy kynde y maye nouzght.* Which is to say: I drew you forth [*eduxi*] from an egg, but I couldn't draw you away from your nature; and so the whole business was shattered.

Thus does the Lord have His chicks in the nest of the church, chicks who do not defile but honor her. But the buzzard, i.e., the Devil, has his own chicks in among these. And, through all sorts of vices, these defile the church. Therefore the Lord will pitch them out of the nest, will cast them into the pit of hell. There, they will be most horribly shattered.

More broadly, this exemplum directs its force against court attendants who envy their brothers and slander them. For, at length, such natures defile the whole court.

11   The Cuckoo and the Sparrow

Against all who rise up in opposition to their benefactors

The cuckoo once placed an egg in a sparrow's nest. And the sparrow indeed nurtured the cuckoo's chick. Then, when he had grown to quite a size and the sparrow came to offer him some food, he opened wide his mouth — and gulped and devoured the sparrow.

Thus many men, though reared and promoted by others, rise up against their benefactors and harass them in various ways. So it is with clerks; once elevated among the canons and archdeacons, they set upon their superiors. For such are the sons of the cuckoo. And when these sons have power, they devour their parents, and brother devours brother simply to get possession of property. Such men are called Sons of Nero — the Emperor who murdered his mother, and his master Seneca as well.

A curse on nurturing such sons! Isaiah 1:2: "I have brought up children, and exalted them; but they have despised me."

12   The Tortoise and the Eagle

Against the curious

A tortoise, dwelling in places which were damp and deep, asked the eagle to carry him up into the heavens. For he wanted to see the fields, meadows, mountains, and glades. The eagle consented and carried the tortoise on high, and he told the tortoise: "Now you are seeing the things you've never seen: mountains, valleys, and glades." Replied the tortoise: "How well I can see! But still, I'd rather be in my hole." "It is quite enough," the eagle said in return, "that all these things have been laid before your eyes." Then the eagle dashed him down into a fall, and the tortoise was completely shattered to pieces.

MYSTICALLY—someone is dwelling, sheltered under a humble roof; he wants to move up and soar upon the streams of the winds. He asks the eagle, i.e., the Devil, to somehow raise him aloft. At length — through all sorts of straight and crooked dealing, through deceits — he makes his ascent. And thus the Devil carries him up. After a while, he perceives the peril of his situation and decides he'd rather be under his humble roof. Then the Devil makes him fall unto his death, into the pit of hell, where he is completely shattered to pieces.

So it goes for fools winging nimbly toward the firmament:
They fall from places prominent, to the depth of evils' torment.

13   The Stork and the Wolf

Against cruel lords who reward their servants evilly

Once upon a time the wolf was strangling on a bone, and a doctor had to be sought. The wolf's servants said to him: "The stork has a long bill, so he'll be able to extract the bone from your throat."

The stork was located, and was promised great rewards. So he came and drew forth the bone from the wolf's throat. Then, he expected his reward. Now the wolf, not wanting to give anything to the stork, said to him: "When I had your head inside my mouth, wasn't I in a position to kill you? And isn't that enough for you — just knowing that I let you live?"

So it is for rustic fellows and the poor. Once they provide services, they're unable to enjoy the slightest reward. For their lord lets them know: "You are *my* man! Isn't it something great that I'm not flaying you? That I'm letting you live?"

14   A Certain "Bird of Saint Martin"

Against those whose daring in deeds doesn't match their words

There lives in Spain a bird called the "Bird of Saint Martin," merely a small wren. It has legs that are slender (in the manner of a finch) and long. Under a scorching sun, on a day near the time of the festival of Saint Martin, it chanced that he threw himself down on his back — close to a tree — and stretched his legs upward. As he did this he said: "Look! Now, should the sky fall, I could hold it up on my legs." And then a single leaf fell nearby; and terrified, the bird flew off exclaiming: "Oh Saint Martin! Why don't you protect your little bird!?"

Such are the many who believe for a while — but who, in a time of trial, draw back. Such was Peter, who was pledged for Christ's sake to go both to prison and unto his death. Yet when he saw that his Lord was being abused, to the maidservant's words he replied: "Woman, I do not know what you are saying; I know him not" (see Luke 22: 57–60). Likewise, the sons of Ephraim practiced bending and shooting their bows, then turned their backs in the day of battle (Psalms 77:9). This can be adapted to soldiers of a certain kind. When their heads are well-lubricated with wine and ale, they boast of their power to withstand and war down three Franks apiece. But when they are thirsty and see the lances and swords about them, then they say: "Oh Saint Martin, protect your little bird!" That is: "*O sein Martin, eide nostre oiselin.*"

15   The Weeping Bald Man and Some Partridges

Against rulers feigning justice

A bald man, his eyes streaming with tears, was killing partridges. And one partridge said to another: "Behold the man — how good and

saintly he is!" And the other asked: "Why do you call him good?"
"Don't you see," replied the first, "how he is weeping?" To this, another answered back: "Don't *you* see how he is killing us!? This man's
tears are damnable—for while weeping, he is annihilating us!"

Thus many bishops, prelates, and great men seem to pray beautifully and give alms—weeping all the while. Yet they flay and annihilate those who are simple and subject to them. Such men's prayers and tears are damnable!

16   The Bird Called "Break Bone"

Of the danger of being in power

There lives a bird who is known as "Break Bone" or *Freinos* because, using his beak, he breaks open bones and eats the gluten and marrow. When a bone is too hard for him to crack, he carries it up into the heavens and lets it fall right onto a rock. And thus the bone is broken to bits.

This is how the Devil acts. When he can't break a man of great constancy, he raises him up into the heights of worldly honor, and then lets him fall—so that the man is completely broken to bits. And as one's ascent is steeper, his fall is proportionately deeper. A stone falls to a greater depth from on high than when dropped from the lowest point. Thus perverse kings, perverse bishops, and rich men—those dwelling on high—fall further into the depths of hell than do the poor.

17   The Eagle

On behalf of celestial contemplation, Amen

When the eagle has chicks, she turns their heads up toward the sun. She saves and nurtures that chick who gazes at the sun's direct rays.

But anyone unable to contemplate the sun is cast out of her nest.

Thus the Lord has chicks in the church. Those who know God, and know as well the divine matters we need to contemplate, *those* He nurtures and saves. But those too ignorant to look on any except earthly things, those He casts into outer darkness.

18   The Stork and His Wife

This exemplum demonstrates that change of place
does not produce holiness

Once upon a time, a stork was quarrelling with his wife and plucked out her eye with his bill. The stork, embarrassed that he had inflicted such a serious injury, started to fly away toward another region. Now a raven intercepted him and wanted to know the cause of his journey. The stork told how he had plucked out his wife's eye with his bill. Then the raven replied: "Don't you still have the same bill?" The stork said yes, this was so. "So what's your reason for fleeing? Since, wherever you are, you always carry your bill with you?"

Thus there are men who have committed many sins. And these men flee into another region—or into the cloister. Nevertheless, included as a part of what they are, they always carry their bill (i.e., their malice, the instrument of sinning, the Devil).

Their clime they alter, not their souls,*

and when they have been perverse in affairs of the world, they are perverse or far worse within the cloister.

Matthew 23:15: "Woe to you scribes and Pharisees, hypocrites! Because you go round about the sea and land to make one convert; and when he has become one, you make him twofold more a son of hell than yourselves."

19   The Heretic and the Fly

They say that a heretic in around Toulouse got up onto a platform and preached that the true God did not make the visible world [*mundus*], i.e., that He did not create either animals or other material things. "Why," he asked, "should a good God have made the fly, seeing that it is a foul [*inmundum*] animal?"*

And a lone fly came along and bit the heretic in the face. With his hand, the heretic swatted at the fly. The fly simply settled down on another part of his face and, again, the heretic swatted at him. He pranced about on the heretic's face with such insistence, now here and now there, that the heretic—unexpectedly tormented—cast himself into a headlong fall and was broken to pieces.

Behold how the fly both proved that God made him and, also, vindicated the injustice done to his creator.

82

20   The Phoenix

That as death draws near, men ought to multiply their good deeds

When the time of his death draws near, the phoenix (who is the one bird of his kind on earth) customarily gathers aromatic fruits and branches; then, out of these, he makes his nest. The nest is set afire and the phoenix is burned to ashes. And from this conflagration another phoenix arises.

Likewise, when death draws near, the just man especially ought to multiply his good deeds—and ought to end his mortal life amid them. And then another life shall rise from these good deeds, a life blessed and immortal.*

21   The Toad's Son and the Slippers

Against the falsification of rational judgment by affection

It happened that the animals announced a council meeting. The toad sent his own son as a delegate. But the son forgot his new slippers. So the toad tried to find a fleet-footed animal, someone who could make a dash to the council. The hare, so he thought, was a good runner.

The toad therefore called in the hare and, once the fee was agreed upon, told him that he was to carry the new slippers to his son. The hare responded with a question: "How am I supposed to pick out your son in such a gathering?" And the toad told him: "The most beautiful amid all the animals, *that* is my son." Said the hare: "But is your son a dove? Or a peacock?" "Of course not," answered the toad, "for the dove has black flesh, and the peacock has ugly legs." Then the hare said: "So what qualities do make your son stand out from the rest?" To this the toad replied: "He who has a head like mine, a belly like mine, legs and feet like mine — that is my beautiful son! He is the one to whom you should take the slippers."

The hare arrived at the council with the slippers and told the lion and other beasts how the toad commended his own son over the other animals. And the lion remarked: *"Ki Crapout eime, Lune li semble."* Which is to say:

If someone has a frog as mistress, he sees her as Diana the goddess!*

22   Young Man, Old Woman   🌿

I observed the affection of a certain young man being held in thrall by a loathsome old woman. The young man queried others. How could he be freed from this woman's love? And someone said: "How is it you desire this woman who is no real beauty?" The youth replied that, to him, she was extremely beautiful.

Likewise, it can happen that some woman has a handsome husband. She nevertheless desires some other man — one who is ugly and crude — more than her husband.

Likewise again, a sinner's soul (which is the bride of Christ) sometimes desires a singular toad more than He whose beauty of form transcends that of the sons of men. For all who engage in fornication, adultery, and deceit relinquish their beautiful spouse and desire a toad. They embrace the Devil and cling to a toad. To such as these, a toad seems more beautiful than the sun or moon — more beautiful than God Himself.

Alas, what error! What blindness! What deception! Oh Lord, illumine our eyes, so that we may perceive [*intelligamus*] you who are the Most Beautiful and desire you who are the intelligence [*intellectus*] over all things. As Augustine says:

You, Lord, made all things. Because you are beautiful, they are beautiful; because you are good, they are good; because you are, they are—and are not evil. As they are truly good, so truly are they as you, the founder of all things—you, in comparison to whom they are neither beautiful, nor good, nor even are.

23   The Cat Who Made Himself a Monk

Against those who solicit honors and favors and worldly dignities, etc.

In a monastic dining hall there lived a cat who had caught and killed all the mice—one huge mouse excepted. The cat thought over just how he might deceive and devour that huge mouse. Finally he shaved a tonsure for himself, put on a cowl, and feigned being a monk. And he sat down and proceeded to eat among the other monks. Seeing this, our mouse—believing that nobody wanted to harm him—was delighted. So he frolicked here and there while the cat, still dissimulating, averted his eyes from this folly. At last, quite carelessly, the mouse pranced in close to the cat. Then indeed the cat boldly seized him with his claws and held him fast. Said the mouse: "Why are you doing something so cruel? Why don't you put me down? Weren't you made a monk?" The cat replied: "You certainly aren't going to speak with such eloquence that I'll put you down, Brother. When I so wish, I am a monk; and when I wish, I'm a canon." And he devoured the mouse.

Thus many (finding themselves unable to get the riches and other things they desire) fast and feign the role of good and holy men, even though they are actually hypocrites and demons giving themselves the *appearance* of the angel of light. While others make themselves monks in order to become cellar masters, priors, abbots, and bishops. And thus they tonsure themselves so that they can seize upon one particular mouse. Then afterwards—when they illicitly have whatever they desired—you'll find yourself incapable of speaking with the eloquence needed to make them put down their mouse.

24   The Spider

Thus the spider spun forth a filament, wove a web, and totally evis-cerated himself—just in order to capture a single fly. At last the wind came along. And it completely ripped up and carried off the web (along with the spider and fly!).

So do members of the clergy, courtiers, and scholars labor—in the cold and heat, through wind and rain, over mountains and through valleys. They totally eviscerate themselves in order to capture some single benefice or single parish—this being the single fly. As Bernard puts it: "An officious prior circles about, follows in pursuit, complies obsequiously, and crawls about on his hands and feet—all in hopes that, somehow, he may lay hold upon ecclesiastical wealth."

25   The Fly

The fly is unpredictable—sometimes biting, sometimes befouling, and sometimes agitating us.

When somebody has a parish, and eagerly and greedily takes it over (being preoccupied with how to preserve and increase his worldly goods), then one is dealing with the biting fly. When he lives luxuri-ously, gluttonously, on a benefice, then one is dealing with the fly which befouls. When he has a great entourage, knights, and ostentatious displays financed by his benefice, then one is dealing with the agitating fly. After a time, the wind comes ripping along and carries off all of this.

The attack of the wind is death, or a fire—an adversity which destroys man's whole position, his whole fortune:

Fortune merely fabricated, by a single syllable is decimated.

This syllable, *death,* totally destroys man's felicity.

Against simoniacs and usurers

The house mouse asked the field mouse what he usually had to eat. The field mouse replied: "Wild beans and, sometimes, dried wheat or barley grains." "Those are quite meagre rations," answered the house mouse. "It's a wonder you don't waste away from hunger."

The woodland mouse then returned the question: "And what do you eat?" "I indeed eat rich morsels and, now and then, even have white bread." Then he added further: "You should join me for lunch. You'll dine on the best." Since this pleased the field mouse, he visited the home of the house mouse. There, men sitting at lunch tossed down morsels and scraps. Said the house mouse to the woodland mouse: "Don't stay standing in the entry hole. Come on in! See how good the things are that they're tossing aside." So the field mouse entered and snatched a single morsel. And a cat pounced after him and, immediately, our mouse leaped back toward the hole.

Then the house mouse said: "Ah, my brother, see what good morsels I eat regularly. You ought to stay on with me for several days." The woodland mouse replied: "They *are* good morsels. But do you daily have such a remarkable kind of partner?" And the house mouse asked what kind of partner he meant. "Why that monstrous mouser," said the woodland mouse, "the one who just about ate me whole." And the house mouse said in reply: "Oh of course. That's how things are. He killed both my father and mother and, often, I have barely escaped myself." The field mouse answered: "Well certainly, I would not wish to gain the whole world if it included a danger that great. You can stay with your morsels. I plan to live better, having my bread and water in security, than I would having every delicacy—while having, also, a 'partner' like that."

I'd rather gnaw a bean than be gnawed by continual fear.

Thus many men—hoping to make acquaintance with rulers of the churches, rulers who are undeserving and are simoniacs and usurers

—eat their meals in the company of a danger just as great. For over the unjustly acquired morsel sits the Devil, the cat who devours souls. They might well prefer eating barley bread, accompanied by a good conscience, over dining on all sorts of delicacies while having such a "partner."

27   The Antelope

There is an animal known as the antelope. Using his horns, he engages the thickets in sword play. After a while, his horns get entangled in the thickets and he therefore can't pull out his head. He begins crying out for help. Hearing this, hunters come and kill him.

Thus do many men play with the affairs of this world—and, in the same way, get entangled. They are held in by so many worldly affairs that no one can pull them away. And demons kill them.

28   An Exemplum: The Serpent and the Crocodile

There is an animal known as the serpent which enfolds itself in mire so that it can, more easily, slither along. And in time, it enters the mouth of the crocodile (when he is sleeping) and makes its way into his belly and, indeed, devours the crocodile's heart. Thus it kills the crocodile.

The serpent signifies the Son of God who took on the mire of our human flesh. He did this so that He might more easily slither into the mouth of the Devil and, thus, penetrate within—there devouring the Devil's heart and killing him.

29   The Fox, the Wolf, and the Well-Bucket

By chance a fox fell into a well-bucket, and down into the well he went. A wolf came along and asked what he was doing down there. "Dear brother," replied the fox, "here I have many fish, and large ones at that! How I wish you could have some of them with me!!" And Isengrim the wolf said: "How do I get down there?" To which our little fox answered: "Up above there's a bucket; get in and you'll be on your way down." For this well ran on two buckets; one came up [*ascendit*] when the other came down [*descendit*]. So the wolf fitted himself into the bucket that was up and descended within—while from below, in the other bucket, the little fox ascended. And when they met in passing, the wolf said: "Dear brother, where are you going?" And the fox replied: "I've eaten enough and so I'm coming back up. But go on down and you'll discover wonderful things." So the wretched wolf went on down and found nothing except water. Then, in the morning, farmers came and dragged out the wolf and beat him until he was dead.

The little fox signifies the Devil who says to man: "Come down to me, down into the well of sin, and you will find delicacies and an abundance of other good things." The fool acquiesces and goes on down into the well of sin and, there, finds no nourishment. In time, enemies come and pull out the impious man, beat him, and kill him. The Devil promised Adam many good things; but in fact he delivers many evils.

30   Three Hunters: The Lion, Wolf, and Fox

The lion, wolf, and fox agreed among themselves to share the task of hunting. The fox seized a goose, the wolf a fat ram, and the lion a scrawny cow. They intended to dine.

The lion told the wolf that the prey ought to be divided. "Let each of us," the wolf replied, "have what he captured: the lion his cow,

I my ram, and the fox his goose." Enraged, the lion swung up his paw and ripped off the wolf's whole scalp with his claws. And then the lion told the fox that *he* could divide the prey.

The fox then said: "My lord, of the fat ram's tender flesh you may devour as much as you wish—and, after that, just as much as you please of the goose; finally, of the cow's tough meat, you may eat in moderation. And unto us (who are *your* men, my lord!) you may give what is left." Replied the lion: "You express yourself well indeed. Who taught you how to divide things up so properly?" The fox responded: "Lord, my brother's blood-red 'cap'—his torn scalp—is a most instructive demonstration."

Thus did the Lord God strike down our first parent on account of the sin of disobedience; and in doing this, He used many afflictions: hunger, thirst, nakedness, and finally death. And Adam's blood-red "cap" ought to scourge us, so that we never would offend God. As Proverbs (19:25) tells us: "From a wicked man being scourged, the fool shall be made wiser." Sometimes the cub gets flogged in the presence of the lion, so that the cub may learn fear and grow gentle.

Thus the Lord God also gave a flogging to the very Threefold Lion itself, so that *we*—the wretched cubs—might learn fear and abstain from sin. God did, I tell you, flog Satan; He flogged the first Adam; and he also flogged the Second Adam, i.e., Christ. Wherefore the voice of Christ unto his Father: "Your wrath has come upon me" (Psalms 87:17)—His voice thus crying out because, under scourges, God exposed Himself to both cross and nails. And He did not spare His own Son.

And yet we wretches have not learned fear. And the Lord can say:

I found every kind of beast to be gentler than you.

Accursed is such a cub who—however much you flog away at the great lions—does not learn fear and refuses to be chastised.

31 A Rat, a Cat, and Some Cheese

Against prelates who give too much power to subordinates

A man had a cheese in his pantry. And a rat got in and began to gnaw away. Then our paterfamilias thought over what he ought to do. Finally, having sought advice, he placed a mouser inside the pantry—and *he* devoured both the rat and the cheese as well.

Thus many bishops place one or another parish within the care of a chaplain who gnaws away at that parish. Finally, such a bishop places an archdeacon in power—an archdeacon who devours both the parish and the chaplain, i.e., both cheese *and* rat.

Thus, when dogs are devouring their kill, the crows wait up in the trees until the dogs — finally satiated — depart. Then the crows come down and devour anything still left clinging about the bones.

Indeed, from time to time, it likewise happens that cardinals, emissaries, bishops, and archdeacons devour chaplains and poor clergymen. Afterwards, the servants and messengers come around; and they completely devour anything still clinging about the priests' bones.

33   The Mouse, the Frog, and the Kite

Against foolish administrators

Once, a mouse wanted to cross the water; and he asked the frog to carry him over. "Hang on tight to my leg," said the frog. "That way, I'll get you to the other side." The mouse did as he was told — and a kite swooped down and carried them both away.

This is what happens when a parish has been given to someone who is foolish and weak. The Devil comes along and carries off both, the chaplain *and* the parish.

34   The Wolf Who Longed To Be a Monk

Against evil habits

There once was a time when Isengrim longed to become a monk. Through earnest pleas, he obtained the consent of a monastic chapter.

And he assumed the tonsure, cowl, and other of their insignia. Then, in time, the monks set him to studying letters. He was supposed to learn the "Our Father." Yet he always responded with "Ram" and "Lamb." They instructed him to look upon Christ crucified and His sacrifice; and, without fail, he turned his eyes in the direction of the rams.

Thus do many men become monks. Yet even having done so, they always say "Ram," always loudly demand good wine, always have their eyes fixed upon some rich morsel—upon their plates. Hence the customary aphorism: *Thai thu Wolf hore hodi te preste tho thu hym sette Salmes to lere, evere beth his geres to the groue-ward.** Likewise, when you want to instruct an adult who is imprudent and irrational, remember that he is not about to give up his settled ways. Adults can be broken with a snap, but they cannot be bent; an old nag certainly doesn't learn how to prance.

Again, all asinine natures follow this pattern, for they never want to put aside their settled habits. So it goes: thrash an ass, wash an ass, punish an ass—you'll never make that ass into a good horse. Hence Jeremiah (13:23) tells us: "If the leopard can change his spots, and the Ethiopian can change his skin, then you too may do good deeds—you, who have long learned to do evil." For every kind of horse naturally maintains unchanged [*retinet in natura*] the things it learned at home. It is just about impossible to let go of habits:

Deep-stained with vices, they cannot put those vices aside.

35 The Complaint of the Sheep

Against wealthy plunderers and extortionists

The sheep complained to the lion about the wolf. They let the lion know that the wolf, both under cover and in broad daylight, was devouring their brothers. So the lion convened a royal council.

He asked the pigs and other animals how the wolf acted around them. "The wolf," said the pigs, "is courtly, open-handed, and generous."* (They said this because the wolf frequently invited the pigs to join in feasting on the lambs and rams that he had seized.) The lion then said: "That isn't what the sheep tell me; let's hear them." "My lord and king," one of the sheep began, "the wolf tore both my parents from me and devoured my son; I myself hardly escaped." The rest of the sheep also cried out in the same vein. And the lion said: "Let judgment be given. Let the wolf be hanged. Moreover, let the pigs—who knowingly ate of such booty—be hanged as well." And his command was carried out.

The wolves are the rich men of this world, who first plunder and ravage Christ's sheep (i.e., poor men) and then give bits of the booty to the pigs (i.e., to other rich fellows who wear them or eat them, so as to gain the admiring approval of men). But the Lord will come to give judgment; the sheep will complain about such wolves, and the pigs may even praise this sort of wolf—yet in vain. For the Lord will order the wolves and pigs hung in hell.

36   The Wolf "Takes Care of" the Sheep

Against evil leaders and others like them

A paterfamilias happened to have twelve sheep. He wanted to make a trip and, so, he turned over his sheep to the care of his companion Isengrim, i.e., the wolf. And his companion swore that he would do a good job taking care of them.

Immediately, the man himself set out on his journey. Isengrim meanwhile thought about his charges—and, on the first day, he dined on his first sheep; on the second day, on another. And he went on this way so that our paterfamilias found only three sheep when he returned home.

He asked his companion what he had done with the rest of the sheep. Isengrim replied that death from old age had overcome them. Then the paterfamilias said: "Give me the skins." And he found the marks [*vestigia*] left by the wolf's teeth. "You are liable for these deaths!" said the paterfamilias. And he had the wolf hung.

So does Christ entrust his sheep to priests for safekeeping. But many priests, either by depraved example or through negligence, destroy His sheep. Because a perverse prelate is guilty for as many deaths as there number exempla of depravity which he passes along to those under him. When the Paterfamilias comes, He will see to it that such corrupt men—or, rather, wolves—are hung in hell.

37   The Wolf and Lamb Who Were Drinking

Against oppressors of the poor

A wolf and a lamb were drinking from the same stream. And the wolf said: "Why are you muddying my water?" "I'm doing nothing of the sort," the lamb replied, "for you are drinking upstream; and the water flows down from you to me." The wolf came back at him: "Curse you! For you are contradicting me!! Who are *you* to be so arrogant?!" And he immediately devoured the lamb.

Thus rich men, for no cause at all—and regardless of how the poor respond—devour them.

38   The Fox Confesses His Sins to the Cock

Against the gluttonous

Once upon a time, a fox had gotten into the chicken coop. Men with sticks came upon him, and lashed him violently—so that the fox barely managed to escape. He beat a retreat as far as he could, threw himself across a haystack, and began to wail mournfully. Then he pled that the chaplain come and hear his sins. Hence came Chanticleer, the cock, who is chaplain of the animals.

A bit fearful of Reynard's well-established ways, Chanticleer seated himself at a good distance. Reynard then confessed his sins and, along with other things, realigned his snout so that it faced the chaplain. And the chaplain remarked: "Why are you moving in close to me?" To this, Reynard answered: "My great illness compels me to do this. Please! Forgive me, and be merciful unto me!!" Reynard then made further confession, mentioning other sins, and — now with his mouth wide open — positioned his entire head directly in line with the cock. And he seized and devoured Chanticleer.

Such as this are those many supposedly-obedient monks and laymen who feign illness and weakness. Yet they are always scheming how to devour their chaplains and superiors.

39   Asses in Lion Skins

Against the slothful

The asses saw that men were treating them cruelly and harshly, through both flogging and overloading them. What is more, they saw that the men were afraid of lions. So among themselves, the asses agreed to get ahold of some lion skins and thus strike fear into these men.

They got the skins. Then clothed in the skins, the asses pranced forth — even did some galloping about. And the men fled, believing that they really were lions.

After a time, the asses began to bray. The men listened attentively and said: "That voice is the voice of asses! Let's move in closer." In a little while, they succeeded. Then — seeing the animals' tails and feet — they said: "There's no question about it. These are asses, not lions!" So they seized the asses and gave them a flogging to remember.

These asses are false men, those who are slothful when it comes to pursuing any form of the Good. At a later time — hoping that deference may be paid them — they adopt the vestment of Benedict. But they often sing out in asinine voices, especially when they talk about *luxuria,* about riches. And then we can say: "Your speech betrays you" (Matthew 26:73). Then we can say that such men come closer to being the Devil's asses than to being monks who follow Benedict's *Rule.**

40   Walter's Search for the Happy Place

There once lived a man named Walter. He longed for a place and condition where he might rejoice forever and suffer no affliction — either of the flesh or spirit. So he set out on his quest. And he found a most beautiful lady whose husband had died.

Walter approached her. Then, when they had exchanged greetings, the lady wanted to know what he was seeking. Walter replied: "I am in quest of two things, namely: a place where I may rejoice forever, a place where I will not suffer at all — in either the flesh or the spirit." "Be my husband and remain with me," replied the lady; "you will thus have all the things you need: homes, lands, vineyards, and the rest."

She showed him an entrance and chamber, both of which pleased Walter. And he asked where he would rest at night. So the lady showed him a bed. Surrounding it were, on one side, a bear — and a wolf on the second, worms on the third, and serpents on the fourth. Walter then asked: "How long will I be dwelling with you? Will I indeed have delights like these forever?" Said the lady: "Not at all! For my husband died and, in time, you will have to also." She continued: "Do you see this bed?" "I see it," Walter responded. And the lady: "The bear will slay you — but whether on the first night or after a year or during the tenth year or later on, I really don't know. Then afterwards the wolf, worms, and serpents will consume you."

"All the other things," said Walter, "are good. But this bed terrifies me. I haven't got the slightest desire to lie regularly in such a

bed—whether to gain you or, even, the whole world." And he made his exit.

Then he came to a kingdom where the king had already died. Said the men of the kingdom: "Your arrival is fortunate indeed. What are you seeking?" Walter answered them: "I am looking for a place where I may be joyful forever and never suffer adversity." "So be our

king, Walter," said the men, "and you will have possession of all good things. Look at that palace! Behold its chambers!" And they showed him (among other things) a bed similar to the lady's; it was even surrounded by the familiar beasts. "Must I," Walter asked, "lie in such a bed?" Their reply left no doubt. Again he questioned them: "Won't these beasts ravage me?" "The bear will kill you," went their response, "and the other beasts will devour you and all of your possessions. That's how it goes with all kings. But when? We don't know." Then Walter himself replied: "A dominion like this is perilous. That bed really makes me shudder and, therefore, I must take my leave."

He set on his way again and came to a special place filled with gorgeous palaces, palaces resplendent with gold columns and gold beams. The citizens of the place welcomed him — and they wanted to elevate him to lordship over all this golden splendor. But they also showed him the bed we have been noting. Whence, terrified by the bed, Walter again took his leave.

At long last he came to a place where he found an old man sitting at the foot of a ladder; the three-rung ladder was leaning up against a wall. The old man asked Walter what he was seeking, and Walter told him. "I am," he said, "looking for the place where I can forever rejoice and suffer no affliction." The old man said: "If you use this ladder to ascend the wall, then there you'll find what you're seeking." So Walter made the climb, and he found it.

MYSTICALLY— take any worldly man you like; he seeks these three things, or some part of them. He seeks (1) a beautiful woman, on account of his licentiousness [*luxuria*], or (2) high position, on account of his vanity [*vana gloria*], or (3) gold and silver, on account of his greed [*avaricia*]. Yet if he looks carefully at the bed on which he must lie, he swiftly flees from all such things. For at the head of the bed stands the bear, i.e., death, who spares no one — death, of whom Hosea says: "I will meet them as a bear that is robbed of her cubs, and I will rend the inner parts of their liver" (13:8). Just as the bear that is robbed of her cubs spares no one — this on account of her great rage — so neither does death.

Similarly, the wolves are kings' kinsmen and officials, who devour all the dead man's goods. Whether he is saved or damned, they couldn't care less. And the worms chew up and devour the body. And the serpents are demons who carry off an impious man's soul, swallow it down, even assail it with varied tortures. Whatever may come of the

99

rest, God protect us from the serpents! Now of these three we read in Ecclesiasticus 10:13: "When an impious man dies, he shall inherit serpents, beasts, and worms." This man without piety gets sectioned into three parts. The serpents (i.e., demons) carry off his soul; the beasts (i.e., men whose lives are bestial — wolves, to be plain) carry off his worldly goods; and the worms get his cadaver.

Whence a certain magician, a master of the evil arts, met some monks who were carrying off a dead usurer and his coins. The magician inquired as to what they were carrying. And they told him: "This man's body, plus the coins that he gave us." "Not so fast!" came the magician's retort; "for he was mine. But rest assured that you and the worms will keep the cadaver. His money? *I* will take that — and demons will carry off his soul."

Do therefore as Walter did. Climb up Jacob's golden ladder — the ladder whose first step is contrition of heart, whose second is true confession, whose third is full penance.* If you will make the ascent up these rungs, you shall be transported unto the glory of eternal life — where, without end, you shall rejoice and not suffer affliction.

May our Lord Jesus Christ lead us all unto this glory!

41   Two Brothers

Against flatterers

There once lived two brothers whose itinerary took them past a monastery. And the second of them declared: "I'll wager you. I'll turn a bigger profit with lies than you will with truth!" "And I'll wager you!!" the first answered back. Having managed this solid agreement, the liar broke in upon the religious community of apes. And the apes asked him: "How do we appear to you?" To this the liar replied: "Of all the creatures upon the face of the earth, you are the fairest. Indeed, it is to you that men are compared. Never have I seen such a handsome congregation." And he praised them without limit. Now, on account of such words, the apes heaped him with honors and gave him gold and silver.

Then the upright brother came along. And the apes asked how the members of their community appeared to him. He responded by saying: "I have never seen a congregation so unsightly, so foul." As a result, the enraged apes gave him an incredible beating—one so bad that he barely escaped:

And sometimes it's perilous to utter words completely true.

So it goes with anyone who flatters prelates and speaks of all they do as good. When you've got prelates who will consign a thousand souls to torture at the hands of their own kinsmen, and flatterers who will declare that these prelates are doing good deeds—then you've got flatterers who receive praises at court, who are enriched, and called upon for wise counsel.

But let Christ come, let John the Baptist come, or let Peter come and speak the truth. The flatterers will throw him out and drive him away from every good they own. For to them, living means being weighted down with worldly goods. Thus many a man profits more by croaking like a raven than by singing sweetly like Philomel.

42   The Dispute of the Wasp and the Spider

How prosperity deceives human beings, and so on

The wasp said to the spider: "You're worthless! You spend all your time in a hole. In just one day, I fly further than you could go in ten." And the spider replied: "I'll make you a bet!"

"What'll you wager?"

"A gallon of wine."

To which the wasp replied: "Let's first have our drink. And whoever loses can pay for the wine." He went on: "Let's have our drink in this tree." "Nothing doing!" said the spider; "but, for your pleasure, I have readied a bright and beautiful parlor. Together, let's sit down here and drink." (This is why spiders' webs are called "parlors" in the Lombard language.)

The wasp went down into the parlor — that is, into the web of the spider. And immediately his feet and head were enmeshed — and so he tried to use his wings to get free, and could not. And he said: "Damn such a 'parlor,' I can't get out!" "Indeed," said the spider, "you'll never get out alive." And he came right up to the wasp and devoured him.

This "parlor" is a gorgeous woman, the pleasant things of this world, the refined opulence of wealth — the things we usually speak of as Parlors of the Devil. And the Devil devours all who thrust themselves amid these. Hence Job 18:8: "He has thrust his feet into a net, and walks in its meshes."

43   The Beetle

Against those who savor earthly over spiritual goods, and so on

A beetle once flew over trees wrapped in flowering herbage, over apple orchards, over roses, over lilies and other flowers. In time, he landed on a dunghill made from the droppings of horses and cattle. And there he came upon his wife, who wanted to know where he had been. The beetle reported to her: "I circled about the earth, flew all the way across her. And I saw the flowers put forth by earth's vegetation, by roses and lilies. Yet nowhere did I ever see such a pleasant place [*amenus locus*], a place so delightful, as this manifest dunghill."*

So it is with many clerics, monks, and laymen. They hear the lives of the saints, make their way over lilies of the valley, over roses of the martyrs, over the violets of confessors. Yet to them, nothing seems as peaceful (indeed, as pleasant!) as a harlot or a tavern or the violence of factions — all of which, taken together, are a reeking dunghill and a congregation of sinners. Whence Ecclesiasticus (9:10) says: "Every woman who is a harlot shall be trodden on as dung in the way."

Such a beetle, such an impious person, is accursed and unnatural. He is someone who (rather than savoring Christ) savors the dung of sin, the places of the Devil. He is someone who (rather than savoring the life and exempla of the saints) savors swallows' droppings. As Augustine writes: "Their taste is corrupt at heart, on account of the burning fever of their iniquity."

44   The Eagle and Dr. Raven, M.D.   ❧

Against ignorant prelates

Once upon a time, the eagle felt a pain in his eyes and called for the raven, the physician of the birds. He sought advice. What could he do about the pain? And the raven told him: "I am going to apply the best herb available. It will cure your eyes."

"If you manage this," the eagle replied, "I'll make sure you get the highest possible fee." The raven accepted this offer. He blended together some onion and excrement and put the mixture into his patient's eyes—and the eagle was blinded. Then the raven went and devoured the eagle's chicks and, next, set upon the eagle herself with blow after blow. And the eagle cried out: "Your 'medicine' is damnable! For now I can't see anything at all. What's more, you devoured my chicks!!" "As long as you could see," the raven replied, "there was no way I could relish those chicks—even though I really wanted to. So now my desire has been fully satisfied."

MYSTICALLY—the eagle is a prelate who keeps his eyes open, so that he can care for his chicks, for the flock entrusted to him. Yet the desire of the Devil is to kill and devour the Lord's flock. Therefore, as long as a prelate has his eyes, he frustrates the Devil's desire. But the Devil makes a plaster from a collection of worldly things. And he thrusts it into prelates' eyes—so that they cannot look upon heavenly things. Such blinded prelates' whole study concerns manor houses, lambs, cattle, and returns on investments. Why? Because their spiritual eyes have been extinguished.* As a consequence, the Devil seizes and devours their chicks—and also attacks the eagle itself, lashing it up one side and down another.

Naas the Ammonite desired to enter into a treaty with the men of Jabes Gallad, so that he could pluck out their right eyes and thus disperse them in peace (see I Kings 11:1–2). Naas is called "the serpent." For the ancient serpent strives to do just this: pluck out the spiritual eyes of prelates and other clerks—so that they do not have the power to reflect upon heavenly things, but only (with their left eyes) upon the things of this earth. And many go along with this, for there are many monks.

45   A Hunter-Soldier Hears a Beast Fable

Against the worldly wise

A certain soldier asked a scholar: "What sort of joy will we find in paradise?" And the scholar replied: "Such joy as the eye has not seen nor the ear hear, such joy as has never arisen within the heart of man. Such are the things which God has prepared for those who love him" (I Corinthians 2:9). And our soldier, a layman who truly loved to hunt with hounds and hawks, queried further: "Will paradise contain hounds and hawks?"

To this, the scholar said: "It is not fitting for dogs to enter into a place as pleasant [*locus tam amenus*] as that!" "Nonetheless," said the layman, "if it had included hounds and hawks, my desire to journey there would have been even greater." And the scholar-clerk responded with this tale:

> The lion, in company with the other beasts, once celebrated a great banquet. He summoned many beasts and supplied them with varied kinds of meats and a wide array of delicacies. Once they had feasted, the animals turned back toward their own homes. Thus, while on his way back, the wolf came upon a pig eating grubby refuse. And the pig called out to him: "Isengrim, where

are you going?" "I'm coming back from the lion's noble banquet,"
replied the wolf; "and you? Weren't you there?" Then the pig asked:
"You can't be telling me, can you, that the lion served up wonderful dishes and all sorts of delicacies?" Said the wolf: "There were,
to say the least, many such—all of them wonderful and well-
prepared." And the pig asked: "Didn't he serve any refuse? That
is, daily fare?" The wolf then replied: "Curse you! What *are* you
asking? For a banquet like that it would hardly be fitting to have
set out foods so vile!!"

Such are the many who value nothing but refuse—nothing except their cut of luxury, or their good wines, or their delicate meats.
Of such men Hosea remarks: "The Lord loves the children of Israel,
and yet they look to strange gods and love the husks of the grapes"
(3:1). That is to say, they love refuse. For the dregs (i.e., refuse) in a
mug of beer are equivalent to the husks of grapes in wine.
Men like this love things that are vile. They love their sins.

A farmer captured some beetles and hitched them, along with his nag, to a plow. And another fellow said: "Why did you ever tie creatures like that to your plow?" "Because," the farmer replied, "anything that doesn't drag me backwards helps to keep everything moving along." Again and again he lashed the beetles onward. Yet whenever these beetles came upon cow droppings, there they always took up residence and totally refused to obey our farmer.

Such are the many men whom God urges on — even drives onward with lashes. In spite of all this, they never pull themselves free from the slime of sin. Concerning men of this sort, Amos (4:10) makes report: "'I sent death upon you in the way of Egypt; I slew your young men with the sword; and I made the stench of your camp rise up into your nostrils. Yet you did not return to me,' says the Lord."

47   The Bees and the Beetles

Against the worldly wise

Once upon a time, the bees invited the beetles to lunch. The beetles accepted and, when the guests were seated at the table, the bees served up honey and honey comb. But the beetles ate sparingly and left in haste.

On another occasion, the beetles invited in the bees. When they were seated at the table, the beetles set cows' dung before their guests. Now the bees didn't want to eat that and, so, took their leave.

The bees are doctors of the church, contemplatives, who invite in impious men and set before them combs of honey — i.e., the Lord's precepts as well as His law, things far sweeter than honey or honey combs. But these impious men eat little or nothing; and when they, in turn, ask someone in, they set out cows' dung — that is, foul [inmunda] words and deeds, binges of drunkenness, and gluttony. As a result, just men are sometimes corrupted — since "depraved communications corrupt good morals" (I Corinthians 15:33). And there are many people in this world who have to be drunk or gorged or engaged in something perverse — lest they do something even more grasping, just to get the same kick. Whence Augustine: "Unless I am castigated, I will do something even more wicked." And Seneca: "If you want to keep company with those who are going to make you better, then ask in people whom you yourself can change for the better."

48   The Ass and the Pig

Against pigs and all who cherish carnal pleasures

An ass frequently witnessed bread and servings of food, as well as slops of refuse and the like, being given to the household pig. He also witnessed how the pig did no work at all — except that, when he had eaten his fill, he went to sleep. "This pig has things pretty good," thought the ass to himself. "He eats and drinks well and doesn't do any work, while I labor all day and eat frugally. I'm going to pretend that I'm ill."

He did so, and lay down in repose. His lord and master whipped him, but of course the ass didn't want to get up. Instead, he moaned. "Our ass," said the lord to his wife, "is sick." His lady replied: "Since he is, let's give him bread and meal — and let's also bring him some water." And this is precisely what they did. The ass ate sparingly, at first — then later on, he took his fill and got fat. And he told himself: "Now I'm really living the good life!"

Next, when the pig was fattened up, the lord of the house called in a butcher — equipped with both ax and knife — to slaughter the pig. Using his ax, the butcher killed the pig with a blow to his head. Then, with his knife, he slit the gullet and drained the blood.

The ass, seeing this, was terrified — fearing that they would slaughter *him* once he had been fattened up. And he said to himself: "I would rather work and lead my former life than be slaughtered like that!" Then he left the stable and pranced about in front of his lord. Seeing this, the lord restored him to his former duties. And in time, our ass died a good death.

The pig signifies the rich — those who dress themselves in fine style and who eat well and do no work. These are clerks and usurers, the pigs of the Devil into whom a foul [*inmundus*] spirit has entered, a foul spirit which has cast them into the sea — i.e., into the bitterness of sin and, finally, into the bitter sorrow of hell. The ass (on whom Christ rides) is the just man, wherever we find him — whether dedicated to work in his study, or in a cloister, or in the field. And it is better for us to work at carrying Christ into the heavenly Jerusalem than to be like the Devil's pigs that are cast into hell. There, the ax of damnation lands on their heads. Such as these "have no part in the work of men; hence they will not be scourged like other men" (Psalms 72:5) but like demons. "Therefore," as Isaiah prophesies, "the sovereign Lord, the Lord of hosts, shall send leanness among his fat ones" (Psalms 10:16).

49   The Chick, the Hen, and the Kite

This is told of those who do not hear God's call

The hen frequently gathered her chicks under her wing, particularly as a protection against the kite. One time, the kite came swooping down over her chicks, so she called out to them. They huddled in under her wings — all but one, who had found a little worm and was pecking away so that he could eat it. Meanwhile the kite returned, and seized the unprotected chick.

Thus does the Lord call unto us — so that, fleeing from sins, we may flee in under the wings of His protection. But many men, the Devil willing, do not flee to Christ. Instead, they stay right there with their grubworm of sin, with a prostitute or with drunkenness or with covetousness. And the kite (i.e., the Devil) comes and seizes so foolish a chick — concerning whom Job observes: "Worms are his sweetness" (24:20). For to an impious man, nothing is so tasty as the worms of sin!

But let us flee in under the wings of the Crucified One — thinking in Him, merging with Him, imitating Him. And so we shall be saved. For He is our protector, and all else.

50   The Banquet of the Lion, Cat, and Some Others   🦋

Against all whose way of life is foul

It happened that the lion invited the animals to a great dinner. A mouser was one of the recipients of this invitation. And the lion, wanting to satisfy each guest, asked the mouser what he liked to eat. And his reply? "Rats and mice." The lion thought this over and decided it would be degrading—unless everyone were served the same course. So after a while, he had a common course of rats brought in; and the cat ate it up with relish. The rest of the animals murmured among themselves, saying: "Fi! Fi!! What *are* we being served?" And because of this, the entire banquet was defiled.

Thus do many men plan great banquets. Certain cats, so it always turns out, are present. Nothing pleases them unless they get to have the degradations of drunkenness. And the civility of these banqueters holds up (and I mean the civility of all of them, willing and unwilling alike) until nightfall—when everyone can guzzle. Can fill his belly with drink and his soul with the Devil.

51   The Goose and the Raven   🦋

Against those overburdened with sins

A fat, heavy goose asked a raven to help him so that he could fly and look down upon the mountain peaks and tree tops. The raven nodded agreement and lined up his feet so that the goose could boost himself onto his back. But the goose weighed so much that the raven couldn't do anything. "Why," said the goose, "aren't you taking me up?" And the raven replied: "No matter how hard I struggle to get you up, you're carrying so much fat that I don't have the strength to lift off!"

52   "On Behalf of a Sinner": A Just Man Entreats the Lord

Likewise, a just man offered up prayers on behalf of a sinner—since the sinner had asked him to do it. The sinner later returned to him, saying: "My lord, I don't think your prayers are doing me any good; for I am still sinning and still stumbling, so to speak, as before." And the just man replied: "Come with me." They set forth together and, at one point, a money bag slipped from their horse. The just man said to the sinner: "Let's pick up the bag." "Okay," came the sinner's reply.

The two of them reached down. The sinner struggled to lift the money bag. The just man kept pulling the other end toward the ground. And he said to the sinner: "Why aren't you hoisting it up?" "I can't," he said, "because you keep pulling down!" The just man answered him: "That's just what you do to me. Through prayer, I struggle to lift you upward. But you're always dragging downward, toward the earth, for you're always sinning. Yet should you resolve to struggle along with me, together we might raise you upward."

53   A Poor Fool*

A certain fellow passed some time in the presence of the pope, some in the presence of the emperor, some in the presence of kings and princes. At length, in his travels he came upon a particular pauper. The poor man invited the fellow to stay with him. And to this the traveller replied: "Why should I stay with you? Especially since I have abandoned so many of noble station? I think *you* are a fool!"

Thus it is with worldly riches. To an extent, they want to pass some time with men of wealth. Yet even if they dwell with the wealthy for a while, I just can't be convinced that they want to tarry forever.

54   A Magician*

A certain magician spent time appearing before kings and princes. And he dazzled all of them blind.

If someone like this wants to enter your home, do not admit him. Most certainly don't let him enter, but drive him away—for what he really wants is to take away your eyesight.

Now this insolent vassal goes by the name of Robert the Rich. It is his riches which dazzle the eyes of rich men blind. Do not admit these riches—for kings wage wars for the sake of lands and riches, and they perpetrate murders on account of riches and their love of them.

55   Playing Chess*

Against nobles glorying in their station

It is the same with rich men as it is in a game of chess, where chessmen are taken from a pouch and arranged on a board. We call some chessmen kings, some knights, some rooks or castles, and some pawns or footsoldiers.† And our rich men play with such; the one who can conquer another gets hailed as courageous [*probus*]. Then the pieces are swept, all in disorder, into a bag.

So every man comes forth from one pouch only, from his mother's womb. Afterward, everyone plays a game—each with the other. One of them is winning his game with another and, finally, checkmates. At last they are gathered up and, again, jumbled into a bag.

Thus it is that, in this world, one plays with another; one loses, another turns a profit, and another is checkmated. Any man who can conquer another gets hailed as courageous and renowned [*probus et inclitus*]. Yet finally they are all thrown into the same bag—that is, their bodies are cast into the earth and their souls into hell. There, there is no order but, rather, the endurance of sempiternal horror.

56   The Wild Colt

A wild colt throws himself into the water or into a pit, unless he is held back by a bridle.

Assuredly, your fleshly nature will thus cast you into the pit of sin and hell (through drunken binges, fornications, and the like) unless you apply the bridle—evidently, the bridle of Christ's restraining nails. If you wrongly rein the bridle toward the table (i.e., toward a great feast) then you must not be forgetful of Him while at table, lest your horse throw you.

Constancy is necessary, lest you be a soldier who falls from his chariot at the buffeting of a breeze. Such winds are the words of slanderers, of flatterers, of men who incite you to wrath; and anyone hearing these words, *if* he is a fool, falls into anger or hatred or sadness. Such a man is not constant. Be therefore constant and firm, lest you fall and flee from the chariot of charity. "Whatever shall befall the just man, it shall not make him sad" (Proverbs 12:21).*

57   The Kite and the Partridges

Once upon a time, the kite was taking stock of his wings and feet and talons. Then he said: "Am I not as well armed as *Nisus,* the Hawk? I have wings, feet, and talons as fine as his. Why shouldn't *I* be out seizing partridges!?" And he knew of a place where many partridges regularly strolled about. Indeed, he mounted his attack—so that he seized one partridge with his beak, two with his wings, two with his feet, and then (when he couldn't hang onto them all) he lost them all. For as the saying goes, "whoever grabs all, loses all."

As far as the rest of the partridges go, the kite wasted no more effort—so that he still would have energy for capturing birds of the woodland.

58   The Fox's Tricks—and the Cat

Against attorneys, etc.

The fox, Reynard, met Tib the Cat; and Reynard said: "How many tricks or schemes* have you learned?" And the cat responded: "In fact, I know only one." "What's that?" asked Reynard. "When the dogs are chasing me," he replied, "I know to get up into the trees and escape."

Then the cat quizzed Reynard: "And you? How many do you know?" The fox said in reply: "I know no less than seventeen tricks; and they give me a full bag. Come along with me and I'll teach you my schemes, so the dogs will never catch you." The cat nodded his assent and, together, the two of them set out.

The hunters and their dogs were following them, and the cat said: "I hear the dogs; now I am scared." "Don't be afraid," Reynard told him; "I'm really going to teach you a way you will escape." And the dogs and hunters drew near. "For sure," the cat then said, "I'm not going on any further with you. I intend to make use of *my* scheme."

With this, he scrambled up into a tree top. The dogs left him alone; but they chased after Reynard and, finally, seized him — one by his legs, one by his belly, one by his back, and one by his head. And the cat, sitting on high, called out: "Reynard, Reynard! Open your bag! All those tricks aren't worth even an egg to you."†

By the cat, we understand simple men who know only a single scheme, namely, to spring into heaven. By Reynard, we understand attorneys, casuists, tricksters who have seventeen tricks — as we phrased it above, a full bag. The hunters and hell hounds come, and it is men whom they hunt. But just men spring into heaven. The impious, tricksters, are seized by demons. And then the just man can say: "Reynard, Reynard! Open your bag!! All your tricks together can't free you from the demons' teeth and claws."

59   The Raven and the Dove's Chick

Against bailiffs and lords*

Once upon a time, the raven seized the young chick of the dove. Then the dove came to the raven's nest, begging for return of her chick. And

114

the raven asked: "Do you know how to sing?" Replied the dove: "I know how—though not very well." "So," said the raven, "sing!" The dove therefore sang as well as she knew how.

"Sing better," commanded the raven, "or you'll never have your chick." And the dove again replied: "I neither can, nor have I learned how to sing better." "Well then," the raven declared, "you're not going to have your youngster." And the raven and his wife together devoured the chick.

It is just the same when wealthy lords and their bailiffs seize the cow or sheep of a simple peasant, then levy a charge of crime or fraud against him. Seeking the hostage or the terms of its freedom, the simple man comes before the powerful. He pledges five coins—more or less, up to the very limit of his ability. "My brother," the bailiff says, "you don't know how to sing better than that? Unless you can sing more sweetly, you won't have the hostage back." "Indeed," the simple man replies, "I haven't learned how to sing better—nor can I, for I am needy and poor. I just can't give you more."

Then the rich man either keeps the animal hostage or, otherwise, butchers it. And it is thus that he devours the poor peasant.

60 The Hoopoe and the Nightingale

Against luxuries—and concerning the religious who flee from them

The beautiful hoopoe, dressed out in an array of colors and crested with exceptional splendor, addressed the nightingale: "You spend the whole night singing and hopping up and down upon the rough branches. Come. Rest yourself in my nest." The invitation pleased the nightingale, and down she went [*descendit*] into the hoopoe's nest. Yet once there, she found fetid dung and, so, couldn't rest at ease. Away she then flew, declaring: "I'd rather hop upon the rough branches than rest amid such dung."

The hoopoe who builds her nest upon dung signifies a lustful woman, a dissipated nobleman, those who often enough possess beds that are fetid indeed — splendid and plush with the dung of sin. The nightingale signifies religious men and women upon their rough branches, i.e., living amid the austerities of religion and praising God in nightly songs. These religious would rather hop and exult upon such rough branches than rot in the stench of luxury — as was the case with a particular Cluniac monk.*

A stranger woman actually came to him by night, asking what she might possess by living with them. "You must, then, come over here," the monk said in reply. And he proceeded to stretch himself out on top of glowing embers. At this, the woman strove with words to get him up from the embers. But he had no desire to arise, and said to her: "I am doing what I am doing in order that *you* may long for it." The abbot of the monastery, witnessing this struggle, began chanting the fifteen psalms *Ad Dominum.*†

Some time later, when this same abbot was laboring at the point of death himself, people asked him whom they should consider appointing as the new abbot, after his death. He answered: "The monk who lay within the fire and was not consumed by it." Now upon hearing these words, everyone standing about thought that the abbot was crazy. So, at last, he told them the story about the monk mentioned above.

Such an event actually happened in our own time, in the case of a preaching brother in Spain. A woman threatened to kill herself unless she could possess what he had. And the brother marked out a place, and there kindled a great funeral pyre. Then he stepped within, and told the woman that she too should enter the fire — if she wished to enjoy its pleasures with him. And thus the woman departed, filled with confusion.

61 The Rich Man Who Owned Many Cows*

There was a rich man who had many cows. And nearby lived a certain widow who owned a single, fat cow. Desiring it, this rich fellow told his servant: "See that widow! She has the fattest cow I've ever seen. Go and bring it to me."

Acting on the command of his lord, the servant brought him the cow. Then the rich man ordered it killed, had one part boiled and the rest roasted, and had the meat carried in for his luncheon. But choking at the moment he took a bite from the first morsel, the rich man died.

Whence Isaiah (33:1): "Woe to you who plunder! Shall not you yourselves also be plundered?" This rich fellow got the cow by plundering, and the Devil plundered his soul.

62   Direct Simplicity in Paying One's Debts

Folk tell a tale of some simple men from Wilby who were up against the deadline when they had to pay off the tax owed to their lord. And they didn't have a messenger who could quickly take care of the matter. "Now that the due date is almost here," they asked one another, "what shall we do?" Several of the men then said: "The hare is clearly a speedy animal. Let's hang a pouch, the payment stuffed inside, around his neck; and let's order him to bear it swiftly to our lord's court." This is precisely what the men did. And the hare? As fast as he could, he

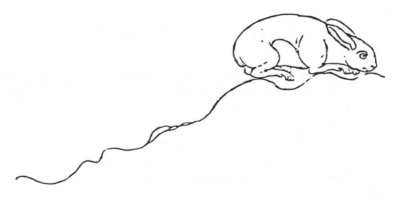

bounded off to a forest glade—with, of course, the pouch and payment! So the men never found out where he had absconded.

Many men do as these. When officials come—from the court, or from the Canons Regular of St. Anthony, or from Roncesvalles—these officials promise many things.* In hope of money, they multiply many lies. And then, believing in them, men give over alms in abundance. Yet having the alms in hand, such officials mount their horses and speed away like the hare—so that the alms-givers don't know where these officials have absconded. They most likely squander the alms in vulgar dives—on that very night! Whence Augustine tells us: "Hold to the certain; turn away from the uncertain. Give alms to those you're certain of—to your neighbors, to humble paupers whom you know to be in need, and especially to your intimates in the faith."

Also like the above are some princes. When the destruction of their own people is imminent, they freely dole out assistance to foreigners who then speed away with the gifts (they run like the olive tree in season).† Nobody knows where they abscond.

In that princes like these are thus afflicting their own men, they are like witches (who injure their own sons). In that they give away food to outsiders, they are like hens (who rear up the children of the duck). Indeed they are like sparrows (who, to their own destruction, nurture the son of the cuckoo)!

63   The Industriousness of the Ant   🔲

Against the useless accumulation of goods

The ants gather corn together into a pile, so that they can survive through the winter. And then the hogs come along, scatter the whole pile, and consume the grains.

From time to time, multitudes of men gather together goods in abundance. And then bandits, either the prince's bailiffs or his relatives, come along and consume the whole—whence the industrious men leave their riches to strangers (see Psalms 48:11).

118

Against those who envy the funerals of the great

It so happened that the wolf had died. And the lion assembled the beasts and commanded observance of full funeral rites for him. The hare carried the holy water, the hedgehogs the candles. The he-goats rang the bells, while the badgers dug the grave. The foxes bore the coffin of the deceased. *Berengarius,* the bear, celebrated the mass—with the ox reading the gospel and the ass the epistle. Once the mass had been celebrated and Isengrim buried, the other animals feasted lavishly—thanks to the remains from the wolf's larder—and agreed that they wanted similar funerals for themselves.

Indeed, it often enough happens thus. Upon the death of some rich plunderer or usurer, an abbot or prior calls together an assembly of the beasts—i.e., of those who live bestially. Such truly is frequently the case in great assemblies of Black and White Monks.* One finds there nothing but beasts: lions in pride, foxes in deceit, bears in voraciousness, he-goats in the stench of *luxuria,* asses in stubborn sloth, hedgehogs in asperity, hares trembling in fear when there was no cause for fear (see Psalms 13:5).

But as to this fear, how are we to understand it? They fear to dismiss secular matters where such dismissal should not be feared, and they do *not* fear to dismiss the things of eternity where such should especially be feared.

Our beastly monks are oxen in earthly labor, since they labor more

strenuously for the sake of worldly than heavenly things. They are not at all the oxen of Abraham, sent by God, but bears of the Devil who refuse to come unto the heavenly banquet (see Genesis 21–25:7).

As we read in Micah 7:4: "He who is best among men is like the brier; and he who is righteous is like the thorn of the hedge." So it often is. And where there is a great congregation, scarcely one just man can be found. And he who is the best among them, stings the congregation's members and fights like the brier — that is, his strategy is like the thistle's and the thorn's.

65   Dog Dirt

Against evil companions and the like

Now there was a dog who wanted to take a crap right on top of a cluster [*congregatio*] of rushes. And one rush gave that dog's rear a good, stinging thrust. Then the dog retreated a fair distance and bayed at the rushes. The rush answered back: "I'd rather have you bay at me from a distance than defile me in close."

Thus it is better to expel fools and evil men from a fellowship (granted that *their* baying is accomplished through slander) than to be defiled by their actual companionship.

As we read in Ecclesiasticus 13:1: "Whoever touches pitch is defiled by it."

66   The Unicorn and a Man

Against those who dwell in sensual pleasures

A unicorn was following a certain man who, as he fled his pursuer, came upon a tree loaded down with beautiful fruit. Below the tree

120

was a pit filled with serpents, toads, and reptiles. Also, two worms—
one white and the other black—were knawing away at the tree. Even
so, the man climbed up into it and dined upon the fruit, all the time
delighting in the tree's leafy branches. To those two worms who kept
on knawing, he paid no attention. And the tree fell. And the wretched
man plunged down into the pit.

MYSTICALLY—the unicorn is death, whom no one can elude.
The tree is the world, whose fruits are diverse pleasures: foods, drink,
beautiful women, and the like. The leafy branches are eloquent words.
And the two worms knawing at the tree are day and night—which consume all.

The wretched man, not thinking ahead, delights in these fruits.
Hence he is inattentive. And, hence, he falls into the pit of hell—
where there live reptiles of diverse kinds who torment the wretch,
through all eternity.

> Anyone that's always hasty is hardly settled in safety.

67   The Fox

> And this one applies to all who pay back good with evil

One day, the fox wished to cross over the water in a ship—and, for
this, he promised a sailor payment. So the sailor used his boat to ferry
the fox across the river, then requested payment. "I'll pay you hand-
somely," announced the fox—and proceeded to pee all over his own
tail and, then, shake it in the sailor's eyes. "You've given me," blurted
the sailor, "a horribly disgusting 'payment.'"

Whence people commonly say: "Whoever serves an evil man, does
himself a disservice."

> Give a dog passage aboard your stern,
> he'll pay you nothing in return.

This tale treats those who never learned to bear adversity

The ape eats the kernel of a nut with gusto, on account of its sweetness. But when he gets a taste of the shell's bitterness, he gives up on the meaty kernel within and throws away the entire nut.

So it goes with men who are stupid—since the joyous pleasure of heavenly life lies concealed under the bitterness of our present suffering. Yet it is on account of this bitterness—because he doesn't want to fast, remain vigilant, or bear up under the least bit of bitterness—that the fool both dismisses and misses the sweetness of eternal life. As Gregory puts it: "The fool prefers perpetual punishment over temporary perseverance in adversity."

69   The Turtle   🐢

Against the weight of riches

The turtle carries his house upon his back. In consequence he seldom processes forth, and he does only a modest day's work.

Of this sort are rich men and bishops, who—with their four-horse chariots, their appurtenances, and their silver vessels—make processionals bearing their entire household. In consequence, they come to paradise but slowly. So, truly, "when riches abound, do not set your heart upon them" (Psalms 61:11). Saint Paul, however, is not advising us to revile those *spiritual* riches through which we may grow to merit the kingdom of heaven (consider I Timothy 6:17–19). Yet, to again recall I Timothy, he does give us warning: "All who wish to become rich in money fall into varied temptations and, thus, into the snares of the devil" (6:9; but see 6:10 also).

GLOSS: The Apostle is not rejecting riches but, rather, their spe-

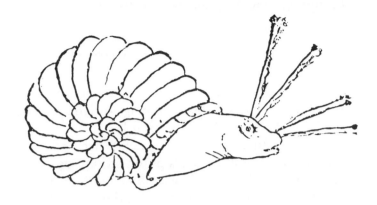

cific disease — namely pride. For the rich man sees himself surrounded with many people, he sees his beautiful vessels, and he sees himself owning fat horses and the like. Then he grows proud. And here is the very disease, the worm of worldly pleasure. Further, the worm knaws away at a lofty tree until it comes crashing down. In just this way, the worm of pride knaws away at men of prominence and pride until they fall into the pit of hell. Even so, there are many who possess riches but neither love them nor set their hearts upon them — except in the act of giving these goods to the poor.

70   Likewise Concerning the Snail*   🦋

Likewise, the snail stretches forth two "horns." But whenever a bit of chaff or a thorn touches them, he draws in both and ensconces himself within his shell.

So it goes with our horned bishops.† When touched by the slightest tribulation or conflict, they draw in their "horns." And as often as they flee, just that often do they ensconce themselves within their chambers and fail to take their stand upon the battlements before the house of God.

71   The Spider, the Fly, and the Wasp

Against rich men who assault the poor, etc.

When a fly comes into her web, the spider courageously strides forth and seizes the fly and kills it. When a droning wasp comes along, making an awful racket, the spider flees down her hole.

So it is with certain bishops and prelates. When a poor and modest man falls into the net of the bishops (on account of some wrongdoing or false charge) they eagerly seize him and have a great feast. But when a rich man comes along, shouting threats, then the bishop or prelate hides himself. Thus Hosea (13:1) reports: "When Ephraim spoke, dread seized Israel"—that is, when a rich man threatened, dread seized the cowardly prelate.

72   The Fox

When the fox gets hungry, he feigns death. How? He lies down on level ground and sticks out his tongue. Then a raven or kite happens along, believing that he has come upon prey. So he dips down to grab the tongue—and is himself grabbed and devoured by the fox.

Thus does the Devil feign the appearance of death (which itself can neither be heard nor seen) and stick forth his tongue. That is, he sets out every wrong which is dainty and desirable: a beautiful woman, delightful food, tasty wine, and the like. And when a man wrongfully grabs for them, he himself is grabbed by the Devil.

73   Another, Similar Exemplum

Similarly, somebody slices a round of cheese and puts a piece in a trap. When the rat smells it he steps into the trap, seizes the cheese, and is seized by the trap itself.

So it goes with all wrongdoing. The cheese is cut whenever a woman is done up and dressed so that she can entice and seize upon foolish rats. Whenever you seize a woman through adultery or the like, you yourself are seized by the Devil. Hence we have this gloss on the Psalms: "The prize you desire lies within a trap. Seize what is another's and you are seized by the Devil."

74 The Fox and the Hens

The fox, hungering and shivering with the cold, went to the chicken coop and begged the hens to open up. "We don't want to," they told him. "After all, you're our enemy, the one who has always hurt us." And he replied: "I swear—and this by all the saints—that I shall do you no evil."

"We don't believe you!"

"You've got every reason to have faith in me," the fox told them, "since now, exhausted by starvation and cold, I must die. And if I do, God will charge *you* with my death."

Guided by piety [*pietas*], the rooster and his hens opened the door. And the fox came inside and rested there quietly for a little while. Finally warmed up and without any memory of the oath he had sworn, he seized a first hen, then killed and ate her—then moved on to another. And so the fox threw everything into disorder.

Now the fox is anyone who is both poor and a deceiver. This man, without an interest in anything except eating well, begs to have the door of the cloister opened; he claims that all he wants is a simple life among simple monks, and that otherwise—if he continues in his worldly life—he will certainly perish. Finally, he claims that God will demand his soul from the monks.

Moved by pity [*misericordia*], the cloister's religious invite him in. Throughout the probationary period, he keeps his peace. Once he has made his vows, he will throw all the brothers into disorder. How? By extorting many meals and many clothes; by envying some of the brothers and degrading others; by grovelling before some, by drawing others into sin, and by slandering yet others.

Against hypocrisy and treachery and the like

The fox was so notorious that the sheep took exceptionally good care of themselves. This meant that they neither wandered outside their proper bounds, nor went beyond the gaze of the dogs who watched over them. "I know what I'll do," thought the fox, "I'll put on a sheep-skin and sally forth among the other sheep. And then, when the time comes, it is lambs and sheep that I'll be in a position to dine on." This is exactly what he did.

It is like this with many religious who have white vestments (religious who are the sheep of Christ). These are false prophets who come in sheep's clothing but, inwardly, are rapacious wolves and fraudulent foxes (cf. Matthew 7:15). These are false monks, false preachers, false religious who seek nothing more from rich men than lands, vineyards, and money—and who harass their own neighbors more than anyone else. Whence, rather than have such a religious for a neighbor, I would prefer a pagan or a Jew. For if I were able to make myself believe that white vestments would make me saintly, then I'd load my neck with as many as I could bear.

76　The Fraudulent Scheme of a Count

Against guile and hypocrisy

A certain count was accustomed to plundering the public roadway. But by now, men had their defenses ready; and whenever men saw him coming in the distance they either fled or, as often as they could, seized arms and defended themselves. Our count, however, wrapped himself and his men in the habits of Cistercian monks—then came up behind a company of merchants.

Glancing back, the merchants saw men wrapped in the vestments of sheep,* and they exclaimed: "Here come worthy men, we can proceed safely." And little by little they made their way along.

The count and his men followed right behind, then gleefully threw aside their habits and burst upon the merchants and stripped them of everything.

Certain monks do the very same. They come upon a wealthy man who is in poor health. And if they can, under the guise of safety, they strip him of all his goods.

77   A Disputation

Once upon a time a white sheep, a black sheep, an ass, and a he-goat were arguing about religion.

The white sheep said: "Look at the whiteness of the skin I wear. This signifies the purity and innocence I possess within myself. Also, I accomplish more than everybody else."

"Granted my external blackness," said the other sheep, "within myself, however, I am beautiful — even though I am black, foul, and despicable in the eyes of the world. Indeed, I myself look down upon this foul world and despise it."

Then the ass spoke up: "I certainly am holier yet. For I bear the cross upon my shoulders. I imitate Christ. And I call out in a loftier way than others."

"But *I*," the he-goat proclaimed, "am holier than anybody else. I wear a hair shirt, made from the hairs of she-goats. And I have an overgrown beard which I have *never* shaved, for fear I might seem beautiful in the eyes of the world."

MYSTICALLY — these four animals include nearly every branch of the regular clergy. The white sheep signifies all who wear white vestments, as for example: Cistercians, Premonstratensians, Trinitarians, and the like. The black sheep signifies all who wear black, for example: the Black Monks and canons.* The ass with the cross upon his shoulders signifies all who extend the cross before them, for example: the Knights

Hospitallers, the Knights Templar, and the like. And the bearded goat signifies Grandmontines and Cistercian converts† with those shaggy beards that they won't let anyone shave.

Whenever they gather together, they argue among themselves over which of the religious orders is better. But unless they value something as holy *besides* their white and black habits, the white and black sheep count among those of whom the Psalmist (Psalms 48:15) speaks: "Like sheep, they are placed in hell; death shall feed upon them." And the same holds for the Templars and Hospitallers. Unless, in both the spirit and the flesh, they keep a grasp upon some other cross—so as to crucify the flesh away from the vices of luxury and gluttony, and the mind from the lusts of greed and pride—they are merely asses of the Devil or of hell, regardless of the kind of cross they carry and regardless of how much and how loftily they "bray" their proclamations. Things fall out similarly with those who wear beards. They can wear any type of beard imaginable, but they shall never enter into glory unless they have grace in their heart and live lives transparently good to both God and men. So goes the verse:

If being bearded could make anybody blesséd,
He-goat piety would best all worldly sanctity.
A saint's not made by a robe, white or black,
Nor can asinine crosses produce justice men lack.

78   The Harrow and the Toad

One day, a harrow was drawn right over a toad. And one tooth of the harrow struck him on the head—while another got him in the heart, another in the kidneys. The toad exclaimed: "May God bring destruction upon all lords!"

Any chaplain can tell the same story. An archdeacon seeks patronage and a court official, boots. The squires seek slippers and the grooms, a linen vestment or money. Likewise, bailiffs and sub-bailiffs and servants and porters of the king or of a viscount seek to get theirs from some pauper. And that's when the poor man can exclaim: "May God bring destruction upon all lords!"

79   The Falcon and the Kite

> This one applies to everyone whose forcefulness and
> audacity are merely physical

Once upon a time a falcon seized a kite and clamped down hard, using only one of his two claws. "You wretch," taunted the falcon, "aren't your body, head, and beak as massive as mine? Aren't your claws and talons as strong? I've got you in my grasp and, soon, will kill you. Why are you letting this go on?"

The kite replied: "I know perfectly well that I'm as strong as you, and that the parts of my body have just as much force as yours—but it's my heart that fails me."

Thus many men are as forceful as others, as powerful as others, and as richly endowed when it comes to laying out expenditures. But what they *don't* have is heart. Again, there are many who can fast and hold to the rigors of religious life just as well as others. But they too don't have heart.

80   The Mice and the Cat

The mice once held a conference to discuss how they could defend themselves—in advance—from the cat. And a certain mouse, a wise one, said: "A small bell could be tied onto the cat's neck. That way, wherever he may saunter forth, we'll be able to hear him and be on guard against his wiles." This advice pleased everyone. Then one other mouse spoke up: "Who will tie the bell onto the neck of the cat?" And yet another of the mice replied: "Not I! For certain!!" "Nor I," came a further response. "I should not wish to draw near to anything *that* threatening—even to gain the whole world."

So it often happens that clerics and monks rise up against a bishop or prior or abbot. And they tell one another: "If only a fellow like this could be driven out, if only we could have another bishop or abbot!" Indeed, everyone might find this a pleasant thought. Then, after a time, they ask: "Who is standing up in open opposition to the bishop? Who will bring the charge against him?" The rest of them reply, terrified, "Not I! Nor I either!!" And it is thus that men of lower station [*minores*] allow those higher up [*maiores*] to live on and prevail over them.

81   Of the Rose and the Birds: Why the Owl Doesn't Fly by Day

And this tale applies to all who strive to possess honors

Gathered in a flock, the birds one day came upon a rose—indeed, the most beautiful primrose. Then they fell to arguing. To whom should it be given? And they announced their decision: Let the most beautiful primrose go to the most beautiful bird.

Again they argued, this time over who among them was most beautiful. Some said that it was the parrot. Others said it was the dove—and yet others, the peacock. Then the owl came along and declared that he was the most beautiful and ought to have the rose. At this, all the birds were moved to laughter, and they said: "You are the most beautiful in your irony, because *you* are the ugliest of all!"*

The birds postponed definitive sentencing until morning. Now the owl, of course, sees clearly in the night. And, while the rest of the birds were sleeping, he stole the rose. When the theft was discovered in the morning, the birds did pass sentence: Let the owl never fly by day. Let him not live among the other birds. (But let him use his eyes very clearly in the dark!) If he dares come out by day, however, let all the birds set upon him, screaming and inflicting wounds.

This very rose is an ecclesiastical benefice, the care of souls, which God values above all else. Thus it is that the rose is the flower of flowers, just as man or the soul is the worthiest of all created things. So who deserves this rose, this office of care? Certainly, the most beautiful of the birds—the one who has the picture of virtues within, the beauty of good deeds without. But along comes the owl, the bird who is ugliest—i.e., impious in vice and defiled by evil deeds. He declares that the rose ought to be his. Then just men double over in laughter and ridicule—and, consequently, adjudicate a decision refusing him any benefice. Yet while the just men are sleeping, back comes the owl —the son of darkness who sees clearly by night: i.e., who best knows how to handle the business of dark places, how to despoil simple men and farms and land, to get and keep great sums of money, to flatter bishops. This is how such men labor to receive benefices from their bishops. And they do not enter in by the door (that is, through love of Christ) but by another way—their deeds thus making them thieves and robbers.

It is much the same with a monk who knows quite well how to handle worldly matters and spread lies, and who within a cloister acquires kinds of authority and high offices. Such men are not choosing Christ but Barabbas (see Matthew 27:16–21). Now Barabbas was a robber; and indeed the worst of robbers succeed in getting benefices from kings, from the Romans, and from others as well.

But what will happen on Judgment Day? Doubtless, all the angels (both good and bad) and all just souls will—with screams and tortures —set upon such an owl. For the most severe judgment will come upon those now in high places: the powerful shall be powerfully afflicted, and yet stronger torments will crush the strong. On that day, sentence shall be handed down: Never, in any manner, shall the owls fly among the birds of heaven. But they will dwell perpetually in outer darkness where there shall be weeping and gnashing of teeth (see Matthew 8:12).

Against those who do not fulfill their vows

The mouse once fell into the froth which had formed on top of some fermenting wine or ale. Passing by, the cat heard the mouse squeaking that he couldn't climb out. So the cat asked: "What are you bawling about?" "I haven't got the strength to climb up," he replied. Said the cat: "What will you give me if I pull you out?" And the mouse answered back: "What's your price?" "If I free you from this mess," the cat asked, "will you come to me when I call?" The mouse replied: "I give you my solemn promise!" "Swear to me," the cat commanded. And the mouse made his vow. So the cat pulled him up and allowed the mouse to go his way.

Then one day the cat was hungry, and he made his way to the mouse's hole and called upon the mouse to come to him. "I'm not going to do it," the mouse replied. Said the cat: "Didn't you swear to me?" "Dear brother," he answered, "I was intoxicated when I made my vow."

So it is with many men. When they are ill or in prison or endangered, they make pledges and promise to reform their lives — to undertake fasts and the like. Yet once they escape the danger, they're not interested in fulfilling their promise, and they say: "Since I was in danger when I made my vow, I'm not bound by it."

83   The Flea

People tell this story as follows. An abbot captured a flea and, having done so, announced: "Now I've got you! You've hurt me lots of times — often routed me from my sleep. I will never let you loose. Instead, I'm going to kill you on the spot."

"Oh Holy Father," the flea implored him, "considering the deeds for which you intend to execute me, place me in the palm of your hand—so that I'll be able to freely confess my sins. Once I've made my confession, then you'll be in a position to kill me."

Moved by *pietas,* the abbot placed the flea right in the middle of his palm. Immediately the flea hopped free and, with a skip, made his escape. In a commanding voice, the abbot called upon the flea. But the flea hadn't the slightest interest in returning.

There are many men who are like this. When held in captivity, they'll promise anything for the time being. Yet once they break free, they pay back nothing.

84 Alexander: A Man in Danger

Many tell the tale of one Alexander, a man assigned to duty at sea. Alexander made a promise to God: if God would guide him to port, then he would be forever good—and *never* do anything to offend Him.

Then, when he was actually in port and harbored in a secure place along the river bank, he declared: "Jesus, Jesus! I have indeed deluded You. Even now, I haven't the slightest interest in 'being good.'"

85 The Granary

People tell the tale of a storage barn, set on fire while filled with grain. Everyone expected this granary to burn to the ground. But when he saw the fire, the barn's owner cried out: "Lord God, if You put out this fire, then—for love of You—I will distribute the grain to the poor." And immediately the fire was extinguished, the grain freed from destruction. Yet even so, the man did not keep his vow; he did not give the corn to paupers.

Why? Men will believe, just to fit an occasion—then beat their retreat at a moment's temptation.

86　The Pelican

And this applies to Christ's Passion

When the pelican's young chicks raise their beaks and strike at him,
he kills them. Afterwards, when he realizes that his brood of chicks
is dead, he is moved by piety. Hence he draws forth blood from his
own side and strews it upon his young ones. Then they come back
to life.

Likewise Adam and Eve struck out against the Lord when, violating His command, they ate of the forbidden fruit. And enraged, the Lord struck back at them and killed them—whence they turned dead in soul, mortal in body. Then the Lord was moved by pity.* And he allowed blood and water to be drawn forth from His side. He strewed this upon His chicks—that is, over the human race—and thus they were brought back to life. He sprinkles the water, whence they are baptized. He sprinkles the blood whenever they are saved in the faith of His blood, the faith of Christ's Passion, and whenever His blood is received in the Eucharist. So the verse:

As blood which the pelican strewed, worked to save his youthful brood,
So does Christ save our human race by the blood shed through His grace.

Whence Christ's own voice: "I have become like a pelican of the lonely desert" (Psalms 101:7).

87   The Battle of the Wolf and the Hare

That we should flee from lust and worldliness

A wolf and hare were face to face, blocking each other's way. And the wolf declared: "More than anything else, you're fearful. Don't you ever risk fighting with any animal?" "Of course I do," replied the hare, "indeed, even with you—though I'll grant that you've got a big body, while I'm on the small side." Indignant, the wolf snapped back: "I'll wager you, indeed I'll make a bet of ten gold coins to one, that I can conquer you!" "That arrangement is certainly agreeable with me," said the hare, "as long as I know your wager is guaranteed."

So both of them exchanged pledges. Then, having done this, the wolf and hare stationed themselves on a field, ready to fight. The wolf dashed straight at the hare, intent on seizing and devouring him. But the hare took to flight and the wolf, being strong, pursued him. Yet the hare kept up greater speed.

The wolf? Exhausted by now, he put an end to his pursuit and threw himself down on the ground. He simply couldn't run any longer. "Now you've been conquered," the hare said to him. "Conquered and laid low upon the earth." The wolf replied: "In that case, don't you want to look out for me?" "You're certainly correct," the hare told him. "After all, what fight could we have had—seeing that you're three times bigger than I am? Why, with your mouth open you could bite off my whole head. I don't do *any* fighting—*except* with my feet, *except* by fleeing!! Using this tactic, I have fought against the dogs . . . and won! So now that you've been conquered, pay up what you owe." Hence this contest was brought to a close. And the lion pronounced judgment that the wolf was conquered.

So it is when a man wants to fight against lust, against the world. He fights with the greatest assurance, and has the greatest certainty of conquest, when he flees. Thus we read in I Corinthians (6:18): "Flee fornication." Regarding which Augustine comments: "With the rest of the vices, to be sure, we can expect pain. But from this vice, flee. Don't even draw near it." Wherefore another remarks: "In this sort of combat, one's fighting gets braver and better by fleeing. And thus lusty Venus is vanquished. When we fly, we make her flee!"

David, had he only been far removed from Bathsheba—so that he could not have looked upon her—would not have been conquered (see II Kings 11). Likewise, Samson might not have sinned and might not have lost his eyes had he only fled from Delilah (see Judges 16). If you draw near to a beautiful woman, she will devour you as would a wolf. The Devil makes his entry simply—through a touch, through sight, through laughter.

88   The Man Who Cradled the Serpent

That a man shouldn't trust his enemies

One day, the serpent was writhing about on the frozen earth. He was very cold. Now a certain man saw all this and was moved by compassion [*pietas*] and, so, took up the serpent and settled him in his bosom to get warm. But once the serpent had warmed up, he bit the man —hard!

"What reason did you have," the man exclaimed, "to wickedly bite me like this? After all, I was the one who gathered you into my bosom, and did it for your sake." Then came the response: "Don't you know that there is eternal enmity between my kind and Man? And don't you know that, for me, hatred of Man comes naturally? Don't you know that a serpent in the bosom, a mouse in a basket, a fire in your midst—all these repay their hosts with evil?"

When they can, captive Saracens slay their lords and escape. So it goes with a perverse man as well. Granted, he may accept a benefice from someone he hates; but then, forever after, he'll injure his benefactor at the slightest opportunity. As a poet says:

I'll hate when I can—then when I can't, I'll grudgingly love.*

It is much the same when someone has an evil nature; every time he can, he'll exercise it. So never draw in as a brother someone naturally perverse. You should never believe that he's on your side!

89 A Man Without Gratitude

A certain man granted one of the king's servants a great favor. This very servant, in turn, singled out and brought an accusation against the man. Hence he was summoned to court and formally charged. Then the man discovered who had filed this action against him. And he called the royal servant over and asked him: "Didn't I do a service for *you*, to the very limit of my powers? I certainly did nothing at all to displease you. So why are you now making this effort to get me condemned?" The other replied: "I know perfectly well that you rewarded me and did me no evil. But such is simply our nature upon this earth

—namely that we always return evil to those who have endowed us with goods."

This is the nature of the Devil who, always, inflicts evil on his friends rather than on others. And he saves his worst rewards for those who serve him.

90   The Panther

This applies to pleasant words and good repute

The panther is an animal which sends forth a good fragrance. Hence savage animals such as the wolf and the leopard and the like (animals which ought to do the panther harm) follow her and do not attack—all because of her good fragrance.

So, too, there live men who are just as gentle in word and deed. Even so, they have enemies who hear and see them. Yet on account of such men's pleasant conversation, their enemies—banishing their own wrath and hatred—follow these men and cherish them. Thus Proverbs (15:1) tells us: "A mild answer breaks up wrath, but a harsh word stirs up fury."

91   The Dog and the Scrap of Meat

Against all who cherish vanities and abandon solid truths, etc.

One day, a dog was crossing a stream while carrying a scrap of meat in his mouth. Seeing the shadow of his scrap and noting that it appeared bigger, he immediately dropped the meat so that he could grab for the shadow. And — just as quickly — the shadow disappeared! Hence he lost his scrap of meat for the sake of a shadow.

Thus there are many men who have the assurance of grace, the solid foundation of all the virtues (the foundation being God Himself). And seeing the shadow of this world — seeing, that is, lovely foods, women, and dignities — they cling to these worldly things. As for this, the Book of Wisdom (5:9–14) teaches:

> All those things are passed away like a shadow, like a messenger who runs onward, and like a ship that passes through the waves . . . or as when a bird flies through the air, of the passage of which no mark can be found . . . or as when an arrow is shot at a target and the divided air presently comes back together again. . . . Such things as these, the sinners said in hell — for the hope of the wicked is like dust, which is blown away with the wind. Or it is like a thin froth that is dispersed by the storm, like smoke that is scattered abroad by the wind, and like one's memory of a guest of a single day that passes by.

Behold, men lose what is good — what is secure and unchangeable — for the sake of this shadow. And so they are deprived of *both* substance and shadow.

Or, as Jeremiah (2:13) reports: "They have forsaken me, the fountain of living water, and have dug themselves cisterns . . . that can hold no water at all." Which is to say, they labored so that they could have transitory things — those things which hold no true refreshment. They drop the rose for the sake of the thorn, the seed for the chaff, the sun for the moon, the wine for its dregs, the olive oil for its sediment, life for death, a thick fur for a fuzzy willow.

A man who does this sort of thing is false. As Augustine puts it: "If you desert He who made you and love the things which He made, in this desertion you are false." Such desertion is spoken of as idolatry. Thus, writing his letter to the Romans (1:25), St. Paul speaks of men "who changed the truth of God into a lie, and who worshipped and served the creature rather than the Creator — He who is blessed forever."

Against the desire for great things which arises from envy

The frog saw a cow ambling along in a field. Now our frog wondered to himself whether he might become as great as that cow. And he called his sons about him and exclaimed: "Behold the height of distinction and grandeur that is possible, if only I can come up to the cow's great magnitude!" Then he inflated himself and was puffed up as much as he could manage.

And now he asked his sons: "Have I reached the point where I'm as great as that cow?" "You," his children answered back, "aren't even as great as the cow's head!" "So be it," said the frog. "Then I'll just puff myself up further." Inflating himself to enormous size (he was in quite a fit!), right down the middle he split.

Thus there are many men who see bishops, abbots, archdeacons — officials who, so to speak, approximate cows — ambling along with a show of great ostentation. Such onlookers wonder to themselves just how they may become as great as these officials. And at length they make the attempt. In consequence they come — spiritually and physically — to their deaths.

93   The Soldier's Son

I observed a certain young man whose father was the very best of soldiers. And the youth, to whom nature had denied great bodily strength, wished to imitate his father. So in time the youth was injured in a tournament and, in consequence of this, died.

Similarly there are laymen who observe other laymen dressing well, eating in high style, riding great horses, and enjoying companionship with princes. So in time they strive with the others to be rewarded equally well. And in consequence, they die.

Brother, if you were made to be such as a great ox, then give praise to the Lord. If you were made a frog (that is, a poor or modest man), be content; don't ask to be made into an ox. Let the Lord order His republic as He wishes, humbling this man and raising up that one. Whence Ecclesiasticus (6:2) admonishes: "Do not extol yourself in the thoughts of your soul, lest your strength [*virtus*] be quashed by folly."*

94   The Mouse Who Wanted To Marry

> Against all who go forth in pride: "lofty" thinkers,
> "wise" men, and the like

Once upon a time a mouse wanted to get married—and she decided to acquire the strongest possible husband. Then, in private, she began to wonder who would be the most vigorous of all. At length she decided that the wind seemed best, for the wind lays low cedars and fortified towers and family dwellings.

Our mouse therefore sent her messengers to the wind, so that he might become her husband. But the wind put questions to the messengers. "Why does she want to marry me?" The messengers answered: "Because, among all created things, you're the strongest." "On the contrary," the wind replied, "the turreted citadel of Narbonne is stronger than I am; for reckoning from this moment, Narbonne has stood firm against me through more than a thousand years. It tears my men to shreds, shatters them to bits—yet I've never been able to overthrow it."

The messengers turned back, carrying home the wind's response. On hearing it, the mouse said: "Given the greater strength of the towered citadel, it then is the one I want for my husband." She relayed this message to the tower and, in turn, the tower asked: "Why do you want to marry me?" And the mouse answered him: "Because of all things, you are the very strongest—stronger even than the wind." Then the tower replied: "Without a doubt, the mice possess greater strength than I! For all day long, they're burrowing onward—and they're causing me to crumble. Indeed, they're building a roadway right through me." And so, having received such advice, it was most fitting that our mouse united herself with another mouse.

Thus many men focus their deliberations on hard questions and promise to work wonders. Yet:

The mountains labor, and bring forth a ridiculous mouse.*

Likewise, the king of Israel addressed Amasia, king of Judah. And the king of Israel (IV Kings 14:9–10) spoke as follows:

> A thistle sent to a cedar tree, which is in Lebanon, saying: "Give your daughter to my son as a wife." And the beasts of the forest, that are in Lebanon, passed by and trampled down the thistle.
> You, Amasias, have beaten and prevailed over Edom, and your heart has uplifted you. Be content with this glory and sit at home! Why are you provoking evil, such that you risk a fall — and the fall of Judah along with you?

But Amasias did not wish to rest at peace. So war began, and the people of Judah was cut down. And truly, Joas, king of Israel, captured Amasias, king of Judah, and subjected him to many evils.

So it goes with many men. They undertake lofty plans and fall so horribly. As St. Jerome writes to Eustocium: "It would have been better [*rectius*] for her to have submitted to marriage with a man, and to have walked on the level ground, rather than strain for the heights and fall into the depths of hell."† Moreover, it is dangerous to boast pridefully about one's good deeds and virtues. As we read in I Machabees 6:43–46, Eleazar (wanting to make an everlasting name for himself) positioned himself under an elephant and killed it. And then the beast fell upon him and he died. Thus Gregory makes the comment: "He dies, since he is underneath the very enemy he destroys; he who is not raised up by the sin which he overcomes, dies." To again quote Gregory: "Whoever pays tribute to himself for what he achieves, is convicted of denying the grace of his Author. Because of this, one ought not glory in one's virtues or good deeds — for it is dangerous to glory in evil."

Elevated, men fall; inflated, they burst; elated, they're punished.
These words, therefore, retain: God shatters all who are vain.

Against flirtations

A certain cat had a beautiful wife. But she did not think very highly of her husband, and she roamed about with other cats. Now her husband complained to his friends about his wife. In turn, one of the friends advised him: "Scorch her coat in a number of places—then she'll stay at home!" And when the husband did as his friend advised, the beautiful cat stayed in the house and no longer roamed about.

Thus many men have beautiful wives, sisters, and daughters; when these women have beautiful tresses and beautiful clothing, they venture forth from their homes. And they go making visits to neighbors —to the men no less than the women. They roam about the streets.

They come to look at others, and to be looked at themselves.*

Thus "Dina went out to see the women of that country" and was herself seen and ravished.† Hence every paterfamilias ought to knot up the hair of these women into a bun and scorch it. And he ought to dress them in skins rather than in precious garments. For thus they will stay at home.

96   A Certain Lady

A certain lady was asked why she dressed so lavishly. And she answered: "I don't do it to please the world—certainly not. I do it, rather, to please my husband."

He spoke up at this point: "That is false, lady! To the contrary, when you're in a crowd of people, *then* you dress lavishly. But when you're at home, face to face with your husband, you dress in rags. And you leave your lavish things hanging on the clothes pole!!"

That we should stop problems at the very beginning, etc.

The stork came to the serpent's hole and called upon him to come out. The serpent answered back: "Who are you!? You who dare to disturb me?" And to this she replied: "I am the stork, and I am quite willing to do battle with you."

"Wretch," the serpent shot back, "seeing that you have legs which are fine and fragile, a neck which is slender and long, why do you want to fight with me? Especially since I was the one to conquer the strongest of all the animals — namely Adam, the first man whom God made, and his wife as well? And since, moreover, I have annihilated multitudes in the desert? Even an entire one hundred storks like you couldn't manage to exterminate a single man. So! Just how is it you presume to do battle with me?"

"Merely come forth from your hole and you'll see," the stork answered. The serpent was overwhelmed by rage. Hissing and opening wide his mouth, he came forth — looking as though he wanted to devour the stork completely.

Immediately the stork let him have it with her beak — right on the top of his head. And immediately the serpent slumped downward (still speaking as death was settling in): "Oh, see! Now you've annihilated me!" "Indeed I have," the stork remarked. "And if Adam and other men had known just where your life and strength is centered, and had used my tactic, *they* would have struck you on the head. And thus not a single one would have been conquered by you."

So here we see what a man must do — armed, of course, with a tactic [*ars*] such as this:

> Stop the beginnings; the medicine is prepared too late
> When evils have grown strong because of long delays.*

When you note the first stirrings of *luxuria* or rage, resist immediately. Immediately dash these fledgling impulses against the rock. Now it is Christ who is the rock. All this is to say: "Kill those early stirrings through the love of Christ."

144

For if you allow them to grow until your whole body is burning with the fire of *luxuria,* you'll lack the forces needed to put it out. Because, by then, those small stirrings have grown so much that they can field great champions. So at the beginning, such vices — like coarse string — are easily undone. And yet, when they have grown, they will yield hard bonds which cannot be broken.

Whence the Lord, addressing the ancient serpent: "I will put enmities between you and the woman; she shall crush your head" (Genesis 3:15). The woman is the Blessed Virgin, the holy church, every faithful soul who must crush temptation at the very beginning — as though this temptation were the serpent's head.

This is how the ancient serpent is conquered!

98   The Peacock Stripped of Its Plumage

Against vainglory, and like vices

The peacock — a bird truly adorned by his plumage and distinguished from the others by variegated hues, one who is kindly and courtly — arrived at the birds' convention. Coming up to him, the raven asked for a gift of two feathers. The peacock said: "And what will you do for me?" The raven replied: "With my high voice, I'll acclaim you publicly in the courts of the birds." The peacock granted him the feathers.

In much the same way, the crow then sought and obtained some feathers for *him*self. The cuckoo did likewise, and many of the other birds as well. The result? Our peacock was left without any of his plumage.

This very peacock was responsible for sheltering and protecting his own young chicks, as well as others. But he simply couldn't, since he didn't have any feathers. Then cold weather came upon him and he perished. And the chicks withdrew from him and, as best they could, managed to live on.

Thus it is whenever kings or counts or knights or bishops own many villas, castles, fields, and vineyards; they are like the peacock —

well adorned with many different feathers. Then flatterers, Hospitallers, Templars, monks, and canons come up to such a peacock. They woo him for lands, vineyards, castles, gifts—all the time, promising him ceremonial acclamations,* masses in his honor, and prayers.

When the foolish peacock goes along with such nonsense, he gives others his holdings—the very things he and his dependents need to live. Now the king of Aragon† did this sort of thing. The result? His successors couldn't do what was fitting. They could not maintain troops, nor fight off their enemies, nor defend their kingdom.

We sometimes see knights do the same sort of thing. They give so much to those in religious life that they are left without any of their plumage. And their heirs are disinherited.

99   The Toad and the Frog   🖋

Against avaricious and greedy laymen

The toad (who lived on dry land) asked the frog (who made his home in a stream) to give him some water to drink. "As you please," responded the frog—and he gave the toad as much water as he wanted. Then the frog himself got hungry and, so, asked the toad to give him a bit of earth. "I shall not, indeed, give you anything," the toad replied. "For even I, fearing the possibility of a shortage, always stop eating *before* I'm satisfied."

Men, at least many of them, are like this. They are so panicky in their greed that they expect the loaves of bread to be mouldy, the bacon rancid, the pastries stale. They themselves are unable to eat. Nor are they able, even in honor of God, to give away the food. They live in fear that the earth may yield them nothing but a shortage.

These men are toads of the Devil. So Habacuc (2:6): "Woe to him who heaps up that which is not his own." He says blessings over things that are not truly his, for he does not dare spend the wealth. "He stores up; and he does not know for whom he shall gather these things" (Psalms 38:7).

146

Likewise, a dog is following along with two men. There's no way of knowing to whom he belongs. But when the two men go their separate ways, the dog follows his master.

In relation to their owner and to the world, riches are like this. And when their owner passes away, riches remain with the world—they're here to stay. It is therefore obvious that riches are followers of the world. So in Habacuc (2:6): "For how long does he load himself up with thick filth?" Because whoever greedily gathers riches together, builds a wall of filth between himself and God—between himself and that heaven he never will be able to enter.

If only covetous men could know of or really believe in the things about to come upon them, they might then weep and howl. St. James' Epistle (5:1–3) thus declares: "Come now, you rich men. Weep and howl over the miseries which will come upon you. Your riches have rotted, and your garments have become moth-eaten. Your gold and silver are rusted—and their rust will testify against you and will consume your flesh as does fire."

101   The Ass and the Lion

Against all who desire to dwell at the courts of the great, etc.

The lion, king of beasts, once called in all of his subordinates—so that they could serve him in various ways. The ass presented himself, stating that he knew how to sing and warble supremely well. "Then let us hear you," said the lion. And the ass opened his mouth . . . and brayed dreadfully! "Wretch," said the lion, "you lied to me. Why? Since your 'tone' is just terrible!! It would be better suited for routing me from my slumber than for putting me to sleep. You must leave my court, *without* delay!"

So many men may long to present themselves at the courts of kings and princes. But because they're awkward, they are driven out.

There are many who yearn to stuff their bellies from the pigs' troughs, yet nobody provides for them. Now the pigs' troughs are the delicate foods of rich men and gluttons—i.e., of the pigs of the Devil. Multitudes of monks, scholars, clerks, and laymen yearn to stuff their bellies in this way, and nobody provides for them. Thus their heart is always returning to the world, and the world rebuffs it. They love and long after this world; but even so, the world has no concern for them. Therefore let them turn again to their Father, let them come to Christ, and He will not spurn them—will, indeed, embrace them and command a great feast. He will slaughter the calf and prepare a royal meal—for "there is greater joy in the kingdom of heaven over one sinner who repents than over ninety-nine just men who have no need of penance."*

So if you are an ass, namely a simple and awkward man, be content. Do not seek to become a courtier. Peter spent but one night at the court of Caiphas—and then he denied Christ.† Yet so long as Peter dwelt in the "court" of Christ, he continued as a just and holy man. For in worldly courts, it is the Devil who sits enthroned—surrounded by men rich in concealments, so that he can slaughter the innocent.

Alas! How many have a greater desire to join the court of a Herod or a Caiphas than the court of Jesus Christ. For, as the Truth Himself says in Luke 22:25–26: "The kings of the Gentiles lord it over them; and they who have power over them are called beneficent. But it is not so with you. On the contrary, let him who is greatest among you become like the youngest—and him who is chief among you, like the servant."

Oh, if only we may live as the oxen of Abraham—or as those asses who feed beside the oxen! (see Job 1:14).

102   The Dogs, an Ass, and His Lord

Against worthless servants

A certain paterfamilias kept dogs. And whenever he returned home from business, they were always making a fuss over the man—stroking him with their paws [*pedes*] and nuzzling him. Seeing this, the ass thought to himself: "I should give my lord this special sort of attention." So one day the lord returned home from his business affairs; the ass ran to meet him, wanting to provide a special welcome. Then the ass raised his rear hooves [*pedes*] and gave his lord a sharp kick in the face and chest. And the lord, enraged, ordered the ass to be whipped (almost to the point of death) and shoved back into the stable.

Thus many men long to assume this or that position, a position which they don't at all know how to handle. So it is that some want to be priests, archdeacons, even bishops—yet are, nevertheless, still asses when it comes to songs of the lyre and asses when it comes to an actual position. For they are ignorant of how to sing, how to read, how to preach. They're the opposite of everything we would hope for. Through perverse deeds, and with all the force they can muster, they kick the Lord in His face. But the Lord, enraged, orders such asses to be whipped —to be shoved down into the prison of hell forever.

103   The Cheese and the Raven

Against vainglory

Now Aesop tells the tale—how:

"The raven's beak kept a grip on his cheese—it couldn't slip," and how the fox, longing to eat the cheese, told the raven: "How well your father used to sing! I would truly like to hear *your* voice!!" At this, the raven opened his mouth and sang. So the cheese dropped to the ground, and the fox ate it up.

Thus do many men carry the cheese. This cheese is the food (namely patience, grace, and charity) which should nourish the life of the soul. But the Devil comes along. And he incites them to deeds of vainglory, so that they will sing: promote themselves into some lord's patronage, ostentatiously adorn the hems of their garments. Thus, because they seek the glory of the world—not the glory which comes from

God—they let patience and all the rest of the virtues drop away. Hence David, because vainglory moved him to order a census, saw a great number of his people drop dead.*

104   An Athenian

It was a custom among the Athenians that anyone who wanted to be thought of as a philosopher should be flogged, vigorously. And if he bore up patiently, then he would be esteemed a philosopher.

Now one man was being thoroughly whipped. Then *before* judgment had been pronounced whether he should be held a philosopher (indeed, immediately following the whipping), he started shouting. "I am more than worthy," he exclaimed, "to be called Philosopher!" And another answered him: "Brother, you might have been—if you could have kept quiet."

105   The Stork and the Cat

That a serious man is guided by his vocation,
rather than by words of praise and blame

It is better to imitate the stork who was carrying home an eel for herself and her young ones to eat. Now the cat—who relishes eating fish, even though he doesn't at all like to get his feet wet—saw her. And he said to the stork: "Oh, you are the most beautiful of birds! For you have a red beak and the whitest of feathers. Is that beak of yours as red on the inside as outside?"

The stork didn't want to reply at all, nor did she want to open her beak — since she certainly didn't want to lose the eel. Our mouser, now enraged, lashed out with denigrating taunts. "You," he told the stork, "are either deaf or mute. Aren't you even able to respond, you worthless wretch? Do you actually eat serpents some of the time — *serpents?* Creatures that are poisonous and most unclean? Every worldly creature chooses worldly things — but you select those that are foul and filthy. Therefore," the cat pronounced in capping his oration, "it is you who are the filthiest of all birds."*

The stork made no response, but kept a grip on the eel and held fast to her way.

Thus a just man is neither exalted by praises nor downcast by vituperation. Let other men say whatever they wish. Just don't lose the eel. Hold fast to charity and patience. Proceed on your way in silence and you shall be saved.†

106   The Cloistered Life: A Further Treatment of the Same Theme

There lived a man who wanted to lead a cloistered life. The abbot, showing him a heap of bones of the dead, said: "Eulogize and pronounce blessings upon these bones." So the man extolled and blessed them. Then, once he'd done this, the abbot questioned him: "Did you say blessings over the bones?"

"I blessed them," he replied.

Then the abbot asked: "And what reply did they give?"

"Nothing," answered the young man.

Once again the abbot spoke up: "You should curse and vehemently berate them." And the young man did so — pushing all his capacities to their very limit.

Then the abbot questioned him: "Did you curse them?"

"Yes," the youth answered, "I cursed them."

"What was their reply?" asked the abbot.

And the young man said: "Nothing."

"Brother," the abbot told him, "if you want to become a monk, it is necessary for you to be like these bones — so that you may respond, to both blessings and curses, with *Nothing*." For as Isaiah (30:15) counsels: "Your strength shall be in silence and in hope."

Amos 5:13: "Therefore, the prudent man shall keep silence, for it is an evil time" — because *we* are living in an evil time. Whence one man's lamentation:

> For being born, woe to me! Alas the day of one's birth!
> Alas mortality!
> Woe to me that I survive! Alas and woe, no longer is
> Eve's son alive!

It was unforseen tragedies such as this which moved Boethius to ask: "Who possesses a happiness so secure, so fixed that he never complains about the condition of his life?" * As for me, I look upon my days one by one — and every day I hear things that make me unhappy.

107   The He Goat Who Wanted To Take a Ride

Against those having no respect for their lords

Once upon a time, a he-goat was appointed the ass's servant; and he observed that the ass was both simple and humble. So our goat climbed up on the ass and wanted to take a ride.

The ass, enraged, drew up his hind feet and sent himself tumbling to the rear — he fell, indeed, squarely on his back. This squashed and killed the goat. And the ass merely remarked: "When an ass is your lord, don't think you can ride him."

In like manner, many men observe that their lords are simple, aged, blind, or inept. Hence they scorn and laughingly mock them.

108   An Aged Father, His Son, and the King

In this way, a man with an elderly father ordered him to tend the sheep—even though the father once was a knight! Hearing how this man was mistreating his own father, the king threw the son into jail.

109   An Aged Father and His Son

Against all who fail to honor their fathers

Another fellow had an aged father who suffered from chronic coughing. "This crude peasant," the son complained, "why he's debilitating us all with his hacking and spittle. Wrap him up in this old sheep skin and dump him out—someplace far from here." And the father died from the cold because he had nothing adequate to wear.

This cruel son had a little boy of his own. And his young son got ahold of an old hide and hung it up on the wall. Now his father asked just what he planned to do with it. "I'm saving it for you to use when you get old," answered the boy, "since that's what you did for your own father. So from you, I'm learning what's necessary to handle *your* old age."

In Ecclesiasticus (8:7) we read: "Do not despise a man in his old age, for we all will grow old."

And this fable treats greedy men (who are entrapped by everything)
and, also, those who abandon themselves to excessive pleasures

The wolf happened to meet the fox. He asked: "Where are you coming
from, my friend?" And the fox replied: "I'm returning from a fish pond;
I caught really excellent fish there, and ate just as many as I wanted."
"How did you catch them?" asked the wolf. "Oh, I just let my tail down
into the water and held it there for a long time," the fox replied, "and
those fish — either believing that my tail was something they could feed
on, or that I might be dead — clung to it. And so I hauled them up
onto the shore and ate them." "Do you think," asked the wolf, "that
I could catch fish that way?" The fox answered him: "You can indeed.
After all, you're stronger than I am!"

Hence, marching in quick step, the wolf made his way to the pond.
He let his tail down into the water and held it there for a long time —
in fact, since the weather was turning cold, he held it that way until
it was frozen in place.

After a long wait, the wolf decided to haul up his tail — believing
that a whole school of fish was clinging to it. But he couldn't; his tail
was held fast in the ice. He was imprisoned there until morning. Then
some men came along and beat the wolf — nearly to the point of death.
And when he had managed to escape (but only barely, having lost his
tail in the process!) he cursed the "friend" who had promised fish, yet
provided blows and wounds and, almost, death.

Thus many men promise riches to their friends and children. And
they make them into usurers, simoniacs, and bandits — and so provide
them with eternal punishment. It is said of such men and their promises: "They sacrificed their sons and their daughters to demons" (Psalms
105:37).

This fable is appropriate, moreover, to those who let themselves
slip down into the waters of sensual pleasure. They linger for so long
amid these pleasures that they get frozen in and imprisoned — the consequence being that they're unable to escape. For "the Gentiles have
stuck fast in the destruction which they prepared. Their foot has been
caught in the very trap which they themselves hid" (Psalms 9:16). To
recall the words of Augustine: "Pleasure binds them, such that they

154

do not dare to break free from that love and turn to truly useful things [*ad utilia*]. For if they made the attempt, it would mean deep sorrow to desert the things that give them pleasure. And it is this sorrow which blocks their escape."

111   The Fly and the Ant

> Against all who sin and lay themselves open to sin
> after receiving the consecrated host

Once upon a time, the fly was arguing with the ant — the fly asserting that he was the nobler and purer of the two. "For I quite regularly partake of the meals of bishops and rulers and other rich men. I drink out of their cups. Indeed," the fly proclaimed, "I sometimes prance about on the face of the king." To this, the ant answered: "I am nobler and purer than you. On account of your foul deeds, everyone loathes you, and they harass you and drive you off. For granted you sometimes may dine upon the dishes of the rich — *other* times you still end up filling yourself with the most disgusting spittle, with varied kinds of rot, with the droppings of oxen and other animals. I, however, simply dine on grain that is wholly clean. So it is obvious that you're the filthier of us — indeed, the filthiest of all flying creatures."

Sentence was handed down in favor of the ant.

Now the fly, partaking sometimes of filth and sometimes of purity, suggests one sort of priest — one who follows the exemplum of the apostles (who are called "rulers of the earth") and also the exemplum of the rest of the saints, one who gathers in for himself the most delicate dishes: namely, the Eucharistic host and the blood of Christ. Then soon after, priests of this sort take deadly refreshment from the vilest of the droppings of dissipation and gluttony, from the rest of the vices. They rise into heaven, then dive down into the abysm (Psalms 106:26).*

155

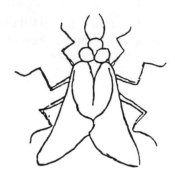

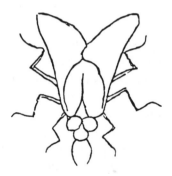

Hence of priests, Ezechiel (22:26) tells us: "They have defiled my sanctuaries; they have put no difference between holy and profane, nor have they distinguished between the polluted and the pure, and I was defiled in the midst of them." Behold how God Himself, He who cannot be contaminated, asserts that such priests *do* defile Him —for, insofar as He dwells in them, it is He whom they defile.

It is likewise with laymen. At Easter and Pentecost† they receive the Eucharist, and quite regularly hear the divine services. Then soon after, they give themselves over to dissipation and gluttony and to other filthy pleasures. They desert the church for some prostitute, that which is purest for that which is most foul,‡ God for the Devil. Such laymen are the Devil's own flies, whom the spiders of hell shall devour. Therefore, model yourself on the ant; gather in grain that is completely clean; put it away in the storage chest of heaven, so that you may live through

156

winter on all you gathered during summertime. So admonishes Proverbs 6:6–8: "Go to the ant, O sluggard; consider her ways and learn wisdom. It is she who—although she has no guide and no master and no captain—provides her food for herself in the summer, and gathers her food in the harvest."

Let us, in consequence, gather in our grains—i.e., good deeds purified from the filth of dissipation and gluttony, from the worm of care and greed, from the pall of pride and vainglory. These grains are stored away in the heavens when, out of a yearning for the highest good, we perform good deeds. God allows us to bequeath such "grains" to our Heavenly Fatherland—so that we may, in that very place, find true and sweet and unfailing refreshment, through our most illustrious Lord Jesus Christ.

Here End Master Odo's Parables
In Praise Of Him Who Is Both
Alpha and Omega

Appendix to *The Fables*
An Explanatory Note

The "Alternate Prologue" and six fables translated in this appendix are all found in manuscripts which Léopold Hervieux *did* use to supplement his readings of fables in MS. Corpus Christi 441. (Cf. the five fables taken from non-supplementary manuscripts and discussed in a note to Fable 3 of this translation.)

Neither the "Alternate Prologue" nor any one of the six, however, corresponds to a particular fable in the Corpus Christi manuscript.

Therefore, they have no place *within* an edition representing that manuscript. Hervieux communicated this judgment by numbering them in such a way that they appear as "add-ons" (see *Les Fabulistes Latins,* IV, 250–55).

In his edition, Odo's *Fables* truly ends with LXXV—this translation's Fable 111. Yet the fables in Hervieux's appendix are numbered LXXVI through LXXXI (translated fables 112 through 117). So even if they are not essential to a translation based on Hervieux's edition—and even though stylistic and other internal indications show that Odo himself viewed LXXV (or 111) as his work's concluding piece—that same translation would also be incomplete without them.

I present these *"Fabulae Quaedam inter Odonianas in MSS. Codicibus Dispersae"* in the order of Hervieux's text—first, the "Alternate Prologue," then the six additional fables (112–17).

Alternate Prologue to *The Fables of Odo of Cheriton**

The Blessed Basil assembled his young men and gave them instruction. He taught them about the soul's moral purity and the body's freedom from passion—about the way of gentleness, about measured speech, about well-ordered expression, and about the kinds of food and drink which do not inflame one. He taught them the practice of silence toward those above them, attentiveness in listening to the wise, subjection to men of eminence, unfeigned charity toward their peers and those of lesser station. He taught them to say little but understand much, to avoid rashness in words—and *not* to be windy in disputation, nor easily given to laughter; he taught them to adorn themselves chastely (yet not to dispute seductively attired women), to have a downcast visage and a soul turned upward toward heaven—to flee the conflicts of disputation (certainly not to usurp a master's authority), and to regard all the honors of this world as but nothing.

Even so, where someone can progress by other means, he may expect the reward of good deeds in the presence of God—in Christ Jesus, our Lord.

The birds one day came upon a nest, one woven from roses and perfumed with flowers. And the eagle declared that this nest should be awarded to the noblest bird.

So he convened an assembly of the birds of the heavens. And he asked all those listening to him to say which bird was noblest. The cuckoo answered him: "Kuk, kuk."

Then next he wanted to know which bird was the most beautiful. The cuckoo responded: "Kuk, kuk."

The eagle then turned to the question of which bird could sing the best. Again the cuckoo answered: "Kuk, kuk."

With this, the eagle became indignant. And he said: "Cuckoo, you wretch! You are always praising yourself. Therefore I am promulgating the highest condemnation against you. In consequence, you will never have *this* nest — *nor any other!*" And this is the reason that the cuckoo always deposits her eggs in the nest of some other bird.

In the same vein, many men are always commending themselves and exalting their own work. For when you ask those in religious life, which is the better of the orders, they reply: "The Franciscans!" "No, it's the Cistercians!" "*Ours* is better than the others!!" Even the Dominicans talk this way. And so it goes with all the others, as well, all of whom say: "Kuk, kuk!" — thus heaping praises on themselves. Likewise, many masters of learning declare that their theological compilations [*sententiae*] and their treatises are better than those written by others. It's the same with soldiers and every other class of men, too. They're always singing: "Kuk, kuk."

But men who are just and humble always disparage themselves. Whence Gregory's observation: "As the merit of one's deeds truly increases, in the view of the humble man himself, the same deeds' importance *de*creases." So it is when we are seeking our own glory; we take no care to please Him who looks upon us from heaven. Also we read, at 31:27–28 of Job: "I have kissed my hand with my mouth — which is the very greatest iniquity." For whoever heaps praises on his own deeds, kisses his own hand. And this is the greatest iniquity. Augustine thus remarks: "A man who longs for human praise is not someone you should defend against vituperation, nor is he someone you should rescue from the judgment of men, nor someone you should free from damnation." Again, Augustine also writes: "Everyone recounts their own merits!" And Gregory: "Such men do not see their own merits, which they exhibit for others to look upon." The same commentator adds: "Hence the mind becomes worthier, yet it seems unworthy to itself." Whence the Truth Himself instructs us, saying (Luke 17:10): "When you shall have accomplished all these things that you are commanded to do, say: 'We are unprofitable [*inutiles*] servants. We have done that which we ought to.'"*

113   Philomel and a Bowman

A certain bowman seized a small bird by the name of Philomel. Just when he was preparing to make his kill, she was given the power of speech. And Philomel said: "What good will it do you if you kill me? Doing that certainly won't enable you to fill your stomach. On the other hand, if you'd like to let me go, I can grant you three guiding precepts which—if you observe them diligently—will thereafter put you in a position to enjoy great advantage [*utilitas*]."

Thoroughly stupified by the bird's speech, the bowman promised to let her go if she would deliver these precepts. And she then told him: "Never strive to grasp anything which cannot be grasped. Never sorrow over anything lost and beyond recovery. Finally, never believe an unbelievable claim. Be a faithful custodian of these precepts and, then, all will be well with you."

And as he had promised, the bowman set her free. Hence, soaring through the air, Philomel cried out: "Alas to you, Oh man! How bad was the advice you got from me—and how great was the treasure you lost today!! For within my bowels is a pearl which beats the egg of an ostrich for size."

Now on hearing this, our bowman was overwhelmed with sorrow that he had ever set her free. And he strove to get Philomel into his grasp, crying out: "Come into my home. There, I will show you the fullest humanity—then freely send you fourth bearing honors." To which Philomel replied: "Now I've learned for certain that you're a fool. For you have failed to pluck any fruit at all from the precepts I delivered. You are sorrowing that I am lost and beyond recovery. And you attempted my seizure, even though it's not within your power to get a grasp on me. And above all, you believed that I actually carry a pearl of such extraordinary size within my bowels. What is more, you believed this when in fact I can't extend myself (and I do indeed mean my whole self!) to the size of an ostrich egg."

Such therefore are fools — men who believe in idols because they worship creatures in themselves, men who believe that they are the custodians when it is they themselves who are held in custody!

114   A Certain Man Flees the Unicorn

There are folk who yearn for bodily pleasures and permit their souls to be destroyed for a goblet of wine. They are like a particular man who — when swiftly fleeing the sight of a unicorn, lest it devour him — fell down into a huge pit. As he fell, he managed to get a grasp on one small tree with his hands and, also, to wedge his feet into a hollow of the same tree (a hollow, however, that was slippery and didn't give firm support).

Indeed, looking down he saw two mice — one white and the other black — who were incessantly knawing away at the base of the tree he was grasping. And they were already so close to getting all the way through that they could cut it down completely. Then, at the bottom of the pit, he saw as well a horrid dragon — breathing forth flames and lusting to devour him with open mouth. Now above the hollow of the tree where his feet had gotten a hold, he saw ten adders' heads jutting forth. And then, raising his eyes, he saw how small his little tree with its honeyed boughs actually was.

Yet forgetful of the peril he was in — surrounded by, on all sides! — he completely gave himself over to the honey's sweetness.

MORALITAS: The unicorn embodies the figure [*figura*] of death, that death who always lusts to pursue and get a grasp on a man. The pit is the world, filled with every sort of evil. The small tree, moreover,

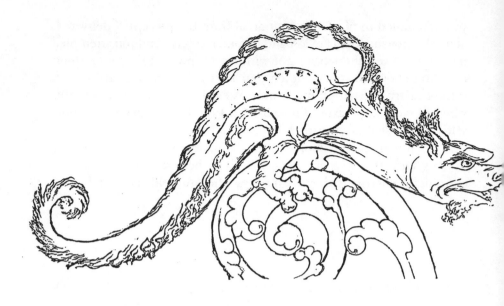

is every man's life which is incessantly being eaten up by the hours of day and night—namely, by the white mouse and the black. And with their cutting away, they are getting in close to that hollow—the very hollow where every man has wedged a foot. The ten adders' heads are the human body, composed of ten elements whose action surrenders the disordered ensemble of the body to dissolution. The horrid dragon is the mouth of hell, lusting to devour everything. Finally, the sweetness of the little boughs is the false pleasure of the world—the pleasure by which a man is seduced, so that he hardly notices his peril.

115   The Mouse and His Sons

A certain house mouse had sons who were bold indeed. When he was coming forth to feed, the sons dashed out ahead—each bumping into the other. When the mouse was in fact returning home, all of them took to flight. Then one day, when the mouse was coming forth to feed, a mouser came along. He was anticipating the sons' exit from the mouse hole.

And he seized one, and then another — and he devoured every last one of them!

Such are many men who do not want to obey either mother church or their parents or their masters. Instead, they prance boldly about. Thence the mouser — that is, the Devil — comes forth against them . . . *tempting* them. And he devours them all, down to the last one, and casts them into Gehenna!

116   The Lord Theodosius, Bishop of Sion

Lord Theodosius, Bishop of Sion, one day came down to the River Rhône in order to watch his fishermen. After awhile, when they were hauling in the net, they thought they had caught an enormous fish. But they discovered that they had a huge cake of ice — rather than a fish.

Now the season was autumn, and they were happier to have the ice than a fish, anyway. For their bishop was suffering from feet that felt as though they were on fire. So they placed the ice cake underneath his feet. And this greatly alleviated his suffering.

It just happened (after he had been standing on the ice for a time) that he heard a man's voice — speaking from inside the ice cake. The bishop adjured this spirit that he ought to reveal his identity. To this oath, the spirit replied: "I am an individual soul, and within this icy cold to which I am condemned, I suffer affliction on account of my sins. Yet I can be liberated if you say mass for me on thirty continuous days."

Led by the influence of *pietas,* our bishop set out upon his thirty-day labor. And when he had worked through to just about the halfway point, it happened (due to the working of diabolical suggestion) that nearly all his city's citizens had set to waging war against one another. Whereupon our bishop was summoned to calm down the conflict.

He came forth in public wearing his sacred vestments. Yet, thereby, he interrupted the course of his thirty-day labor — so that afterwards

163

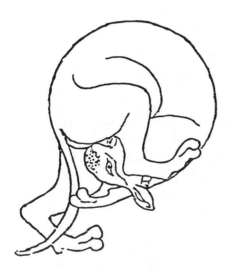

he had to start all over again. From the very beginning. And this time, when he had completed about two parts of his undertaking, a massive army set siege to the city. Hence, routed from prayer, he cut short his performance of the mass.

Then, when he again came back to his labor, he started its thirty days' course from the beginning, once more. And he kept going successfully until he got to the thirtieth mass. Yet when he now wanted to celebrate this final mass, the entire village — including the bishop's own household — appeared to be in flames. At this, the bishop's assistants told him that he should abandon the mass and flee. He then replied that, even if the whole village had to be burned down, he could not abandon his labor. He went ahead and celebrated the mass.

And at its conclusion, the cake of ice turned back into water and the soul within was set free. As for the fire which all believed they had seen, it dropped away like something imagined and brought them no curse at all. Amen.

117   The Wolf, the Fox, and the Ass

Once upon a time, the wolf was hearing confessions from the animals. And when many of them had confessed great sins to him, the fox at last came and told him that he had seized and eaten multitudes of hens without blessing them — and likewise with other prey.

Then, at the conclusion of this proceeding, there came along an ass. He confessed, saying: "I stole one small portion of a sheaf of hay which fell from a certain man's cart. And I did this because I was suffering from hunger."

Then the wolf said to the fox: "You did not sin, because seizing hens is an action that is inborn and natural to you. But this ass — who stole from another — is cursed!" And the wolf ordered the ass whipped, indeed making it clear that he deserved *hanging!!* But the fox was sent away, uninjured.

Notes to the Translation

FOR EACH of Odo's fables I give, after the number and title assigned it in this translation:

1. the Latin title from Hervieux's edition (*Les Fabulistes Latins,* Vol. IV, pp. 173–255),
2. the number or number-superscript designation which identifies the fable in Hervieux, and
3. the number given to the fable by Perry (in *Aesopica,* Vol. I, pp. 625–44)—*if,* in fact, that particular fable is a part of his edition; Perry prints only about one third the number of fables in Hervieux. (This is not a simple matter of good or bad editing, but of editions compiled in accord with very different principles and purposes.)

These references are, in a number of cases, followed by documentary and/or informational-critical annotations (signaled by asterisks in the texts of the fables). Each such note is intended to help readers develop a fuller appreciation of particular fables and, more broadly, of Odo's powers as a narrative artist. However, such information and critical commentary have only been provided where the limits inherent in translation seemed to make them necessary.

     1. "How the Trees Elected a King" (*Qualiter elegerunt sibi regem ligna*), Hervieux I.

     2. "The Ants" (*De Formicis*), Hervieux Iᵃ.

     3. "The Frogs Elect a King" (*Qualiter Rane elegerunt sibi regem*), Hervieux Iᵇ.

     *This particular fable does not occur in the manuscript on which Hervieux based his edition (MS. Corpus Christi 441), nor does it appear in any of the other manuscripts he used to supplement his readings of fables in that manuscript. It comes from British Museum MS. Harley 219. However, Hervieux printed it as an entry in one of his appendices (see IV, 248–50)—along with four other fables, designated as

I^d, XXXVI^b, XXXVI^c, and XLII (this translation's Fables 5, 53, 54, and 61). Because my translation aims at making Odo's achievement available to a range of readers, I have put my renderings of all five *"Odonis de Ceritona Fabulae Quaedam in MSS. Codicibus Dispersae"* back into the body of *The Fables,* and I have placed each fable at that point in the sequence required by Hervieux's own number-superscript designation. Yet for the sake of accuracy, I have signaled each such repositioning by a note (such as this one) indicating the manuscript of origin. Where fables (this translation's Appendix excepted) lack manuscript designations, their origin is always MS. Corpus Christi 441.

4. "The Chicks Elect a King" (*Qualiter Pulli elegerunt sibi regem*), Hervieux I^c.

5. "The Birds Elect a King" (*Qualiter Volucres elegerunt regem*), Hervieux I^d. *British Museum MS. Harley 219.

6. "An Abbot, Food, and Some Monks" (*De Abbate, cibo et Monachis*), Hervieux I^e.

7. "The Hawk, the Dove, and 'the Duke'" (*De Niso et Columba et Duce*), Hervieux II; Perry 588.

8. "The Hornet" (*De Scrabone*), Hervieux II^a.

9. "The Crow" (*De Cornice*), Hervieux III.

10. "The Buzzard and the Hawk's Nest" (*De Busardo et de nido Ancipitris*), Hervieux IV.

11. "The Cuckoo and the Sparrow" (*De Cucula et Burneta*), Hervieux IV^a.

12. "The Tortoise and the Eagle" (*De Tortuca et Aquila*), Hervieux V.

13. "The Stork and the Wolf" (*De Ciconia et Lupo*), Hervieux VI.

14. "A Certain 'Bird of Saint Martin'" (*De quadam ave Sancti Martini*), Hervieux VII; Perry 589.

15. "The Weeping Bald Man and Some Partridges" (*De oculis Calvi lacrimantibus et Perdicibus*), Hervieux VIII.

16. "The Bird Called 'Break Bone'" (*De ave qui dicitur frangens os, Freinos*), Hervieux IX.

17. "The Eagle" (*De Aquila*), Hervieux X.

18. "The Stork and His Wife" (*De Ciconia et Uxore*), Hervieux XI; Perry 590. *Horace, *Epistles,* I, xi, 27.

19. "The Heretic and the Fly" (*De Heretico et Musca*), Hervieux XII.

*This fable derives much of its force from Odo's handling of the distinction between *mundus* and *inmundus*—*mundus* here denoting "the world," but in other places sometimes functioning adjectively in characterizing things as "worldly," even "(morally) beautiful"; *inmundus* almost always characterizing things as unclean, foul, and (given frequent punning usage of the distinction) as "(morally) ugly" because they are too deeply "inmattered"—too deeply embedded *in* the earth, *in* the world, *in-mundus.* Because the *mundus-inmundus* distinction, whether stated fully or partially (with the opposing term merely implied), is critical to many of Odo's fables, I have attempted to preserve it—rendering *mundus,* with as much consistency as idiomatic English allows, by some variant of "world" or "worldly" and *inmundus* as "foul." However, readers should know that "worldly" and "foul" sometimes translate other Latin terms. Thus, though I could not keep the Latin pun alive in English, where the full *mundus-inmundus* contrast is crucial to understanding the impact of a fable's issue(s), I have, as with "The Heretic and the Fly," supplied the Latin term(s).

The twelfth-century theological context of this particular fable is nicely summarized by G. R. Evans (though without explicit reference to Odo) in *Old Arts and New Theology* (Oxford: The Clarendon Press, 1980), p. 180: "A topic of some interest to dualists and orthodox Christians alike was the reason for the creation of noxious things. The existence of reptiles and insects which sting or bite man and poison him, seemed to them strong evidence for the view that material things could not be the creation of a good God."

20. "The Phoenix" (*De Fenice*), Hervieux XIII.

*In Hervieux's text, this fable is followed by the following statement — set in boldface and obviously not intended to be read as part of either "The Phoenix" or the subsequent fable: **Deinde est de uolatilibus; sequitur de gressibilibus.** This may be translated: "From here on we are done with flying creatures; what follows concerns those that move upon the earth."

The distinction between flying creatures and creatures that move upon the earth derives from Genesis 1:20–28. And it seems likely that the inscription reflects an early intent to divide up the fables into two groups, following the biblical distinction. The biblical context which the inscription invokes is of considerable importance; in Odo's fables, creatures biblically destined to *be* ruled by Man (their ruler) provide the rule and measure by which human actions are judged. The measured "take the measure" and the ruled "give the rule." But even the most casual reader will see that the inscribed statement does not divide Odo's work into two sections concerned with two classes of creatures — *even if* such a division was part of Odo's original plan.

21. "The Toad's Son and the Slippers" (*De Filio Bufonis et sotularibus*), Hervieux XIV; Perry 591.

*The main narrative line of this little piece is rather easily rendered in English. But because of a scientific tradition embedded in common Latin yet lacking a ready counterpart in common English, the philosophic aspect of the narrative (the significance of its focus on "the *qualitative*") is too easily lost — as might be said of this translation's Fables 1, 3, 4, and 5, as well. (Cf. the grammatical paradox which animates Fable 6 — what is the comparative of a superlative? — a paradox which *translates* without commentary.)

To clarify, the story of the toad and his son turns upon the way in which qualitative judgments are influenced by one's emotional attachments or internal circumstances. When the hare asks the toad what qualities make his son stand out, Odo's actual text reads: *Qualis est igitur filius tuus?* The question is readily recognizable as the third of the widely used analytical-rhetorical sequence: *an sit? quid sit? quale sit? cur sit?* And this third question, *quale sit?*, is usually translated "of what sort/ quality is it?" Of course, the toad's son being the fable's concern, the hare is really asking "of what sort is *he*?"

In any case, the toad gets the point, for his reply is qualitative: "He who has a head like mine, a belly like mine, legs and feet like mine [*quale est meum*]. . . ." Moreover, this thrust is re-emphasized when the hare tells the regal lion and his subjects "how [*qualiter*] the toad commended his own son over the other animals." Here, the word rendered as "how" communicates more than exasperation with the toad's emotionally induced blindness. It also refers back with precision to the toad's double falsification: (1) his falsification of his own and his son's qualities, on the one hand (he identifies these with the beautiful), and (2) his falsification of the distinctive qualities of other animals, on the other (he absurdly identifies the dove with blackness and the peacock with ugliness). This multiple mendacity, even if unintentional on the toad's part, argues for the validity of the aphoristic leonine verse that Odo uses to cap this particular tale.

22. "Young Man, Old Woman" (*De Juvene et Vetula*), Hervieux XIV[a].

23. "The Cat Who Made Himself a Monk" (*De Cato qui se fecit monachum*), Hervieux XV; Perry 592.

24. "The Spider" (*De Aranea*), Hervieux XV[a].

25. "The Fly" (*De Musca*), Hervieux XV[b].

26. "The House Mouse and the Field Mouse" (*De Mure domestica et silvestri vel campestri*), Hervieux XVI.

27. "The Antelope" (*De quodam animali quod vocatur Antiplos*), Hervieux XVII.

28. "An Exemplum: The Serpent and the Crocodile" (*De Ydro et Cocodrillo exemplum*), Hervieux XVIII.

29. "The Fox, the Wolf, and the Well-Bucket" (*De Vulpe et Lupo et situala putei*), Hervieux XIX; Perry 593.

30. "Three Hunters: The Lion, Wolf, and Fox" (*De Leone et Lupo et Volpe et Venatoribus*), Hervieux XX.

31. "A Rat, a Cat, and Some Cheese" (*De Caseo et Rato et Cato*), Hervieux XXI; Perry 594.

32. "The Dogs and the Crows" (*De Canibus et Cornicibus*), Hervieux XXI[a].

33. "The Mouse, the Frog, and the Kite" (*De Mure, Rana et Milvo)*, Hervieux XXI[b].

34. "The Wolf Who Longed To Be a Monk" (*De Lupo qui voluit esse monachus*), Hervieux XXII; Perry 595.

*Since this English proverb is not translated by Odo, I give it in *modern* English—varying Hervieux's rendition (see IV, 22–23, n.4) only slightly: "Though the wolf were hooded as a priest, and though you set him to learning the psalms, his glances are always toward the grove."

35. "The Complaint of the Sheep" (*Quod Oves sunt conqueste Leoni de Lupo*), Hervieux XXIII; Perry 596.

*These are the characteristics of heroes and noble leaders (King Arthur as portrayed by Geoffrey of Monmouth, for example) in medieval romances, histories, and biographies. Cf. Fable 55, below.

36. "The Wolf 'Takes Care of' the Sheep" (*Quidam commendavit xii Oves compatri suo Lupo*), Hervieux XXIII[a].

170

37. "The Wolf and Lamb Who Were Drinking" (*De Lupo et Agno bibentibus*), Hervieux XXIV.

38. "The Fox Confesses His Sins to the Cock" (*De Volpe qui confitebatur peccata sua Gallo*), Hervieux XXV; Perry 597.

39. "Asses in Lion Skins" (*De Asinis indutis pellibus leoninis*), Hervieux XXVI.

*The *Rule* of St. Benedict (480–543) is a compilation of precepts intended to govern monastic life. It was adopted by many Western orders.

40. "Walter's Search for the Happy Place" (*De Guatero querente locum ubi semper gauderet*), Hervieux XXVII.

*Odo: *scalam . . . cuius primus gradus est cordis contritio, secundus uera confessio, tercius plena satisfactio.* For an embodiment of this sequence (contrition-confession-penance) in a popular drama of the Middle Ages, see *Everyman,* lines 537–727. The relevant scriptural text is Genesis 28:10–17. Jacob, in a dream, sees a ladder or *scala* whose top touches heaven, a ladder on which angels are ascending and descending. Upon awaking, Jacob says: "How terrible is this place! This is none other than the house of God, and the gate of heaven [*domus Dei et porta caeli*]." The bearing of this upon our fable's conclusion does not, I suspect, require much commentary.

41. "Two Brothers" (*De duobus Sociis, uno verace, alio mendace*), Hervieux XXVIIᵃ.

42. "The Dispute of the Wasp and the Spider" (*De contentione Vespe et Aranee*), Hervieux XXVIII; Perry 598.

43. "The Beetle" (*De Scarabone*), Hervieux XXVIIIᵃ.

*"Pleasant place," *amenus locus,* is a loaded term. Just as medieval authors of romances, political songs, histories, and the like turned portraits of their characters on certain conventions, so they rendered settings (often using them as commentary on the characters) with another convention, "*descriptio* of place." Rhetorical handbooks and *artes poetriae* gave instructions, plus exemplary models, showing what to include in one's description of a *locus amoenus.* (It should be a verdant glade, should contain flowers, be transversed by a brook — gently babbling — and wafted by soft breezes, be filled with songbirds, etc.) This is the type of "pleasant place" the beetle's reference here — and the scholar's in Fable 45 — are intended to call to the reader's mind. Of course, even for a reader unaware of the "technical" character of "pleasant place," the beetle's comment can only seem absurd, ironic, and humorous (though the joke is serious).

For further discussion of this descriptive convention, see: Ernst Robert Curtius, *European Literature and the Latin Middle Ages,* trans. W. Trask (New York: Harper Torchbooks, 1963), pp. 183–202; John Finlayson, "Rhetorical 'Descriptio' of Place in the Alliterative *Morte Arthure,*" *Modern Philology* 61 (1963): 1–11; Theodore Silverstein, "The Art of *Sir Gawain and the Green Knight,*" *University of Toronto Quarterly* 33 (1964): 258–78.

44. "The Eagle and Dr. Raven, M.D." (*De Aquila et Corvo medico*), Hervieux XXIX; Perry 599.

*Odo: *oculi spirituales sunt extincti.* This concern for the eye's moral-spiritual function may be seen as going back to Jesus' words in the Sermon on the Mount; see Matthew 6:22–23.

For a useful discussion of some of the matters related to medieval extension of concepts such as "spiritual eyesight," "moral eyesight," etc., see David L. Clark, "Optics for Preachers: The *De oculo morali* by Peter of Limoges," *Michigan Academician* 9 (1977): 329–43.

45. "A Hunter-Soldier Hears a Beast Fable" (*De Milite venatore* and *De Leone qui invitavit bestias*), Hervieux XXX and XXXª, respectively.

Though Hervieux (IV, 205) gives these fables separate numbers and separate titles, he presents their two texts as one. I have simply given the "two" a single title and translated the text(s) as actually printed, i.e., as one continuous narrative.

46. "The Beetles and a Farmer" (*De Scrabonibus et Rustico*), Hervieux XXXI.

47. "The Bees and the Beetles" (*De Ape et Scrabone*), Hervieux XXXII.

48. "The Ass and the Pig" (*De Asino et Porco*), Hervieux XXXIII; Perry 600.

49. "The Chick, the Hen, and the Kite" (*De Pullo Galline et Milvo*), Hervieux XXXIV; Perry 601.

50. "The Banquet of the Lion, Cat, and Some Others" (*De Convivio Leonis et Catti et aliorum*), Hervieux XXXV; Perry 602.

51. "The Goose and the Raven" (*De Auca et Corvo*), Hervieux XXXVI; Perry 603.

52. "'On Behalf of a Sinner': A Just Man Entreats the Lord" (*De quodam Justo rogante Dominum pro quodam Peccatore*), Hervieux XXXVIª.

53. "A Poor Fool" (*De quodam Stulto*), Hervieux XXXVIᵇ.
*Bibliothèque Mazarine MS. 986.

54. "A Magician" (*De quodam Incantatore*), Hervieux XXXVIᶜ.
*Bibliothèque Mazarine MS. 986.

55. "Playing Chess" (*De Scacis*), Hervieux XXXVIᵈ (but see note immediately below).

*Printed by Hervieux (IV, 210) as XXXVIᵇ, though clearly intended to bear the designation XXXVIᵈ (see IV, 42 and 470 — and for the actual XXXVIᵇ, see IV, 249).

†Odo: *Quidam dicuntur reges, quidam milites, quidam duce ̄, quidam pedones.* "Duke" (from Latin *dux,* pl. *duces*) is the obsolete English term for the rook or castle in chess. For Odo's original audience, I would add, the transition from the game of chess to the "game of life" would have been easy and unforced — since all the pieces in the game of chess bear the names and parallel the functions of "classes" of actual people in medieval society. What is more, Odo's "application" asserts that such people (especially rich men) are popularly acclaimed for virtues which are distinctly, recognizably "heroic" — even though it is these very "virtues" which the fable exposes as illusory.

Cf. the pigs' praise of the wolf as "courtly, open-handed, and generous" (*curialis, liberalis,* and *largus*) in Fable 35. And regarding "popular acclamation" for one's "virtues," see Fable 98 and my accompanying note discussing *laudes* ("acclamations," "praises").

56. "The Wild Colt" (*De Pullo indomito*), Hervieux XXXVII.

*With reference to the "style" of this fable's final paragraph (the translation's rhythms and alliterations imitate characteristics of the actual Latin text), see Fable 111 and the attached note on the "poetics" of prose.

57. "The Kite and the Partridges" (*De Milvo et Perdicibus*), Hervieux XXXVIII; Perry 604.

58. "The Fox's Tricks—and the Cat" (*De fraudibus Vulpis et Catti*), Hervieux XXXIX; Perry 605.

*Throughout the translation of this fable, "scheme" and "schemes" consistently render the Latin *artificium* and *artificia.* Those in possession of such *artificial* schemes contrast to those virtuously simple men who have but one scheme or artifice—those whose "artifice" is singular rather than plural and, therefore, *natural* (i.e., in accord with their nature and with Nature).

†The reference to eggs in this taunt has much the same significance as in the saying, "to take eggs for money"—i.e., to value or accept as valuable something of little value (see *Brewer's Dictionary of Phrase and Fable*, centenary edition, rev. Evans [New York: Harper and Row, 1979], "Egg"). If "eggs" is dropped from Tib's sentence (against Perry's judgment in *Aesopica*), then his statement would end: ". . . aren't worth anything to you."

59. "The Raven and the Dove's Chick" (*De Corvo et Pullo Columbe*), Hervicux XL; Perry 606.

*In British usage, one kind of "bailiff" (Odo's term is *baiulus*) is the man who acts as agent and/or administrator—by overseeing activities, collecting rents, adjudicating disputes, etc.—for a manor lord.

60. "The Hoopoe and the Nightingale" (*De Uppupa et Philomena*), Hervieux XLI.

*The Cluniacs, so named because they were attached to the monastery at Cluny, were one of the many monastic reform groups which emerged during the Middle Ages. Cluny was founded in 910, and its second and very influential abbot was Odo of Cluny (b.879–d.942)—Odo of Cheriton's patron saint.

A knowledge of monastic reform movements is hardly essential for enjoyment of Odo's art, though it often sharpens one's appreciation. Interested readers will find an overview in Henry Osborn Taylor's *The Mediaeval Mind* (Cambridge, Mass.: Harvard University Press, 1925), 2 vols.; chapter sixteen, "The Reforms of Monasticism," is in I, 369–83. And, for the importance of Odo of Cluny to Odo of Cheriton, see Albert C. Friend, "Master Odo of Cheriton," *Speculum* 23 (1948): 641–58, esp. 643 and 650–51.

†The psalms referred to here (119–33 in the Vulgate) make up the sequence which Odo designates the *xv Psalmos AD DOMINUM*—the sequence also known as the *Canticum graduum* or the *Gradual Psalms.* These psalms function as steps or as rungs of a "ladder" (*gradus*) on which one makes his ascent—upward toward God.

61. "The Rich Man Who Owned Many Cows" (*De quodam Divite multas habente vaccas*), Hervieux XLII.

*British Museum MS. Harley 219.

62. "Direct Simplicity in Paying One's Debts" (*De simplicitate solventium censum*), Hervieux XLII^a.

*Odo: *Sic faciunt plerique: cum veniunt questores de Hautepas, vel Sancti Antonii, vel Runcivallenses, multa promittunt.* Now *questores* can be "officials" of various sorts: tax collectors, pardoners, judges, men questing after various things. Odo's are plainly the kind who want money. But the prepositional phrase following *questores* must have puzzled even Odo's medieval Spanish translator, since he abandons any attempt to render *de Hautepas* (see G. T. Northrup, *El Libro de los Gatos: A Text with Introduction and Notes* [Chicago: University of Chicago Press, 1908], pp. 65–66). It is possible that *Hautpas, Hautepas, Haute pass,* etc.—there are various spellings—refers to a high pass in the mountains. But perhaps a different reading is appropriate here. One literal meaning of *Hautpas* (a French term) is "a high step"—that is, a raised platform or dias, such as royalty and prominent persons are often seated upon; in this fable, it seems to be used as metonymy for "the court" or any center of organized power or activity.

As for the officials *Sancti Antonii,* the next item in Odo's statement, their status is also ambiguous. They might come from a specific place, perhaps the *Sancti Antonini villa* (Saint-Antoine-de-Ficalba) located in southern France—though I cannot say whether this *villa* was, in Odo's day, a settlement known for its money-hungry representatives. I have therefore translated in line with Northrup's suggestion (p. 66, n. 20) that reference is to "the *chanoines réguliéres de St. Antoine* . . . organized in 1070 A.D. for the purpose of aiding those afflicted with the disease known as St. Anthony's fire." In contrast, however, it is improbable that Odo's *Runcivallenses* are anything other than representatives from a place, from Roncesvalles (as Chicagoans are "from Chicago"). Roncesvalles pass was the seat of a famous hospice run by Augustinian canons, and of a monastery which (again I cite Northrup) "had the privilege of soliciting contributions throughout Christendom." The pass was notorious for its pardoners.

Whatever the precise interpretation we give to Odo's references, his point comes across clearly: *questores* (the Spanish version's *demandadores*) are slippery characters—whatever the institution in whose name they make promises and plead and lie. Be warned!

†Odo: *sicut Oliverius currunt.* This phrase appears to reflect a folk saying. The aphorism *Oliverio currente,* "when the [oil from the] olive tree is running freely," designates a season or time of prosperity—a moment when something or someone is "in full tide of fortune." Its Old French counterpart is *olivier courant* (see *Revised Medieval Latin Word-List from British and Irish Sources,* ed. R. E. Latham [London: Oxford University Press for The British Academy, 1965], "*oliv/*"). The application of this to the behavior of Odo's "foreigners"—making off when their fortune is "at full tide"—is pointed and unstrained.

63. "The Industriousness of the Ant" (*De industria Formice*), Hervieux XLII[b].

64. "The Wolf's Funeral" (*De Lupo sepulto*), Hervieux XLIII; Perry 607.

*The Black Monks are the Benedictines; their lives were ordered by the *Rule* of St. Benedict and they wore black habits. The White Monks are Cistercians, *strict* adherents (or so they liked to claim) to the *Rule* of Benedict; they wore white habits.

65. "Dog Dirt" (*De Cane stercorante*), Hervieux XLIV; Perry 608.

66. "The Unicorn and a Man" (*De Unicorne et quodam Homine*), Hervieux XLV; Perry 609.

67. "The Fox" (*De Vulpe*), Hervieux XLVI; Perry 610.

68. "The Ape" (*De Symia*), Hervieux XLVII.

69. "The Turtle" (*De Testudine*), Hervieux XLVIII.

70. "Likewise Concerning the Snail" (*Item de Testudine*), Hervieux XLVIII[a].

*Readers of this fable, that immediately preceding, and the earlier "The Tortoise and the Eagle" (Fable 12) may be puzzled by the jumble of tortoise, turtle, and snail—especially if they have been noting the actual Latin titles, since I render *tortuca* simply as "tortoise" while treating *testudo* as "turtle" in one case (Fable 69) and as "snail" in another (the present fable, 70).

Tortuca, tortoise, probably derives from Late Latin *tartarucha; testudo* is the classical term for the turtle. Odo observes this distinction, though there is no way of telling how precisely he understood it. However, considered by itself, his use of *testudo* appears to reflect a semantic extension suggested by my double translation ("turtle," "snail").

Niermeyer (*Mediae Latinitatis Lexicon Minus* [Leiden: Brill, 1976], p. 1027) treats *testudo* as a variant of *testitudo:* "nave," "vaulted hall," "skull." By today's standards, turtles, and snails hardly belong to the same genus. But both have "vaulted," "domed" shells. This observable likeness is probably the basis for extending *testudo* to mean "snail." Assuming such a metaphorical extension makes sense of the tale and central analogy of the present narrative (Fable 70)—since snails have "horns" or feelers (more properly, in modern terms, "stalks" on the end of which their eyes are located) but turtles do not.

†"Horned" in appearance (and, thus, also seemingly powerful) because of the twin-peaked miter worn as an emblem of episcopal office.

71. "The Spider, the Fly, and the Wasp" (*De Aranea et Musca et Burdone*), Hervieux XLVIII[b].

72. "The Fox" (*De Vulpe*), Hervieux XLIX.

73. "Another, Similar Exemplum" (*Aliud exemplum*), Hervieux XLIX[a].

74. "The Fox and the Hens" (*De Vulpe et Gallinis*), Hervieux L; Perry 611.

75. "The Fraud of the Fox" (*De fraude Vulpis*), Hervieux LI.

76. "The Fraudulent Scheme of a Count" (*De fraude Comitis*), Hervieux LI[a].

*Odo: *illos [homines] indutos vestimentis ovium.* These are vestments "of sheep" because (as we noted in a previous context) the Cistercians were distinguished in appearance by their white wool habits. (As a related matter, it is worth mention that the Cistercians were noted for their sheep-farming.) When the merchants glanced back, they would have seen men dressed in white—and, so, assumed them to be Cistercians. The bandits' "sheepish," white appearance would have reassured the merchants. It would "naturally" have led them to assume that the "Cistercians" travelling behind them were sheep-like in character: gentle. But, to express the point with biblical irony, these "sheep" are more inclined to slaughter others than to be led to the slaughter; their behavior marks them as the proverbial wolves in sheep's clothing.

77. "A Disputation" (*De contentione Ovis albe et Ovis nigre, Asini et Hirci*), Hervieux LII.

*"Black Monks and canons," i.e., Benedictines.

† "Converts," *conversi* to monastic life who, nevertheless, did not take monastic vows. The implication of Odo's comments here appears to be that Cistercians were especially given to taking in such converts, or at least to keeping those taken in notably unkempt. *Conversi:* lay brothers.

78. "The Harrow and the Toad" (*De Traha et Bufone*), Hervieux LIII.

79. "The Falcon and the Kite" (*De Falcone et Milvo*), Hervieux LIV; Perry 612.

80. "The Mice and the Cat" (*De Muribus et Catto et cetera*), Hervieux LIVª; Perry 613.

81. "Of the Rose and the Birds: Why the Owl Doesn't Fly by Day" (*De Rosa et Volatilibus: Item quare Bubo non volat de die*), Hervieux LV; Perry 614.

*These are learned birds indulging in learned wit. My "in your irony" render's Odo's *per antifrasim*, by contradiction. This is a technical term from rhetoric. Quintilian (*Institutes of Oratory* 9:47) treats ἀντίφρασις as a species of irony, remarking that it derives its name from negation, *a negando*. Saying one thing, the speaker communicates the contrary. So Julius Rufinianus' *Figures of Thought* (sec. 12) explains that "*antiphrasis* is a figure of thought in which we deny the very thing we say and, nevertheless, say it" (Halm, *Rhetores Latini Minores* [Leipzig: Teubner, 1863], p. 62). And Odo's own countryman of an earlier century, Bede, provides an explanation which is quite apt to the present fable's use of "most beautiful" to mean "most ugly" or "ugliest." "*Antiphrasis*," according to his *On Schematisms and Tropes*, "is *the irony of a single word*, as when one says: 'Friend, for what purpose have you come?' [Matthew 26:50]"—the irony in Bede's example arising from Jesus addressing Judas, immediately after the kiss of betrayal, with the one word "friend" (Halm, p. 615). Odo's birds dissolve in laughter at the knowledge that their *pulcherrima* ("most beautiful") means—when they apply it to the owl—the contrary, *turpissima* or "most ugly."

This entire fable, consistent with the situation it renders, is filled with rhetorical and legal terminology—most of which can be "translated" quite adequately without the kind of attention a phrase like *per antiphrasim* requires.

82. "The Mouse and the Cat" (*De Mure et Catto*), Hervieux LVI; Perry 615.

83. "The Flea" (*De Pulice*), Hervieux LVIª.

84. "Alexander: A Man in Danger" (*De quodam Alexandro in periculo posito*), Hervieux LVIᵇ.

85. "The Granary" *(De Grangia),* Hervieux LVIᶜ.

86. "The Pelican" (*De Pellicano*) Hervieux, LVII.

*Odo's pelican kills the chicks and then, moved by *pietas*, revivifies them. Enraged (*iratus*), God "killed" Adam and Eve and, then, moved by pity (*misericordia*), "brought [them] back to life." This motivational schema and its terms may be compared, especially, to "The Fox and the Hens" (Fable 74). Behind both fables lies the tradition which depicts men of noble character as marked by their capacity for righteous anger and justice, on the one hand, and for pious compassion and mercy, on the other.

87. "The Battle of the Wolf and the Hare" (*De contentione Lupi et Leporis*), Hervieux LVIII; Perry 616.

88. "The Man Who Cradled the Serpent" (*De Homine qui posuit Serpentem in sinu suo*), Hervieux LIX; Perry 617.

*Ovid, *Amores*, III, xi, 35.

89. "A Man Without Gratitude" (*De Homine ingrato et Socio male remunerante*), Hervieux LIX[a]; Perry 618.

90. "The Panther" (*De Panthara*), Hervieux LX.

91. "The Dog and the Scrap of Meat" (*De Cane et frusto carnium*), Hervieux LXI.

92. "The Puffed-up Frog" (*De Rana inflata*), Hervieux LXII.

93. "The Soldier's Son" (*De Filio Militis*), Hervieux LXII[a].

*Inexplicably, Odo's biblical reference drops the most telling words of Ecclesiasticus' warning: "Do not extol yourself in the thoughts of your soul *like a bull* [or *like an "ox"*], lest your strength be quashed by folly." "Like a bull," *velut taurus*, makes the citation's impact, as part of a poetic argument, all the sharper.

94. "The Mouse Who Wanted To Marry" (*De Mure qui voluit matrimonium contrahere*), Hervieux LXIII; Perry 619.

*Horace, *The Art of Poetry*, 139.

†I quote F. A. Wright's translation (slightly altered) of Jerome's *Ad Eustochium* from the Loeb *Select Letters of St. Jerome* (London: Heinemann, 1933), p. 65. This is Migne's Letter XXII (*Patrologia Latina*, XX, 397–98) in his reprinting of Jerome.

95. "The Cat's Beautiful Wife" (*De pulchra Uxore Catti*), Hervieux LXIV.

*Ovid, *The Art of Love*, I, 99.

†Odo: *Egressa est Dina, ut videret mulieres regionis illius, et corrupta est.* Even though Odo does not identify this by a scriptural reference, it is in fact a close paraphrase of Genesis 34:1: *Egressa est autem Dina filia Liae ut videret mulieres regionis illius;* "and Dina the daughter of Lia went out to see the women of that country [i.e., the Sichemite city of Salem 'in the land of Canaan']." Continuing on in the same chapter of Genesis, the very next verse (34:2)—a verse which is part of the "context" which Odo presumably assumed his audience would bring to their reading of this fable—clarifies the bearing of Odo's paraphrase on the argument of his tale. "And when Sichem, the son of . . . the prince of that land, saw her, he was in love with her—and he abducted her [*rapuit*] and lay with her, ravishing [*vi opprimens*] the virgin."

Regardless of twentieth-century convictions about the powers and freedoms proper to women, the real point of Odo's fable has little to do with recommending their oppression. We would produce a different portrait, but Odo routinely paints virtuous women as weak and vulnerable. Hence, consistent with the point of many other of his fables, this little narrative's argument "against flirtations" argues *for protection* of the weak. Women's weakness includes a tendency to disregard or forget marriage's binding, Natural obligations as a sacrament.

96. "A Certain Lady" (*De quadam Domina*), Hervieux LXIV[a].

97. "The Stork and the Serpent" (*De Ciconia et Serpente*), Hervieux LXV; Perry 620.

*Ovid, *The Remedies of Love*, 91–92.

98. "The Peacock Stripped of Its Plumage" (*De Pavone deplumato*), Hervieux LXVI; Perry 621.

*Here, my "acclamations" renders Odo's *laudes,* "praises" (just as, in this fable's first paragraph, "I'll acclaim" rendered the raven's *laudabo,* "I will praise"). But "praise," *laus* (English "laud," "laudation," etc.) is not just a technical term of rhetoric. In the practical, political application which gives it added meaning, it refers to the acclamations or shouts of popular approval such as a ruler might receive as a sign of enthusiasm for his achievements or, frequently, as a definitive if informal "vote" for his election to a higher position or receipt of a new title, a new honor. Examples of such "election by popular acclaim" are found again and again in saints' lives, imperial biographies and autobiographies, histories, and annals. So it is not just "acclaim" or "praise" in itself which seduces a foolish peacock. It is the hope and expectation of material and social rewards which he thinks will flow from all the things public acclamation *seems* to promise. (Will my readers think it a lapse from scholarly decorum if I remind them that a title on the door is said to rate a Bigelow on the floor? As with so many of Odo's fables, the point seems as pertinent to the twentieth as to the thirteenth century.)

†One of the kingdoms of medieval Spain.

99. "The Toad and the Frog" (*De Bufone et Rana*), Hervieux LXVII; Perry 622.

100. "One Dog, Two Men" (*De Cane et duobus Hominibus*), Hervieux LXVIIª.

101. "The Ass and the Lion" (*De Asino et Leone*), Hervieux LXVIII.

*Odo's text does not set off these words as a quotation. However, the passage in quotation marks is almost a word-for-word rendering of Luke 15:7—a rendering so close that Odo's original readers could hardly have missed its "biblicality"—even without the aid of special punctuation. Further, regarding the slaughter of the "calf" or *vitulus* (the term used by both Odo and the Vulgate), see Luke's telling of the story of the prodigal son (15:21–30, esp.).

†See John 18:25 and ff.

102. "The Dogs, an Ass, and His Lord" (*De Cane et Asino et Domino suo),* Hervieux LXIX.

103. "The Cheese and the Raven" (*De Caseo et Corvo*), Hervieux LXX.

*The reference here (taking Hervieux's *muneravit* as a misprint for *numeravit*) seems to be II Kings 24:1–15, esp. David's command that Joab "number" (*numera*) or take a census of his subjects is motivated by pride in the populousness of his "empire," by the vainglory this fable of Odo's warns against. So God inflicts a pestilence upon David's people, and seventy thousand die. On account of vainglory, David—like the fable's raven—suffers the punishment of loss (not to mention the suffering of his people).

104. "An Athenian" (*De quodam Atheniensi*), Hervieux LXXª; Perry 623.

105. "The Stork and the Cat" (*De Ciconia et Catto),* Hervieux LXXI.

*The cat's oration turns on the familiar distinction between the"world(ly)" and "foul (things)," the *mundus* and *inmundus* (cf. the use of this distinction in other fables, esp. numbers 19 and 111). To give the speech in the actual words of Odo's text: *Vel es surda uel muta. Non poteris respondere, miserrima? Nonne quandoque comedis serpentes que sunt animalia uenenosa et **inmundissima**? Quodlibet **animal mun-***

dum[,] munda diligit, et tu, turpia et inmunda. Igitur es inter ceteras aues inmundissima.

†The impact of this fable is vastly enhanced for a reader who is aware of the extensive, extended use of demonstrative rhetoric during the Middle Ages. This is the rhetoric of praises and blames, and treatises *de laudibus et vituperandis*—the most widely known of which was probably the section *De Laude* of Priscian's *Praeexercitamina* or *Preliminary Exercises* (Keil, *Grammatici Latini*, 8 vols., III [Leipzig, 1859], 430–40, esp. 435–37)—were the common property of medieval readers.

At least equally common were works *actually using* the tactics described by writers like Priscian. These works ranged across a variety of "fields." They include biographies, histories, heroic narratives, sermons, and fables. In works such as these (for example, Einhard's *Life of Charlemagne* or Geoffrey of Monmouth's *History of the Kings of Britain*), the capacity to keep moving ahead in spite of obstacles—guided, all the while, by a constancy and *patientia* which make one immune to both flattery and attack—is praised again and again. Indeed, it is the very thing being praised in this "hagiographic" tale by Odo. So one might say that "praise and blame" is both central to this fable's subject and also, at the same time, a formative principle of its art. Moreover, "praise and blame" is in some sense fundamental to the art of Odo's entire collection. These are after all fables (or *parabolae*) set forth, as the beginning of the Prologue puts it, "in praise of [*ad laudem*] Him who is both Alpha and Omega."

106. "The Cloistered Life: A Further Treatment of the Same Theme" (*De Claustrali ad idem*), Hervieux LXXII.

*Boethius, *The Consolation of Philosophy*, II, prose iv.

107. "The He Goat Who Wanted To Take a Ride" (*De Hirco equitante*), Hervieux LXXIII; Perry 623[a].

108. "An Aged Father, His Son, and the King" (*De Patre sene et Filio suo et Rege*), Hervieux LXXIII[a].

109. "An Aged Father and His Son" (*De Patre sene et Filio suo*), Hervieux LXXIII[b]; Perry 624.

110. "The Wolf and the Fox" (*De Lupo et Vulpe*), Hervieux LXXIV; Perry 625.

111. "The Fly and the Ant" (*De Musca et Formica*), Hervieux LXXV.

*Because of its "poetics" or "style," this is a difficult passage to render. Earlier in Odo's text (see Fable 56 and note) the difficulties were due primarily to patterns of assonance and alliteration. Here, they are due to powerful rhythmic structures embodied in the Latin text. However, it has been possible to find devices which provide an *approximate* sense of the character of the original when that is read aloud.

One should note that the fable's rhythmic passage (beginning: "Now the fly . . ."), elaborate as it is, comes to a conclusion with a biblical aphorism which is contrastingly brief and pointed—yet, like the whole which precedes it, rhythmical. *Ascendunt* ["they rise"] *in celum, descendunt* ["then dive down"] *usque ad abissum.* But for discussion which will enlarge on the matters merely suggested here, see Erich Auerbach, *Literary Language and Its Public in Late Latin Antiquity and in the Middle Ages*, trans. R. Manheim (New York: Pantheon/Bollingen Series LXXIV, 1965), pp. 27–31, and L. R. Palmer, *The Latin Language* (London: Faber and Faber, 1961), pp. 132–35 and 200–205.

†The feast of the seventh Sunday following Easter, Pentecost commemorates the descent of the Holy Spirit on the apostles. See Acts of the Apostles 2:2–4, esp.
‡Odo: *de mundissimo ad inmundissimum . . . transeunt.*

"Alternate Prologue to the Fables of Odo of Cheriton" (*Prologus*).

*Prologus, in Bibliothecae Bodleianae Codice Douce 88, Authentico Prologo Praepositus (Hervieux, *Les Fabulistes Latins,* IV, 250).

112. "The Eagle and the Cuckoo" (*De Aquila et Cucula*), Hervieux LXXVI; Perry 626.

*The bearing of this citation on the fable as a whole is clarified if the passage's context is remembered. Luke 17:9–10: "Does one thank that servant for doing the things commanded of him? I think not. So you also, when you shall have done all these things which you are commanded to do, say: 'We are unprofitable servants; we have done that which we ought to do.'" To recall our fable's words, men who are just and humble "always disparage themselves."

113. "Philomel and a Bowman" (*De Philomela et Sagittario*), Hervieux LXXVII; Perry 627.

114. "A Certain Man Flees the Unicorn" (*De quodam Homine et Unicorni*), Hervieux LXXVIII.

115. "The Mouse and His Sons" (*De Mure et Filiis suis*), Hervieux LXXIX.

116. "The Lord Theodosius, Bishop of Sion" (*De domino Theodosio, Sediensi episcopo*), Hervieux LXXX.

117. "The Wolf, the Fox, and the Ass" (*De Lupo, Vulpe et Asino*), Hervieux LXXXI; Perry 628.

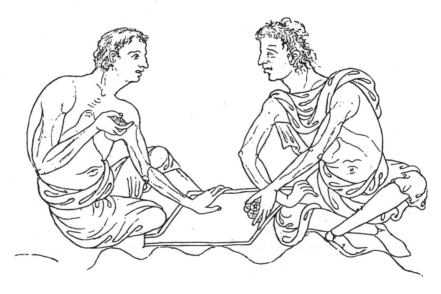

Bibliography

T HIS BIBLIOGRAPHY lists works referred to in the annotations attached to particular fables. It also gives most works referred to in my Introduction (the exceptions being pieces such as Thurber's *Fables for Our Time*) plus others which were used — some heavily — though not actually mentioned, and those works which — although sources of little or no material "information" — provided fundamental insights and sparked my thinking about basic issues. These texts will be of particular interest to readers wishing to consider some of the critical questions raised by my approach to the art of *The Fables.*

Editions

Hervieux, Léopold, ed. *Les Fabulistes Latins.* 5 vols. 1893–99. Reprint. Hildes-
      heim: Georg Olms, 1970.
      Odo of Cheriton's *Fabulae* are in IV, 173–250. The four books of the
      anonymous *Romulus* are in II, 195–245, while the epitome version of
      the *Romulus* (the *Breviatae Fabulae*) is printed on pp. 246–61 of the
      same volume. The text of Phaedrus' fables is in II, 5–81.
Perry, Ben Edwin, ed. *Aesopica.* I. Urbana, Il.: University of Illinois Press, 1952.
      After the first volume, no others were ever published. Perry's selection
      from Odo of Cheriton's *Fabulae* is printed on pp. 625–57.

Background and Critical Resources

Aarne, Antti. *The Types of the Folktale.* Translated and Enlarged by Stith
      Thompson. 2nd revision. Folklore Fellows Communications, No. 184.
      Helsinki: Finnish Academy of Sciences, 1961.

In his preface to the second revision, Thompson writes: "A word is perhaps desirable about the difference between an index such as this and the *Motif-Index of Folk-Literature.* This classification is concerned with whole tales, those that have an independent tradition. And they are confined to narratives of a certain area. On the other hand, the motif-index attempts a theoretical classification of motifs covering the whole world."

Accessus ad Auctores. Edited by R. B. C. Huygens. *Latomus* 12 (1953): 269–311 and 460–80.

Aesop. *Fables of Aesop.* Translated by S. A. Handford. Baltimore: Penguin Books, 1964.

Aesop's and Other Fables: An Anthology. Edited by Ernest Rhys (1913). Reprint with postscript by Roger Lancelyn Green. Everyman's Library, No. 657. New York: Dutton, 1971.

This is a selection of fables, from Aesop's through Tolstoy's. The translations are by various hands, but a small selection from Caxton's Aesop is included. In all, eighteen different sources are represented.

An Alphabet of Tales: An English 15th Century Translation of the "Alphabetum Narrationum" once attributed to Etienne De Besançon. Edited by Mary Macleod Banks. Early English Text Society, Original Series, Nos. 126 and 127. 1904–1905. Reprint (as one volume). Millwood, N.Y.: Kraus, 1975.

Auerbach, Erich. "Figura." Translated by Ralph Manheim. In *Scenes from the Drama of European Literature.* New York: Meridian Books, 1959.

———. *Literary Language and Its Public in Late Latin Antiquity and in the Middle Ages.* Translated by Ralph Manheim. Bollingen Series, LXXIV. New York: Pantheon, 1965.

Augustine. *Civitas Dei.* In J.-P. Migne, *Patrologiae Latinae.* XLI.

———. *The City of God.* Translated by Marcus Dods, with George Wilson and J. J. Smith. New York: Modern Library, 1950.

Ault, Warren O. "The Village Church and the Village Community in Mediaeval England." *Speculum* 45, no. 2 (April 1970): 197–215.

Avianus. *Fabulae Aviani (The Fables of Avianus).* For text and translation see the Loeb Library *Minor Latin Poets,* translated by J. Wight Duff and Arnold M. Duff.

Avianus prefaces his fables with a dedicatory letter to one Theodosius —most likely Theodosius Macrobius. There is, from our point of view, considerable irony in this—given Macrobius' view of "fables" (discussed in my introduction to this translation of Odo of Cheriton). For Macrobius' text, see his *Commentarium,* edited by Jacob Willis, and *Commentary,* trans. by W. H. Stahl.

Babrius. *Aesopic Fables of Babrius in Iambic Verse.*
For text and translation see Perry, Ben Edwin *Babrius and Phaedrus.*
Also see Hull's translation.

————. *Aesop's Fables Told by Valerius Babrius.* Translated by Denison B.
Hull. Chicago: University of Chicago Press, 1960.
This is a straight translation, without accompanying text.

Bacon, Francis. *Apophthegms New and Old.* In *The Works of Francis Bacon.*
Edited by James Spedding, Robert Leslie Ellis, and Douglas Denon
Heath. 14 vols. 1858–74. Reprint. Stuttgart-Bad Cannstatt: Friedrich
Frommann Verlag Gunther Holzboog, 1963. VII, 123–65.
"Julius Caesar did write a Collection of Apophthegms. . . . Certainly
they are of excellent use. They are *mucrones verborum,* pointed speeches"
(from "His Lordship's Preface" to the *Apophthegms*). A *mucro* is not
simply any sort of "point" but the point of a sword or spear. And an
apophthegm is an instrument of "war," of "attack."

————. *De Dignitate et Augmentis Scientiarum.* In *Works.* Text: I, 423–837;
Translation: IV, 273–V, 3–119.
The *De Augmentis* contains (in Book II, chap. xiii) one of the most
powerful discussions of fables, parables, enigmas, and the like, ever written. More than 350 years after Bacon's death, it continues to speak with
great force and suggestiveness.

————. *De Sapientia Veterum (On the Wisdom of the Ancients).* In *Works.*
Text: VI, 617–86; Translation: VI, 687–764.

————. *Maxims of the Law.* In *Works.* VII, 307–387.
Maxims (like fables and aphorisms and parables, etc.) are rated as a
"minor form" in the twentieth century. But Bacon, whose great *Novum
Organum* is written entirely in aphorisms, clearly did not see them as
"minor" or unimportant. Perhaps this is partly because he (like Tertullian) practiced law and, so, understood that aphorisms, etc., could
be instruments of discovery—could be more than clichés, more than
devices for comfortably restating what "everybody knows." Thus, in his
preface to the *Maxims,* he explains: "I could have digested these rules
into a certain method or order, which, I know, would have been more
admired, as that which would have made every particular rule, through
his coherence and relation unto other rules, seem more cunning and
more deep; yet I have avoided so to do, because *this delivering of knowledge in distinct and disjoined aphorisms doth leave the wit of man more
free to turn and toss, and to make use of that which is so delivered to
more several purposes and applications*" (VII, 321). Bacon knew the force
in saying that language and literature are forms of action.

————. *Novum Organum (The New Organon).* In *Works.* Text: I, 119–365;
Translation: IV, 3–248.

Baldwin, Charles Sears. *Medieval Rhetoric and Poetic (to 1400) Interpreted from Representative Works*. 1928. Reprint. Gloucester, Ma.: Peter Smith, 1959.

Barbaro, Ermolao. *Fables* (1422). See *Fabulae Aesopicae,* edited and translated by J. R. Berrigan, for text and translation.

Benedict. *St. Benedict's Rule for Monasteries.* Translated by Leonard J. Doyle. Collegeville, Mn.: The Liturgical Press of St. John's Abbey, 1948.

Berechiah ha-Nakdan. *Fables of a Jewish Aesop, Translated from the Fox Fables of Berechiah ha-Nakdan.* Translated by Moses Hadas. Historical introduction by W. T. H. Jackson. New York: Columbia University Press, 1967.

Bernard of Clairvaux. *Five Books on Consideration: Advice to a Pope.* Translated by John D. Anderson and Elizabeth T. Kennan. Kalamazoo, Mi.: Cistercian Publications, 1976.

Boethius, Anicius Manlius Severinus. *The Theological Tractates,* translated by H. F. Stewart and E. K. Rand, and *The Consolation of Philosophy,* translated by "I.T." and Revised by H. F. Stewart. Loeb Classical Library, No. 74. London: William Heinemann, 1918.

Bohr, Neils. "Quantum Physics and Philosophy: Causality and Complementarity." In *Essays 1958–1962 on Atomic Physics and Human Knowledge.* New York: Interscience, 1963, pp. 1–7.

Booth, Wayne C. *The Rhetoric of Fiction.* Chicago: University of Chicago Press, 1961.

Bowersock, G. W., ed. *Approaches to the Second Sophistic: Papers Presented at the 105th Annual Meeting of the American Philological Association.* University Park, Pa.: The American Philological Association, 1974. Of the several papers in this collection, B. P. Reardon's "The Second Sophistic and the Novel" is of special interest with reference to my introductory discussion of Odo of Cheriton.

Brewer's Dictionary of Phrase and Fable, centenary ed. Revised by Ivor H. Evans. New York: Harper and Row, 1970.

Brumbaugh, Robert S. *Plato's Mathematical Imagination: The Mathematical Passages in the Dialogues and Their Interpretation.* Indiana University Publications: Humanities Series, XXIX. 1954. Reprint. Millwood, N.Y.: Kraus, 1977.

Buchanan, Scott. "An Introduction to the *De Modis Significandi* of Thomas of Erfurt." In *Philosophical Essays for Alfred North Whitehead.* 1936. Reprint. N.Y.: Russell and Russell, 1967, pp. 67–89.

———. *Poetry and Mathematics.* 1929. Reprint. Philadelphia: Lippincott, 1961.

———. *Rhetoric.* A St. John's Manual. Santa Fe: St. John's College Bookstore, n.d. Mimeographed.

———. *Symbolic Distance in Relation to Analogy and Fiction.* Psyche Miniatures, General Series, No. 39. London: Kegan Paul, 1932.

Cicero, Marcus Tullius. *Ad C. Herennium, De Ratione Dicendi (To Gaius Herennius, On the Theory of Public Speaking).* Translated by Harry Caplan. Loeb Classical Library, No. 403. London: William Heinemann, 1954.

———. *De Inventione, De Optime Genere Oratorum,* and *Topica (On Invention, The Best Kind of Orator,* and *Topics).* Translated by H. M. Hubbell. Loeb Classical Library, No. 386. London: William Heinemann, 1949.

———. *De Re Publica and De Legibus (The Republic* and *Laws).* Translated by Clinton Walker Keyes. Loeb Classical Library, No. 213. London: William Heinemann, 1928.

Clark, David L. "Optics for Preachers: The *De oculo morali* by Peter of Limoges." *Michigan Academician* 9 (1977): 329–43.

Clement of Alexandria. *Stromata.* In J.-P. Migne, *Patrologiae Graecae.* VIII, 685–1382 through IX, 9–602.
An English translation of the *Stromata* is available in *The Ante-Nicene Fathers: Translations of the Writings of the Fathers down to* A.D. *325* (Grand Rapids, Mi.: Wm. B. Eerdmans, 1975), II, 299–568.

Clement of Rome. *First Clement.* Translated by Robert M. Grant and Holt H. Graham. In *The Apostolic Fathers.* 6 vols. New York: Thomas Nelson and Sons, 1964–68. II, 15–100.
Clement discusses the "singularity" of the phoenix—a matter relevant to Odo's Fable 20 ("The Phoenix")—in sections 25–26 (pp. 50–52 in the Grant-Graham translation).

Commendation of the Clerk (De Commendatione Cleri). In *University Records and Life in the Middle Ages,* edited and translated by L. Thorndike (Translation: pp. 201–235; Text: pp. 409–433).

Conrad of Hirschau. *Dialogus super Auctores.* Edited by R. B. C. Huygens. *Collection Latomus,* XVII. Brussels: Latomus, Revue d'Etudes Latines, 1955.

Correr, Gregorio. *Fables* (1429). See *Fabulae Aesopicae,* edited and translated by J. R. Berrigan for text and translation.

Coulton, G. C. *Medieval Panorama: The English Scene from Conquest to Reformation.* [1938.] Reprint. Cleveland: Meridian Books, 1955.

Crane, R[onald] S. "Shifting Definitions and Evaluations of the Humanities from the Renaissance to the Present." In *The Idea of the Humanities and Other Essays Critical and Historical.* 2 vols. Chicago: University of Chicago Press, 1967. I, 16–170.

————. "Philosophy, Literature, and the History of Ideas." In *The Idea of the Humanities*. I, 173–87.

Crossan, John Dominic. *In Parables: The Challenge of the Historical Jesus*. New York: Harper and Row, 1973.

————. *The Dark Interval: Towards a Theology of Story*. Niles, Il.: Argus Communications, 1975.

Curtius, Ernst Robert. *European Literature and the Latin Middle Ages*. Translated by Willard R. Trask. Bollingen Series, XXXVI. 1953. Reprint. New York: Harper Torchbooks, 1963.

Dante. *Epistola X/Letter 10* (to Can Grande). Translated by Philip H. Wicksteed. In *A Translation of the Latin Works of Dante Alighieri*. 1904. Reprint. New York: Greenwood Press, 1969, pp. 343–68.
This is Dante's "*accessus*-style" discussion of his *Comedy*. For earlier examples of this approach to literary texts, see *Accessus ad Auctores,* edited by R. B. C. Huygens, and Conrad of Hirschau, *Dialogus*.

DeBruyne, Edgar. *The Esthetics of the Middle Ages*. Translated by Eileen B. Hennessy. New York: Ungar, 1969.

Dewey, John. *Art as Experience*. 1934. Reprint. New York: Capricorn Books, 1958.
Few have ever written about the fine arts with Dewey's elegance and clarity. But see especially his third chapter, "Having an Experience."

Dronke, Peter. *Fabula: Explorations into the Uses of Myth in Medieval Platonism. Mittellateinische Studien und Texte*, IX. Leiden: E. J. Brill, 1974.

Dudo of St. Quentin. *De Moribus et Actis Primorum Normanniae Ducum*. Edited by J. Lair. *Memories de la Societe des Antiquaires de Normandie* 23 (1865): 115–301.

Einhard. *Einhard's "Life of Charlemagne": The Latin Text*. Edited by H. W. Garrod and R. B. Mowat. Oxford: The Clarendon Press, 1925.

————. *The Life of Charlemagne*. In *Two Lives of Charlemagne*. Translated by Lewis Thorpe. Baltimore: Penguin Books, 1969.

Eudes of Rouen. *The "Register" of Eudes of Rouen*. Translated by Sydney M. Brown. Edited by Jeremiah F. O'Sullivan. Records of Civilization, Sources and Studies, LXXII. New York: Columbia University Press, 1964.

Evans, G. R. *Old Arts and New Theology: The Beginnings of Theology As an Academic Discipline*. Oxford: The Clarendon Press, 1980.

Everyman. In *Chief Pre-Shakespearean Dramas*. Edited by Joseph Quincy Adams. Cambridge, Ma.: Houghton Mifflin, 1924, pp. 288–303.

Fabulae Aesopicae Hermolai Barbari et Gregorii Corrarii. Edited and Translated by Joseph R. Berrigan. Lawrence, Ka.: Coronado Press, 1977.

This is a dual-language text. Like the volumes in the Loeb Library, it prints the original text on the left, the English translation on the right. *Fabulae Aesopicae* contains the fables of Barbaro and Correr.

Faral, Edmond, ed. *Les Arts Poétiques du XII et du XIII Siècle.* Paris: Libraire Ancienne Honore Champion, 1924.
This volume contains the treatises on the art of poetry mentioned in my introduction and notes. Some such treatises are now available in English translation (see Geoffrey of Vinsauf, *Documentum* and *Poetria Nova,* and Murphy, *Three Medieval Rhetorical Arts*).

Ferrante, Joan M. *Woman As Image in Medieval Literature: From the Twelfth Century to Dante.* New York: Columbia University Press, 1975.

Finlayson, John. "Rhetorical 'Descriptio' of Place in the Alliterative *Morte Arthure.*" *Modern Philology* 61 (1963): 1–11.

Fish, Stanley E. *Self-Consuming Artifacts: The Experience of Seventeenth-Century Literature.* Berkeley: University of California Press, 1972.
I share most reviewers' reservations about this study. Yet as overstated as many of Fish's central claims may be, his argument is suggestive and deserves consideration.

Friend, Albert C. "Master Odo of Cheriton." *Speculum* 23 (1948): 641–58.

Gadamer, Hans-Georg. "Aesthetics and Hermeneutics." In *Philosophical Hermeneutics.* Translated by David E. Linge. Berkeley: University of California Press, 1976, pp. 95–104.

———. "The Eminent Text and Its Truth." *The Bulletin of the Midwest Modern Language Association* 13, no. 1 (Spring 1980): 3–10.

Geoffrey of Monmouth. *The "Historia Regum Britanniae" of Geoffrey of Monmouth: With Contributions to the Study of Its Place in Early British History.* Edited by Acton Griscom. London: Longmans, Green, 1929.

———. *The History of the Kings of Britain.* Translated by Lewis Thorpe. Baltimore: Penguin Books, 1966.

Geoffrey of Vinsauf. *Documentum de Modo et Arte Dictandi et Versificandi (Instruction in the Method and Art of Speaking and Versifying).* Translated by Roger P. Parr. Mediaeval Philosophical Texts in Translation, No. 17. Milwaukee, Wi.: Marquette University Press, 1968.

———. *Poetria Nova of Geoffrey of Vinsauf.* Translated by Margaret F. Nims. Toronto: Pontifical Institute of Mediaeval Studies, 1967.
Another translator's version is available in Murphy, *Three Medieval Rhetorical Arts.*

Gesta Stephani. Edited and Translated by K. R. Potter. London: Nelson, 1955.

Gierke, Otto. *Political Theories of the Middle Ages.* Translated by F. W. Maitland. Boston: Beacon Press, 1958.

Giles, J. A., ed. *Scriptores Rerum Gestarum Willelmi Conquestoris.* Publications of the Caxton Society, III. London: D. Nutt, 1845.

Goodman, Paul. *Speaking and Language: Defence of Poetry.* New York: Random House, 1971.

——. *The Structure of Literature.* Chicago: University of Chicago Press, 1954. For general remarks on translation (from which I quote at the beginning of my introduction's fourth section) and an illuminating discussion of Dillon's translation of Baudelaire's *La Géante,* see pp. 225–35.

Graesse, J. G. Th. *Orbis Latinus.* 4th ed. Revised and Enlarged by Helmut Plechl and Günter Spitzbart. Braunschweig: Klinkhardt and Biermann, 1971. This is a Latin-German/German-Latin lexicon of geographical names.

Gregory IX, Pope. "The Statutes of Pope Gregory IX on the Reformation of the Monks of the Order of St. Benedict." In *The "Register" of Eudes of Rouen,* pp. 737–46.

Grosseteste, Robert. *On Truth.* In *Selections from Medieval Philosophers.* Edited and Translated by Richard McKeon. 2 vols. New York: Charles Scribner's Sons, 1929. I, 263–81.

Halm, Carolus, ed. *Rhetores Latini Minores.* 1863. Reprint. Frankfurt am Main: Minerva, 1964.

Haskins, Charles Homer. *Norman Institutions.* 1918. Reprint. New York: Ungar, 1960.

——. *The Normans in European History.* 1915. Reprint. New York: W. W. Norton, 1966.

——. *The Renaissance of the Twelfth Century.* 1927. Reprint. Cleveland: Meridian Books, 1957.

——. *The Rise of Universities.* 1923. Reprint. Ithaca, N.Y.: Cornell University Press, 1965.

Heiserman, A. R. *Skelton and Satire.* Chicago: University of Chicago Press, 1965. Heiserman's view of "the satiric object"—i.e., what a "satire" attacks— differs in important ways from that developed by Rosenheim (*Swift*). To say that satire mounts an attack upon "discernible historic particulars" (Rosenheim) is to rule much medieval satire non-satiric. This was my reason for pointing out in my introduction that Odo's fables, when they have "attack" as one of their purposes, take aim at "a generic target or victim: a class of people," etc. But Heiserman puts the point more broadly: "One can legitimately speak of a body of literary works called 'medieval English satire.' All the devices of these works . . . are ordered to mount attacks on recognizable objects that include both abstractions like folly and historical particulars like Wolsey. . . .

"It would seem that satire imposes very few limits on the ingenuity of the satirist. . . . But we have seen that, in the medieval period at least, the objects were themselves conventional and that they were attacked by conventional mixtures of conventions" (p. 305).

Henderson, Arnold Clayton. "Medieval Beasts and Modern Cages: The Making of Meaning in Fables and Bestiaries." *PMLA* 92, no. 1 (January 1982): 40–49.

———. "'Of Heigh or Lough Estat': Medieval Fabulists as Social Critics." *Viator* 9 (1978): 265–90.

Henry of Huntingdon. *Henrici Archidiaconi Huntendunensis Historia Anglorum. "The History of the English," by Henry, Archdeacon of Huntingdon.* Edited by Thomas Arnold. Rolls Series, Vol. 75. London: Her Majesty's Stationery Office, 1897.

Hoare, F. R., trans. and ed. *The Western Fathers.* 1954. Reprint. New York: Harper Torchbooks, 1965.
This is a collection of saints' lives—"sacred" as contrasted to "secular" biographies like Einhard's *Life of Charlemagne*, etc. It prints translations of Sulpicius Severus' *Life of St. Martin* (a truly remarkable work), Paulinus the Deacon's *Life of St. Ambrose*, St. Possidius' *Life of St. Augustine*, St. Hilary's *Discourse on the Life of St. Honoratus*, and Constantius of Lyon's *Life of St. Germanus.*

Horace. *Satires, Epistles* and *Ars Poetica.* Translated by H. Rushton Fairclough. Loeb Classical Library, No. 194. London: William Heinemann, 1929.

Jacobs, Joseph. *History of the Aesopic Fable.* 1889. Reprint. New York: Burt Franklin, 1970.

Jerome. *Selected Letters of St. Jerome.* Translated by F. A. Wright. Loeb Classical Library, No. 262. London: William Heinemann, 1933.

Kantorowicz, Ernst H. *Laudes Regiae: A Study in Liturgical Acclamations and Mediaeval Ruler Worship.* University of California Publications in History, XXXIII. 1946. Reprint. Millwood, N.Y.: Kraus, 1974.

Kretzschmar, William A., Jr. "The Literary-Historical Context of Henryson's 'Fabillis.'" Ph.D. dissertation, University of Chicago, 1980.
See especially chapter 4 ("The Medieval Fable") and chapter 5 ("Remarks on Medieval Genres Adjacent to Fable").

La Fontaine. *Selected Fables.* Translated by James Michie. New York: Penguin Books, 1982.

Latham, R. E. *Revised Medieval Latin Word-List from British and Irish Sources.* London: Oxford University Press for The British Academy, 1965.
This is an enlarged edition of the 1934 *Medieval Latin Word-List from British and Irish Sources* (J. H. Baxter and Charles Johnson, eds.).

El Libro de los Gatos: A Text with Introduction and Notes. Edited by G. T. Northrup. Chicago: University of Chicago Press, 1908. Reprinted from *Modern Philology* 5, no. 4 (1908).

Lutz, Cora E. *Schoolmasters of the Tenth Century.* Hamden, Ct.: Archon Books, 1977.

Mack, Maynard. "A Note on Translation." In *World Masterpieces,* rev. ed. Edited by Maynard Mack, *et al.* 2 vols. New York: W. W. Norton, 1965. I, 1695–1702 or II, 1651–58.
  This "note" appears in identical form as an appendix to both *World Masterpieces* volumes and may, thus, be read in either.

McKeon, Richard P. "Creativity and the Commonplace." *Philosophy and Rhetoric* 6, no. 4 (Fall 1973): 199–210.

————. "Philosophic Semantics and Philosophic Inquiry." Chicago, [1966]. Mimeographed.

————. "Poetry and Philosophy in the Twelfth Century: The Renaissance of Rhetoric." In *Critics and Criticism.* Edited by R. S. Crane. Chicago: University of Chicago Press, 1952, pp. 297–318.

————. "*Pride and Prejudice:* Thought, Character, Argument, and Plot." *Critical Inquiry* 5, no. 3 (Spring 1979): 511–27.

————. "The Uses of Rhetoric in a Technological Age: Architectonic Productive Arts." In *The Prospect of Rhetoric: Report of the National Developmental Project.* Edited by Lloyd F. Bitzer and Edwin Black. Englewood Cliffs, N.J.: Prentice-Hall, 1971, pp. 44–63.

McKeon, Zahava Karl. *Novels and Arguments: Inventing Rhetorical Criticism.* Chicago: University of Chicago Press, 1982.

Manly, John Matthews. "Chaucer and the Rhetoricians." In *Chaucer Criticism.* Edited by Richard J. Schoeck and Jerome Taylor. 2 vols. Notre Dame, In.: University of Notre Dame Press, 1960–61. I, 268–90.

Macrobius, Ambrosius Theodosius. *Commentarium in Somnium Scipionis.* Edited by Jacob Willis. Leipzig: Teubner, 1970.

————. *Commentary on "The Dream of Scipio."* Translated by William Harris Stahl. Records of Civilization, Sources and Studies, XLVIII. New York: Columbia University Press, 1952.

Matthew, D. J. A. *The Norman Conquest.* New York: Schocken Books, 1966.

Mellinkoff, David. *The Language of the Law.* Boston: Little Brown, 1963.

Minor Latin Poets. Translated by J. Wight Duff and Arnold M. Duff. Loeb Classical Library, No. 284. London: William Heinemann, 1935.
  This volume contains, among other works, Publilius Syrus' *Sententiae,* the *Distichs of Cato, The Phoenix* which is often attributed to Lactan-

tius (but see also Clement of Rome, *First Clement* and my note), and, finally, Avianus' *Fabulae.*

Mumford, Lewis. *The City in History: Its Origins, Its Transformations, and Its Prospects.* New York: Harvest Books, 1961.

Murphy, James J. *Rhetoric in the Middle Ages: A History of Rhetorical Theory from Saint Augustine to the Renaissance.* Berkeley: University of California Press, 1974.

Murphy, James J., ed. *Three Medieval Rhetorical Arts.* Berkeley: University of California Press, 1971.

Murphy prints Anonymous of Bologna's *The Principles of Letter-Writing* (translated by James J. Murphy), Geoffrey of Vinsauf's *The New Poetics* (or *Poetria Nova,* translated by Jane Baltzell Kopp—cf. M. E. Nims' translation), and Robert of Basevorn's *The Form of Preaching* (translated by Leopold Krul, O.S.B.).

Nida, Eugene A., and William D. Reyburn. *Meaning Across Cultures.* American Society of Missiology Series, No. 4. Maryknoll, N.Y.: Orbis Books, 1981.

Though focused on biblical translation, this volume treats issues facing the translator of almost any text.

Niermeyer, J. F. *Mediae Latinitatis Lexicon Minus: A Medieval Latin—French/English Dictionary.* Completed by C. Van De Kieft. 2 vols. Leiden: E. J. Brill, 1976.

This is a remarkable volume, useful for many things but especially strong in the terminology of law and political-social institutions. Volume I is the lexicon proper. Volume II, very slender in comparison to the lexicon, is a list of abbreviations for both volumes and an Index Fontium or list of "all the editions of sources cited in the Dictionary" (II, xii).

Olson, Elder. *Tragedy and the Theory of Drama.* Detroit: Wayne State University Press, 1961.

Olson's remarks regarding translation are focused on Aeschylus' *Agamemnon;* see pp. 171–76.

Ordericus Vitalis. *Historiae Ecclesiasticae Libri Tredecim.* Edited by Augustus Le Prevost. 5 vols. Paris: Julius Renouard et Socios for the Société de L'Histoire de France, 1838–55.

Ovid. *The Art of Love, The Remedies of Love* [and other works]. Translated by J. H. Mozley. Loeb Classical Library, No. 232. London: William Heinemann, 1929.

——. *Heroides* and *Amores.* Translated by Grant Showerman. Loeb Classical Library, No. 41. London: William Heinemann, 1914.

Owst, G. W. *Literature and Pulpit in Medieval England: A Neglected Chapter in the History of English Letters and of the English People.* 2nd rev. ed. Oxford: Basil Blackwell, 1966.

Oxford English Dictionary, Compact Edition. New York: Oxford University Press, 1971.
> Because this dictionary's concept of "English" is so inclusive, it treats a range of French and French-derived locutions; this made it indispensable for dealing with a number of matters in Odo's text.

Palmer, L. R. *The Latin Language.* London: Faber and Faber, 1961.

Pedro Alfonso. *The Scholar's Guide: A Translation of the Twelfth-Century "Disciplina Clericalis" of Pedro Alfonso.* Translated by Joseph Ramon Jones and John Esten Keller. Toronto: Pontifical Institute of Mediaeval Studies, 1969.

Perry, Ben Edwin. "An Analytical Survey of Greek and Latin Fables in the Aesopic Tradition." In *Babrius and Phaedrus, Newly Edited and Translated into English. . . .* Translated and Edited by Ben Edwin Perry. Loeb Classical Library, No. 436. London: William Heinemann, 1965.
> The "Analytical Survey" is not only keyed to Perry's *Aesopica.* It also provides summaries of many fables and/or cross references (often extensive) to an extraordinary range of other fable collections and to reference works such as Thompson's *Motif-Index.* Thus the "Analytical Survey" is valuable to anyone interested in tracing sources and parallels — including those in folklore.

Perry, Ben Edwin, trans. *Babrius and Phaedrus.* Loeb Classical Library, No. 436. London: William Heinemann, 1965.
> This volume contains the *Aesopic Fables of Babrius in Iambic Verse* and *The Aesopic Fables of Phaedrus the Freedman of Augustus,* as well as the "Analytical Survey" listed and explained above.

Phaedrus. *The Aesopic Fables of Phaedrus the Freedman of Augustus.* See Perry, directly above.

Physiologus. Translated by Michael J. Curley. Austin: University of Texas Press, 1979.
> This, along with *Theobaldi "Physiologus"* and Pliny the Elder (*Naturalis Historia*) is probably the source, direct or indirect, of most of the moralized animal lore in Odo's *Fables.*

Pirenne, Henri. *Medieval Cities: Their Origins and the Revival of Trade.* Translated by Frank D. Halsey. 1925. Reprint. Garden City, N.J.: Doubleday Anchor, 1956.

Pliny the Elder. *Naturalis Historia (Natural History): Books VIII–XI.* Translated by H. Rackham. Loeb Classical Library, No. 353. London: William Heinemann, 1940.

The entire *Natural History* runs to 37 books (and a number of volumes in the Loeb edition). The listing immediately above, containing Books VIII–XI, prints the zoological portions that are especially important for traditions of animal lore and fable.

Priscian. *Praeexercitamina.* In *Grammatici Latini.* Edited by Hermannus Keil. 8 vols. Leipzig: Teubner, 1859, III: 430–40.

————. *Fundamentals Adapted from Hermogenes (Praeexercitamina).* Translated by Joseph M. Miller. In *Readings in Medieval Rhetoric.* Edited by Joseph M. Miller, Michael H. Prosser, and Thomas W. Benson. Bloomington: Indiana University Press, 1973, pp. 52–68.

Quintilian. M. Fabius. *The "Institutio Oratoria" of Quintilian.* Translated by H. E. Butler. 4 vols. Loeb Classical Library, Nos. 124–27. London: William Heinemann, 1920–22.

Rader, Ralph W. "Fact, Theory, and Literary Explanation." *Critical Inquiry,* 1, no. 2 (December 1974): 245–72.

Randall, John Herman, Jr. *Hellenistic Ways of Deliverance and the Making of the Christian Synthesis.* New York: Columbia University Press, 1970.

Richter, David H. *Fable's End: Completeness and Closure in Rhetorical Fiction.* Chicago: University of Chicago Press, 1974.

Romulus. See Hervieux, *Fabulistes Latins* and explanatory note, above.

Rosenheim, Edward W., Jr. *Swift and the Satirist's Art.* Chicago: University of Chicago Press, 1963.

Sacks, Sheldon. *Fiction and the Shape of Belief: A Study of Henry Fielding with Glances at Swift, Johnson and Richardson.* Berkeley: University of California Press, 1967.

Savory, Theodore. *The Art of Translation,* rev. ed. London: Jonathan Cape, 1968.

Schofield, William H. *English Literature from the Norman Conquest to Chaucer.* 1931. Reprint. New York: Phaeton Press, 1969.

Seneca, Lucius Annaeus. *Moral Essays.* Translated by John W. Basore. 3 vols. Loeb Classical Library, Nos. 214, 254, and 310. London: William Heinemann, 1928–35.
Seneca's *De Constantia* is in I, 48–105.

Sider, Robert Dick. *Ancient Rhetoric and the Art of Tertullian.* Oxford Theological Monographs. London: Oxford University Press, 1971.

Silverstein, Theodore. "Allegory and Literary Form." *PMLA* 82 (1967): 28–32.

————. "*Rex Iustus et Pius:* Henry's Throne and Dante's Christian Prince." In *American Critical Essays on "The Divine Comedy."* Edited by Robert J. Clements. New York: New York University Press, 1967, pp. 125–39. Even for the reader not immediately concerned with Dante, this essay brings together and discusses a range of materials on kingship—thus making it a good introduction to medieval convictions and conventions regarding the proper character of a "ruler."

———. "The Art of 'Sir Gawain and the Green Knight.'" *University of Toronto Quarterly* 33 (1964): 258–78.

Skelton, Robin, trans. *Two Hundred Poems from the Greek Anthology*. Seattle: University of Washington Press, 1971.
Skelton's views on translation are in some ways quite different from my own. I suspect that the differences are, in large part, due to the standing of *The Greek Anthology* among English readers. It is a well-known, frequently translated collection—unlike Odo's. For Skelton on translation, see his volume's introduction, esp. xviii–xx.

Smalley, Beryl. *The Study of the Bible in the Middle Ages*. 1952. Reprint. Notre Dame, In.: University of Notre Dame Press, 1964.

Souter, Alexander. *A Glossary of Later Latin to 600* A.D. Oxford: The Clarendon Press, 1957.

Sprague, Rosamund Kent, ed. *The Older Sophists: A Complete Translation by Several Hands of the Fragments in "Die Fragmente Der Vorsokratiker" Edited by Diels-Kranz*. Columbia, S.C.: University of South Carolina Press, 1972.

Steiner, George. *After Babel: Aspects of Language and Translation*. New York: Oxford University Press, 1975.
This is a study which no one interested in translation, especially its import for understanding "culture" in its broadest sense, would want to miss.

Stenton, Doris Mary. *English Society in the Early Middle Ages: 1066–1307*. 3rd ed. The Pelican History of England, No. 3. Baltimore: Penguin Books, 1962.

Strecker, Karl. *Introduction to Medieval Latin*. 4th ed. Translated and Revised by Robert B. Palmer. Dublin: Weidmann, 1967.
Strecker prints a brief word list/vocabulary (pp. 48/55) which, however limited and idiosyncratic, is often useful.

Sumption, Jonathan. *Pilgrimage: An Image of Mediaeval Religion*. Totowa, N.J.: Rowman and Littlefield, 1975.

Taylor, Daniel J. "Varro's Mathematical Models of Inflection." *Transactions of the American Philological Association* 107 (1977): 313–23.
See Varro, *De Lingua Latina*.

Taylor, Henry Osborn. *The Mediaeval Mind: A History of the Development of Thought and Emotion in the Middle Ages*. 4th ed. 2 vols. Cambridge, Ma.: Harvard University Press, 1925.

Tertullian. *Apology* and *De Spectaculis*. Translated by T. R. Glover. Loeb Classical Library, No. 250. London: William Heinemann, 1931.

Theobaldi "Physiologus." Edited and Translated with introduction, critical apparatus, and commentary by P. T. Eden. Leiden: E. J. Brill, 1982.
See also *Physiologus,* translated by M. J. Curley, and Pliny the Elder, *Naturalis Historia,* translated by H. Rackham.

Theophrastus. *The Characters of Theophrastus.* Translated by J. M. Edmonds. Loeb Classical Library, No. 225. London: William Heinemann, 1929.

Thiébaux, Marcelle. "The Mediaeval Chase." *Speculum* 42, no. 2 (April 1967): 260–74.

Thompson, Stith. *Motif-Index of Folk-Literature: A Classification of Narrative Elements in Folktales, Ballads, Myths, Fables, Mediaeval Romances, Exempla, Fabliaux, Jest-Books and Local Legends.* 2nd ed., revised and enlarged. 6 vols. Bloomington: Indiana University Press, 1955.
For this work, the key phrase is "narrative *elements.*" Cf. Aarne, *Types of Folktale.*

Turner, G. J., ed. *Select Pleas of the Forest.* The Publications of the Selden Society, XIII. London: Bernard Quaritch, 1901.
Turner's introduction ("The Forests in the Thirteenth Century") to his collection of documents is a very extensive and detailed discussion of the forests and Forest Law. Stenton *English Society in the Early Middle Ages* relies upon it for information in this area, as have I in my introduction.

Turner, Ralph V. "The Judges of King John: Their Background and Training." *Speculum* 51, no. 3 (July 1976): 447–61.

University Records and Life in the Middle Ages. Edited and Translated, with an introduction and notes, by Lynn Thorndike. Records of Civilization, Sources and Studies, XXXVIII. 1944. Reprint. New York: W. W. Norton, 1975.

Varro, M. Terentius. *De Lingua Latina (On the Latin Language).* Translated by Roland G. Kent. 2 vols. Loeb Classical Library, Nos. 333 and 334. London: William Heinemann, 1938.
Regarding the fundamental identity of "analogies" and "proportions," consider Varro's X, iii (Loeb text: II, 562–67):
 What is *ratio pro portione?* In Greek, this is called *ana logon;* thus *analogia* is derived from "analogue." If two things of the same genus (even though they may be unlike in some way) belong to the same *ratio,* and if two other things which belong to the same *ratio* are placed beside the first two, then — because these verbal pairs belong to the same *logos* — each one separately is said to be an "analogue." Like-

wise, when the four are set side by side or are "collated," they are said to be an *analogia*. . . .

These phenomena exist in dissimilar things—as in numbers, when you compare two with one and likewise twenty with ten. For twenty has to ten the same *ratio* as two to one. Such is the case with similar phenomena like coins . . . likewise, such is the case with all other things: those which have this kind of fourfold nature are said to be *pro portione*—as is observable in progeny. The daughter is to the mother as the son is to the father and, as matters stand with temporal divisions, midnight is to night as noon to day.

This is something which is used extensively by poets, with extraordinary acuteness by the geometers; and in speech it is used more diligently by Aristarchus than by other grammarians, as when . . .

Wetherbee, Winthrop. *Platonism and Poetry in the Twelfth Century: The Literary Influence of the School of Chartres*. Princeton: Princeton University Press, 1972.

William of Jumièges. *Gesta Normannorum Ducum*. Edited by Jean Marx. Rouen and Paris: Libraire de la Société de l'Histoire de Normandie/ Libraire de la Société de L'Ecole des Chartes, 1914.

William of Malmesbury. *Willelmi Malmesbiriensis Monachi De Gestis Regum Anglorum, Libri Quinque: Historiae Novellae, Libri Tres*. Edited by William Stubbs. 2 vols. Rolls Series, Vol. 90. London: Her Majesty's Stationery Office, 1887–89.

William of Poitiers. *Gesta Guillelmi Ducis Normannorum et Regis Anglorum*. Edited by Raymonde Foreville. Paris: Société d'Édition "Les Belles Lettres," 1952.

Wittgenstein, Ludwig. *Tractatus Logico-Philosophicus*. Translated by D. F. Pears and B. F. McGuinness. International Library of Philosophy and Scientific Method. London: Routledge and Kegan Paul, 1963.

Yu, Anthony C. "The Better Form of Treason: Reflections on Literary Translation." *Criterion: A Publication of the Divinity School of the University of Chicago* 17, no. 2 (Summer 1978):9–13.
The author is the translator of the massive Chinese tale, *The Journey to the West*. But his comments, though made with specific reference to Oriental literatures, address the fundamental nature—the fundamentally democratic nature—of literary translation. "As our academic programs flourish . . . we will certainly witness an even greater number of well-researched and well-documented studies of this figure or that topic drawn from what is probably the longest, single literary culture in the world. Admirable and desirable though this phenomenon may be to the advancement of learning and of academic careers, it is," he

warns (here making the point demanding greatest emphasis), "hardly comforting to those who cherish the conviction that great imaginative writings should be enjoyed by the wider human community as well as by the arduously trained specialists. As long as the wide gulf of language remains unbridged, the text will remain the privileged property of experts."

THE FABLES OF ODO OF CHERITON

was composed in 11-point Digital Compugraphic Garamond and leaded two points by Metricomp,
with display type in Goudy Mediaeval and initial capitals in
Hadriano Stonecut by J. M. Bundscho, Inc.;
printed sheet-fed offset on 55-pound, acid-free Glatfelter Antique Cream,
Smythe-sewn and bound over binder's boards in Joanna Arrestox,
also adhesive bound with paper covers by Maple-Vail Book Manufacturing Group, Inc.;
and published by

SYRACUSE UNIVERSITY PRESS

SYRACUSE, NEW YORK 13210